STREET RETRIBUTION

I0716713

Marc A. Beausejour

S.H.E. PUBLISHING, LLC

STREET RETRIBUTION

Copyright © 2022 by Marc A. Beausejour

This book is a work of fiction. Names, characters, businesses, organizations, places, events, and incidents either are the product of the author's imagination or are used fictitiously. Any resemblance to actual persons, living or dead, events, or locales is entirely coincidental.

For information contact : www.shepublishingllc.com | info@shepublishingllc.com | Tel: 219.515.8032

Edited by D.A. Goodwin | Front Cover photo by ID 48584570 © Ammentorp | Dreamstime.com | Book Photo by LaTisha Guster

Library of Congress Control Number: 2024932786

ISBN: **978-1-953163-96-7 (*paperback*)**

Second Edition : February 2024

1   2   3   4   5   6   7   8   9   10

This book is dedicated to the memory of my grandfather, Joseph P. Beausejour whose journeyed to the spiritual realm on August 5, 2021. I hope I carry the family legacy as you have for decades. Continue to rest in peace and we will meet again.

PREFACE

I'm normally not a fan of writing prefaces before my readers dive into the novels, but I will make an exception in this case. First, I would like to extend my gratitude to all my readers and supporters who have brought, read, and advertised my books over the years. I am grateful that you have taken the time to be a part of my literary community. We've come a long way in this journey; from dealing with Pastor Michael Hillman's personal trials, growing up with Jamal Samuels and Omar Keaton, and learning to cope with loss with Andrea McAfee. You've sat behind bars with Levell Thomas, and you've been spectators to both of Sylvio Dominique's title fights. These characters have become part of my life and as I've grown as an author through the years, they have taken larger roles in these stories and each character has a story that has shaped them at some point. With that said, before you embark on this journey, I encourage my readers to begin reading The Preacher's Web and Adia's Ballad, primarily because all the questions and puzzle pieces that were unexplained in those books will begin to come together in this installment. For those who have not read my books, I would ask that you try to separate the author from the characters. I understand that some of my readers have strong spiritual personal convictions and there are certain scenarios where some characters use foul language and racial slurs which you may find offensive. But please remember that the words and the actions of some of these characters in no way reflect my personal faith and beliefs, nor do they compromise my integrity. If you have read my other books, you will know that in order for me to convey an effective story, I have to tell it in all of its raw form and that includes using the vernacular that many people may find offensive. Not all stories are clean; to find redemption and life, we must walk through the shadow of death and destruction. As you prepare to read this account of a man who once lived a double life as a gangbanger and drug dealer, only to be haunted by his past life many years later, please reflect on a hurdle or an obstacle that has been holding you back for years and believe that you will one day shake yourself loose from the shackles of your struggles and you will be free. God bless you all, and happy reading!

PROLOGUE

TWO BOYS WITH A VISION

JUNE 2000

Officer Jamison made his way around the corridor of the Queensboro Boys Detention Center (QBDC), accompanied by a fourteen-year-old boy. Wearing the tan inmate uniform, while handcuffed behind his back, the boy wore a scowl on his face, shrugging off Jamison every time the veteran officer placed a hand on his back. Under 24 hours ago, the boy was arrested and booked for aggravated assault after brutally beating up another teenage boy in the town galleria. This was not his first offense, which indicated that he had walked the halls of the detention center in the past.

David Anderson was no stranger to the juvenile criminal system. Standing at over six feet tall, husky with brawny arms, he had grown up in an environment where one had to scrap and fight for survival. Abandoned by his parents as a child, David was raised by his grandmother, Willamena Anderson, and she did her best to raise him to be a respectable young man. But David had an unquenchable rage that he unleashed whenever confronted or provoked by another person.

It started at the age of eleven when a neighborhood boy that was playing football with David and other kids decided to be sneaky and run off with David's football. As the boy ran off laughing, thinking there was no way that the pudgy kid would ever catch up with him, an enraged David would proceed to pursue him to the end of the block and not only retrieve his football, but also savagely beat the boy.

Before long, the boy was lying on the asphalt, writhing in pain, and the police were called. David was booked and stayed at the juvenile detention center for nearly a week before being released. Willamena Anderson tried bringing David to church, punishing him for his crimes, and attempted to get him more engaged in school, but all her efforts seemed to be for naught. Although he performed just enough to be promoted to the next grade, David never took an interest in school. By the time he was in middle school, he began to cut classes regularly.

Hanging out with his much older friends, David started to learn the ways of the street, how to deal with drug users and dealers, and how to effectively break into homes when people were away to steal valuables in order to resell them. As David saw it, these people had it made, and they could afford to replace whatever he stole.

They ain't ever had to worry about what they gonna eat or how they survive. I gotta hustle out here to make a living.

But after David's third arrest, Willamena decided to teach her grandson a lesson. She would no longer bail him out or pick him up. She was going to leave David at the detention center throughout his term to show him that she would not always be there.

Maybe that hard-headed boy will finally learn a thing or two in there. But it was a decision that she would soon regret.

Now at fourteen years of age, David was in his third stint at QBDC. He strode quietly as Officer Jamison pointed to his quarters.

"Park it here, Anderson," Jamison said gruffly as he reached for his keys to unlock the cell.

"Fuck you," David muttered silently as he walked into the cell.

Contrary to what people believed, the cells were not as closed and contained like other facilities. This one was the size of a small bedroom, where the young prisoner had space to walk and ponder around. About 16 feet from his bed was a small window view, which allowed David to see the cell next to his own, but he never paid attention to it upon arriving. Still seething in anger, David paced in his cell, thinking his grandmother would spring him.

But two hours passed, then five hours, then eight hours, and before long, David realized his grandmother was not coming to pick him up. He was beginning to lose his mind, and before arriving at any rational thought, he began punching his pillow in fury.

"Damn, bro, what the pillow do to you?" a voice asked from the next cell after David paused from punching his pillow over forty times.

The voice echoed directly from the small glassless window between the cells. Each cell was designed the same way, so the inmates routinely chatted with one another. But David was not keen on making friends.

"Mind yo' damn business!" he replied sharply. Normally, whenever David spoke strongly or issued warnings, people listened. But the owner of the voice kept going.

"I seen you round hea' before. Everybody ova' here keep sayin' not to mess wit' David Anderson, or you'll get yo' ass beat. I was like, okay, I gotta meet this cat."

David looked at the window, where he a saw a thin black boy with cornrows staring back at him. He looked about 17 years old. "If you know what's good for you, you'd listen to them. I ain't the one, B," he replied, hoping his sharp voice would instill fear into the confident stranger.

But the boy kept talking to him. "You got raw anger. I like that. You ain't scared of no one—not the police, correctional officer,s or anyone in this muthafucka. I already know, we gon' be cool."

David shook his head. Why can't this guy take a hint? "Cool? Nigga, I don't even know you like that."

"I feel you, homeboy. So, what you in for?" the boy replied, laughing.

David rubbed his knuckles. If he was going to be stuck here, he might as well talk to the boy. "I got into a fight at the mall galleria. Some clumsy-ass spilled his drink on me, so I rearranged his jaw."

"Damn, man, like that? You raw, son. I like that. Lemme drop some knowledge on you though. Why do you think you're out there pickin' fights? Starting to make a name? It's cuz you lookin' for respect," the boy replied. "You a bulldog, and they look at you like you was a poodle or some shit. Check it out though. When we get up out of here, roll wit' my set. We both know the streets. We both know how to fuck people up if they cross us, but we need to put fear in these people's hearts, you know what I'm sayin'?"

"Nigga, what set are you talkin' about?" David asked, getting angrier by the minute. He hated being confused.

"Ight, come up here for minute. I'll show you what I'm talkin' about," the boy said.

Standing on top of his bed, David looked through the window, and for the first time, he saw the other boy's room. He only had one thought. This dude's sick.

There were countless vivid drawings everywhere, from anime, to illustrations of different people from all walks of life. The drawings ranged from detailed to disturbed, especially one of a man lying on the ground with a bullet hole in his head and the blood pouring out of the open wound.

Noticing that David was paying extra attention to the explicit drawing, the boy said, "This one's my pops, Deon Hill. He rolled wit' the Posse 287s since before I was born. When I was five years old, he was sent with another homeboy to infiltrate the Rolling 45s, which was another warring set. What he ain't know was that the Posse 287s turned they back on him and sent him on a suicide mission. They had a man on the inside, and once my father got into 45 territory, they blasted him. I remember my mama bringing me to the autopsy room to ID him. She shouldn't have bought my young ass, but since she ain't had no one to watch me, she went there wit' me."

David shook his head. No kid should have to see a dead parent. Not like that. Suddenly, David felt remorse for the boy. "Damn, man, that sucks. Sorry you had to go through that," he said.

"Oh, trust me, it ain't over," the boy replied. "I've been lookin' for the assholes for years, but I ain't ever find 'em. What I needed was leverage. I needed connections cuz I ain't trust the Posse anymore, and the 45s ain't nothin' but some punk ass niggas, so I need to create a crew of my own. Level the playing field, you know what I mean?"

"Yeah, but how you gonna do that?" David asked.

"Check this out," the boy replied as he reached into his art collection and pulled out a paper that illustrated blood drops with guns pointing at each other surrounded by dollar bills.

At the bottom of the illustration, David saw a print in large letters: MONEY OVER BITCHES-M.O.B.

"This is how we gon' roll once I get out. I'm gon' recruit, and I'mma take over this game. We gon' run Queens as a family. Sort of like how the Italian mafia run their shit. You down?" he asked, extending a hand through the bars.

Figuring he had nothing to lose, David returned the handshake as a regular dab, but the boy laughed.

"Nah, we gon' do it like this." He proceeded to teach David the handshake that would later become the official greeting of the M.O.B. gang members. "Whoever ain't down wit' us is against us," the boy said.

"Facts. By the way, what they call you?" David asked the boy.

"My fam calls me Dontrell, but I go by Tadarius," the boy replied, and for the next few weeks leading up to their release, they began forming what would soon become the most dangerous gang and crime syndicate in Queens, New York.

May 2017 | Legal attorney Perry Wilcox displayed his visitor's badge at security checkpoint upon entering the Queensboro County Prison in Long Island, New York. Upon receiving the approval for entry, he followed a chief officer to the visitor's quarters where he had an appointment with his defendant. Having practiced law for more than fifteen years, Wilcox was no stranger to the many cases that he would be called upon to represent.

He had defended low account drug-dealers, tax evaders, traffic violators, and repeat offenders. His success-to-failure ratio stood second to none, but he hardly bragged about his successful cases. He had been heavily criticized in the media for representing the lowest common denominator in the eyes of the public, but in Wilcox's point of view, the public had a duty to blame the prosecutors. Maybe if they would have taken their time to study the cases and provided enough incriminating evidence, he wouldn't have been as successful, so if anyone should take the blame for why the criminals he represented constantly walked away scot-free, it should be the prosecution for benign neglect and failure to observe the other factors of the cases.

Wilcox found himself in the midst of a case that had run for thirteen years, and he was defending a prime suspect who was accused and found guilty of orchestrating the murder of 18-year-old Loree McAfee in September 2003. What made the case more challenging for Wilcox was the fact that the man he was defending did not have a spotless record.

In fact, his record was filled with nothing but run-ins with law enforcement as a juvenile, so it made Wilcox's job of representing his client exceedingly difficult. The man was the leader of one of New York's deadliest gangs: M.O.B. This wasn't a regular gang that fought petty wars with other gangs, although there were reported skirmishes in the past, but M.O.B. had grown into an urban conglomerate, having amassed over ninety members in less than two years, connecting with all the major drug imports, casinos, and nightclubs. Its members constantly infiltrated these establishments, and Tadarius Hill stood in charge of the nefarious organization.

Through his many channels, Tadarius had successfully been able to hire Wilcox as his attorney, and they had been mired in countless attempts to file appeals for early release, but all their attempts had failed. His arms and legs covered with tattoos and extremely well versed in weaponry and drug distribution, Tadarius was seen as an extremely dangerous individual.

As Wilcox waited in the visitor's room, the doors suddenly opened, and his client walked in handcuffed and accompanied by two officers. Wearing the prison's orange jumpsuit, Tadarius sat down in front of Wilcox. The gang leader had bulked up during his time in prison, as he had been considered slight in build in the days leading up to his imprisonment.

Tadarius had been transferred since his imprisonment, having been held in Elmira Maximum Security Detention Center in upstate New York before being relocated to Queensboro County Prison due to good behavior and one of Wilcox's many appeals to the New York State Court of Appeals.

But Tadarius wasn't the only member of M.O.B. locked up. Other members had been arrested and charged with being in association with his gang. And during a pivotal trial that took place, a key testimony from a former gangbanger had implicated Tadarius and another member of M.O.B. by the name of Terrell as being the individuals largely guilty for the murder of Loree McAfee.

In Tadarius's eyes, his empire fell apart the moment David got involved with Loree. David and Loree had begun dating that summer, and Tadarius was none too pleased about it. Loree was a well-known gang informant and call girl, and the meeting with David was supposed to be a one-night rendezvous.

Instead, Tadarius's his right-hand man was immediately sprung, and Loree started talking to David about separating himself from Tadarius and M.O.B. Loree and Tadarius frequently clashed, but one day she went too far, and Tadarius was determined to put her in her place.

That bitch had David whipped and said some unforgivable shit. She had to go.

Unfortunately, his plan to eliminate Loree flawlessly without any repercussions backfired, and Tadarius suffered not only the betrayal of his brother, but he also almost lost his life after one of Queen's most dangerous shootouts between M.O.B. and local SWAT team law enforcement.

Tadarius was shot in the leg, and the injury was so severe that he almost lost his leg. After emergency surgery where the bullet was extracted from his leg, he was bound in a cast and was in a wheelchair for almost a year. He regained his ability to walk while in confinement, but to this day, he still walked with a slight limp in his right leg.

While locked up, Tadarius began secretly plotting to destroy everyone who had betrayed him and snitched on him. They were going to pay for what they did to him. After his arrest, the remaining members of the gang scattered across the borough, some renouncing their association to the gang while others remained staunchly loyal.

As he sat across from his lawyer, Tadarius said, "I hope you got some good news for me, Perry."

Wilcox sighed, taking off his glasses. He rubbed his aching forehead, then took out a classified file and placed it on the table.

"Well, I've filed a motion for appeal for early release, and just when I thought we would get an approval, this gets out," he replied, pulling out a printed article that he pushed towards Tadarius.

As the inmate read the article, he felt his anger bubbling within him. Xavier Furrows, a man who happened to be a member of M.O.B. that was locked up for an unrelated case, implicated Tadarius and Terrell as being the masterminds behind Loree's murder. He also testified that Tadarius had murdered another man in 2002 by the name of Theo Brunsen, who was thought to have been missing for years.

Xavier apparently took a plea deal to shorten his jail sentence by outing Tadarius as a murderer and mastermind and linking him to the case. This would be a fatal blow to any chance that Tadarius had for early release.

"So Zay turned on me?" It's okay. I got something for his ass too. They thinkin' I can't get them from here. But they got another thing coming. "Anybody else rolled over?" he asked.

"Well, nobody recently," Wilcox replied. "Listen, Tadarius, you got to stay on the straight and narrow now. Your past is already working against you, and if you step outta line again, there ain't gon' be no second chance."

"Well, what am I supposed to do, let 'em keep me from walkin' outta hea'? You got another thing comin' Perry."

"Look, just lay low for now. We can't have you locked up even longer. I'll keep you posted," Wilcox said as he gathered his things to leave.

But although Tadarius shook his head in agreement, he had no intention of laying low. First, he planned on putting his "brother" six feet under. Then he was going to get Zay. But the goal was to kill Antonio Franks.

CHAPTER 1

MEET ATTORNEY EDWARD REED

OCTOBER 2017

Waking up to the sounds of cars honking and people bustling on Monday morning, Edward Reed rolled in his bed and checked the time on his phone. It was ten minutes before seven, which meant he had just a little over an hour before he had to be at work. After taking a quick shower and grabbing a banana morning smoothie out of the fridge, he dressed in his best pastel shirt and light grey Armani suit topped off with a silver tie.

Always gotta dress to impress. Adjusting his tie, Edward checked his hair in the bathroom mirror. Although he had just been to the barbershop just a week prior, his hair had a tendency of growing rapidly.

Grabbing his hairbrush and trimmer, he shaved the excess hair that had begun growing on his forehead before proceeding to brush his hair until he had a perfect hairline. He applied just a touch of Vitamin D oil on his hair so the waves set into place. His waves and his line had to be on point because it was what attracted the clients, and the ladies were attracted to it as well.

Edward was not known to be superficial when it came to his looks, but life had taught him that the first impression of a person was based off his or her looks. Five minutes later, Edward made his way out of his apartment with his work briefcase in hand. He lived on the Upper East End in Manhattan, just a few minutes off Broadway. Having just moved to the apartment a few months earlier from Jackson Heights, Edward relocated to get within closer proximity to his job.

Working for the Schorr Law Group in Manhattan provided Edward with a bevy of opportunities, from drawing new clients, to the perks that a New York businessman enjoyed when he was off work. The nightlife in New York, in his opinion, stood second to none. Edward had been to various clubs, bars, and overnight spots with his colleagues after a hard day working on affidavits.

Standing at six foot five with a toned body and megawatt smile, Edward rarely left the clubs alone. On most nights, he would be accompanied by a female who was impressed with his suits, his smile, and his easygoing demeanor, and Edward had the wordplay to make women swoon or become suddenly moist in certain areas. But it was not only his looks that attracted women to him. They were also attracted to him intellectually.

Edward graduated from North Carolina A&T State University with a bachelor's and master's in civil law. He was also an Alpha Phi Omega fraternity member in his years at the historically black college. Although law was not considered one of the major programs that was offered at the university, it was the career path that Edward chose for personal reasons.

He started working in a law office in North Carolina upon graduation but began to feel homesick and decided to move back to his birth state of New York. He did not consider it an easy decision, however, because part of him wanted to stay in North Carolina. His college experience, and his first job gave him a chance to start over a new chapter of his life. He wanted to put his high school years as far behind him as possible and escape his familiar confines.

But even though North Carolina had Charlotte—the Queen City—and its share of history, it could not rival his roots in New York, and there was no denying the endless job opportunities that Edward would receive in the city. He was also making good money in his current position, and although it was not a standard six-figure salary, it was enough to pay his rent and help other people, which was the reason that he decided to take up a career in law.

Upon his return to the Big Apple, he had to re-adjust to the city life again, which was not difficult, but his whole agenda was to lay low. Edward had his reasons for wanting to remain under the radar. It was more than ten years ago since the event had occurred, but he had been no stranger to the judicial system. He had been a star witness in a major crime case in which suspected gang members had murdered a teenage girl.

It was not a coincidence that Edward was selected by a defense team to be a witness in defense of a former gangbanger-turned high school football star who was accused of the murder. To his everlasting shame, Edward had once been involved with the very syndicate that was accused of murdering Loree McAfee in 2003. It was this part of his past that he wished to eradicate from his memory bank.

It took Edward years to realize that it was not his fault that his father was a gang banger, a member of the infamous "Shower Posse," who was arrested some years later, leaving Edward's mother Isabelle to raise him. It took him years to realize that it was not his fault that he was introduced into the street life at merely twelve years old and was taught how to handle a gun, load and unload the barrel, lock the clip, and apply the safety.

Edward knew more about firearms and weaponry than most average people knew in a single lifetime unless they were in the army or a member of law enforcement. It wasn't his fault that he was forced to live with his aunt for years, not because his mother was incapable of raising him, but because his life was in great peril.

He was a product of the environment, seen as a traitor because he turned against his environment, and the powers that be would not just let it slide. But that part of his life was over. It was behind him, and Edward was intent on moving forward.

As he drove his blue Toyota Camry, he reflected on the cases that he had to work on once he arrived in the office. Contrary to what television portrayed with its various shows depicting the judicial system at work, the life of a modern-day lawyer was neither glamorous nor interesting in the slightest.

Since beginning at Schorr Law Group in 2015, Edward had been relegated to office work, only taking minor cases such as traffic violations or parole violations. Maybe once or twice, he had dealt in juvenile cases, and all of those cases would be one thing or the other. It was either drug possession or assault and battery. There were no cases of interest, certainly not on the level of the Loree McAfee case, which had, to his surprise, turned cold.

Some years ago, it was reported that Terrell, the man who was initially accused of pulling the trigger on the gunshots that ended Loree's life, was in fact, not the trigger man. Terrell had maintained his innocence and denied any involvement in the murder, but when he was asked who killed Loree, he could not identify the murderer.

Many attempts had been made to re-open the case for further investigation, but the McAfee family had reportedly refused to do so. They strongly believed that Terrell was lying, and he was the man who had killed their daughter. With the advent of forensic science and testing methods, there was no evidence tying Terrell to Loree's murder, and the state was currently mulling over a decision to release Terrell, which Edward knew would enrage the McAfee family.

Edward had internally debated on whether he wanted to be involved in the case once again, but he quickly decided against it. He had already meddled in their affairs once, and he would not test fate to get involved again.

Entering the Schorr building, the secretary, Pamela Duncan greeted him. "Hello, Mr. Reed. Running a little late, aren't we? Mr. Schorr is meeting with the staff on the fifteenth floor."

"Is he really? Damn, I gotta get up there," Edward replied, taking the elevator to the fifteenth floor where he walked across the hall until he arrived in the conference room.

The law group consisted of Daniel Schorr, the founder of the firm, and then there were Sarah Vincent, Hank Kendall, Leon Burrell, Caitlyn Samuels, Jerome Kaplan, and Sheree Grofeld.

Edward arrived only five minutes after the meeting started.

"Okay, now that we got all the stragglers here, we can finally begin," Mr. Schorr said, smiling feverishly at Edwards.

"My apologies, sir," Edward replied as he sat down.

As they unrolled the numbers for the previous month and summarized the success ratio of cases within the last two years, Edward realized that he was near the bottom in terms of ranking compared to his colleagues. He made a mental note of his statistics and resolved to improve on his numbers.

After the meeting ended, the attorneys returned to their respective offices to continue working their cases. Edward's cases included a few traffic citations, entertainment recording contracts and one drug possession case. After a long day of calling his clients, scheduling meetings, and discussing fees, he packed his suitcase and left the building. While waiting in traffic in downtown Manhattan, he decided to go to his favorite bar earlier than usual.

Typically, after a long workday, Edward would return to his apartment, change out of his suit, and go out into the city for a nightcap, which normally included beer, chicken wings, and sports. On the weekends, he would hit the gym, but his apartment had a big enough hall to perform his daily exercises. For a workaholic like Edward, the gym and the bar served as an escape from his workday. There was one aspect that those places had in common: they were great places to meet women.

As a bachelor who was always on the move, he rarely had time to settle down. Not only was he not invested in any long-term relationships, but he also wouldn't turn down female companionship if he was approached by the right woman. Feeling lucky, he managed the rush-hour traffic just long enough to arrive at his favorite location. The Diamond Bar, which was located just half an hour from East Village, was a quaint spot.

Decked with three pool tables, four televisions, and a long bar table, the bar was one Edward had grown accustomed to, along with all its patrons. His favorite bartender, Emile, was experienced and knew just what Edward wanted after a long day of paperwork, phone calls, and conference calls.

Entering the bar, Edward silently hoped there weren't too many people ahead of him to place orders as he was eager to drink and head home for the evening, unless the evening presented an opportunity for him.

"What up, Emile? Lemme get the usual," he said as he sat down on the bar stool.

"Comin' right up, Mr. SVU," Emile joked as he reached into the bar and mixed a special batch of vodka and apple juice.

Edward rolled his eyes at the mention of the dubious nickname. Emile often joked about Edward's profession as a lawyer and stated more than once that Edward should guest star in an episode of Law&Order: Special Victim's Unit.

"By the way, Eddie, when are we gon' chop it up about that parking ticket that I'm tryin' to have expunged?" Emile asked.

"Yo, quit buggin' Emile. You know yo' ass never picked up no damn parking ticket," Edward laughed.

"Dead-ass, bro. The po-po caught my ass parking in a no parking zone, and all I did was stop for a moment to get me a Nathan's dog. Even had my emergency lights on and everything."

"Maybe you should've just parked the car in a legal space before you got your hot dog, man," Edward replied. "I'm a lawyer. I ain't no miracle worker."

"I'm just sayin' man. They stay tryin' to accuse a brotha' of something."

After Emile finished preparing Edward's drink, he paid the jovial bartender. Sipping his drink quietly, he didn't realize that he was no longer sitting alone. A beautiful woman was next to him. She stood about five foot four with slender legs and full pouty lips, and she wore a short brown dress that seemed to rise up just above her knees.

She had just ordered her second round of tequila when she first saw Edward. He did not initially acknowledge her presence before, but he knew she was eyeing him, and if this night ended up like many of his other nights, he was going to sleep very well.

"Yes, you could buy me a drink," she stated, tapping Edward's wrist.

Turning around, Edward smiled as her eyes met his. "You know, normally I don't buy drinks for strangers," he replied.

The woman shook Edward's hand. "Jacqueline Smith, but everybody calls me Jackie."

"Edward Reed, attorney at law."

"So that explains this Armani vibe you got going on here. I was about to say that you were too overdressed for this spot," Jackie replied as she downed another shot of tequila.

"Yo, Emile, lemme get a Martini for the young lady." Turning to Jackie after placing the order, he said, "Nah, this ain't how I normally come here. Typically, I go back to my spot and change before coming back out. Matter fact, I dress more laid back after hours."

"Really? Well, I think your suit makes you look regal, you know, like a young Denzel Washington," Jackie remarked.

"Word? I don't know about all that now. Denzel got the GQ game on lock. But you look especially stunning in that dress." Edward took the chance to look at the exquisite woman before him.

"Thank you. So, what do you do when you're not working?" she asked after Emile provided her drink.

"Normally, I'm just chillin' with friends, or I'm going to the gym. That's pretty much my life right now. I don't got nothin' else goin' on."

"Anybody special in your life?" Jackie asked.

She wants to know if I got a girlfriend or wife. First sign that she wants me.

Edward was no stranger to the game. He knew the routine, and he knew what the endgame was going to be. "Nah, I'm single right now. I really don't have time for a steady relationship. What about you?" he asked.

"I ain't into the whole monogamous relationship thing. I think it's overrated these days. Personally, I think if you vibe wit' someone, and there's a spark, you go for it, and let the chips fall where they may. You know what I'm sayin'?"

Upon hearing the reply, Emile, who had been pretending to wipe down the bar counter, looked up at Edward and gave him a little wink. It was a secret code that he had with Edward, and it told him that Edward pretty much had the night in the bag. He had seen Edward leave the bar with many women who had no thoughts of monogamous relationships either.

"So, did you drive here, or did you take a taxi?" Edward asked as he motioned to Emile for the tab.

Standing up, Jackie gave Edward a full view of her body, which was well-toned from her legs to her chest. She was a free spirit, for Edward could also see that she was not wearing a bra.

Approaching him, she whispered in his ear, "I walked here."

About an hour later, Edward and Jackie were at his front door. As soon as he turned the keys to his apartment, she closed the door behind her and kissed him ravenously. Kicking off her shoes as he worked the zipper of her dress down, before long she was facing him in all her naked glory.

Her exposed breasts, round and soft, were in his hands, and her aroused nipples told him that she was ready for him. Unbuttoning his shirt and undoing his pants, she grabbed his manhood and began stroking it vigorously as they continued kissing. Edward was not a two-minute man, but Jackie's sex appeal had him on the cusp of releasing early, and he could not go out that way.

Guiding her into his bedroom, he softly placed her in bed as he licked her petite body down, causing her to moan uncontrollably. Her moans increased as his hands rubbed her clitoris with regularity, and after a few minutes, his mouth decided to go downtown. After a while, it was her turn, and Edward's eyes closed as he clenched his fists to prevent himself from busting too soon as Jackie's mouth continued working its magic on his erected penis. Finally, he entered her and continued grinding in a rhythmic motion as her moans and his heavy panting filled the air.

"Fuck! Don't stop! Keep going!" Jackie yelled as Edward grinded in and out willingly with the desire to satisfy his female counterpart.

Then Jackie briefly surprised him by pushing him onto the bed and mounting him. For about five minutes, she was riding him with every intention to make him explode. But it was Jackie who ended up exploding unexpectedly, and Edward felt her climax repeatedly.

Finally, Edward could no longer hold onto his seed. He groaned loudly as he finished inside her. Sweating and breathing heavily, Jackie laid down on top of him. Two more hours passed, and Jackie slept blissfully in Edward's arms. But Edward barely slept, and after a while he shifted Jackie over to the other side of the bed.

Walking to the bathroom, he looked at himself in the mirror. Jackie was exactly what the doctor ordered after a stressful day at work, but Edward still felt uneasy. He hoped that he had not caused a feeling of infatuation to rise within Jackie because he did not wear a condom during sex, and he feared that she might one day be pregnant. He could not afford to become a father.

The last thing he wanted to do was grow roots in the city—not while he was working and trying to keep a low profile. Looking at his right forearm, he saw the tattoo of the past that he worked so hard to bury. Bearing blood drops, dollar bills, and the gun emblem of M.O.B., Edward once again saw Antonio Franks.

CHAPTER 2

ANTONIO'S INDUCTION INTO M.O.B.

JUNE 1994

At 4:32 a.m., Phillip Franks arrived at his small two-room tenement in Washington Heights, New York. Making sure he tiptoed quietly so he would not wake his wife, Isabelle, and his five-year old son, Antonio, Phillip made his way into the small kitchen and opened the fridge. Aside from a half-filled carton of milk, a jar of peanut butter, and some Wonder Bread, the fridge was virtually bare. But Phillip was starving, and he knew once his next payday hit, he would have the money to go shopping.

After taking out two slices of bread and spreading peanut butter on them, he made a sandwich with a cup of milk to wash it down. He was so busy chewing that he didn't realize Isabelle had woken up, stirred by her husband's movements in the kitchen. She walked over and stood by the doorway, watching him intently as he continued to eat his impromptu meal. Suddenly, as if on cue, he turned around and saw her staring right at him.

"Isabelle...my bad, I didn't mean to wake you," he explained with his mouth half full.

"I'm sure you didn't, especially after you come waltzing in at half past four in the morning. I didn't know the laundromats closed so late," she replied smartly.

Phillip worked as an attendant at the laundromat on 138th Street for ten-hour shifts. But Isabelle knew that was not all that Phillip did. The laundromat was a day job cover that concealed what his real occupation was. The Phillip that the Heights was familiar with ran the streets well after 11 p.m. as a member of the new Shower Posse gang, the organized Jamaican syndicate that ran Brooklyn, upper Manhattan, Bronx, and Queens.

They were heavily involved in drugs and arms smuggling, and with their empire, they had managed to bring in over $2 million worth of drugs and weaponry. Phillip was a member of the notorious gang, and not only was he trained in guns and weaponry, but he was also a very skilled martial artist, mastering the arts of Judo and Capoeira.

Phillip has had run-ins with the law in the past, but each time police questioned him over a crime, there was never sufficient evidence to put him away. When the drug empire hit a boom in the 1980s, Phillip found success in drug trafficking and made more money in six months dealing with the Posse than he had in one year working at the laundromat. It was also rumored that he fathered four other sons with three women.

But Phillip's lifestyle did not appeal to Isabelle, and she was at her wits end. Having birthed her first and only son—Antonio—in 1989, she gave Phillip the ultimatum: either walk away from the Posse to take care of his family and step children, or she would leave him and take Antonio with her. Phillip did not want his family to leave him, especially with his fortunes changing for the better.

Phillip was half Jamaican, half Sierra-Leonean, but he was born and raised in Jamaica. Isabelle was also Jamaican, but she was raised in Brooklyn, and when she first met Phillip, she had no idea that he was a member of the Shower Posse. Phillip was able to conceal his other life for years. Then the fancy gifts started coming, such as jewelry, new furniture, clothes, and even a nice, albeit small, apartment in the Heights, which was predominantly Dominican.

How could he afford all this? He couldn't have gotten all this money working at the laundromat.

It was only later that Isabelle realized how naïve she was after learning that Phillip was taken by police in connection to a gangland-style shooting that took place outside a Spanish club. Phillip had an alibi that proved he was not present on that day, and without evidence to hold him, he was released from custody and forced to explain his secret life to Isabelle.

There were days where Isabelle wanted to leave him, but they shared a son together, and she didn't want Antonio growing up in a broken home. Now Isabelle stared at her husband intently, waiting for an explanation.

"Isabelle, I was taking care of business, okay? It's no big deal."

"No big deal?" Isabelle asked. "Phil, I've asked you a thousand times to leave that life behind. You have too much to lose now. What if you get caught by the police again?"

"You think I don't cover my tracks when I roll wit' the crew? What kind of fool do you take me for?"

"You really don't want me to answer that question, do you? I mean what is it going to take for you to realize that being with the Posse can end up with deadly consequences? Do you want your son following in your footsteps to become some gang member?" she asked.

Phillip turned away from Isabelle and continued eating his sandwich. "No. I don't want that life for Antonio. But you gotta understand that I do what I do so that he doesn't have to live that life. Isabelle, it's a hard-knock life in these streets. It's usually every man for himself out there. I'm gonna teach Antonio how to be tough and how to survive out here, instead of depending on anyone to help him."

Isabelle shook her head, shocked at how stubborn Phillip was being. "Being tough isn't aligning yourself with drug kingpins and murderers just to create a rep. Being tough is standing up for yourself and doing right by your family. Or maybe you forgot?"

While the couple argued, Antonio heard the commotion. Getting out of bed, he walked past his parents in the kitchen, headed a small black, duffel bag that Phillip had brought with him. Curiosity got the better of him, and he went over to the bag, thinking that his father might have brought him some toys or some fun items to play with.

Reaching into the bag, he took out a very strange toy that he had never seen before. Sleek, black, with a chrome-brown handle, it was very shiny, and the boy began turning it over as his mind struggled to process what the new toy was. Phillip's eyes darted to the bag for all but a split second when his eyes widened in horror as he saw his five-year-old son handling a loaded MAC-10 handgun.

It didn't take long for Isabelle's eyes to follow Phillip's eyes over to Antonio. In horror, she saw her son playing with a gun.

"ANTONIO, NO!!" she yelled as she ran over to a stunned Antonio, who was clueless as to why his mother was in tears as she pulled the gun from his grasp.

"Antonio, listen to me. This is not a toy, okay?" Phillip warned his son, who had begun to cry after his mother pulled the weapon from him.

Hugging him tightly, Isabelle tried her best to comfort him. After three minutes of hugging and tucking him back into bed, she turned toward her husband, enraged. "That's it, Phillip. I can't live like this anymore. Because of you, my son could've shot himself," she choked, holding back tears.

"Isabelle, I'm sorry. I should've seen him heading for the bag. I was meaning to put it away somewhere, but..."

"But what? When were you going to put it somewhere? After he blew his brains out? How could you bring a gun into the house, knowing our son was here?"

"Look, it ain't even mine, okay? I'm holding it for Jasper till he gets out of custody. It's his piece." Phillip was trying to explain his case, but the damage was done.

"Phillip, I think I should go. I think I'm gonna take Antonio to my sister's house in Queens. I can't be around you if you think it's safe to bring guns around my son."

"C'mon, Isabelle, your sister? You know she can't stand my ass. Look, I should've put the gun somewhere else. I get that, but don't do me like that," Phillip begged as Isabelle walked back into their room, sobbing.

Phillip grabbed her arm in attempt to stop her from walking out on him, but she yanked away. "Let go of me, Phil. You've proven to me that you ain't ready to become a father, and you ain't ready to leave this street life behind. I'm not gonna sit here and wait for you to come to your senses and realize there's more at stake than your ego. If you need me, I'll be at Shirley's house by this afternoon. So, I think you better go now. Make yourself scarce until I leave. Then you can leave your guns anywhere you want."

Shaking his head, Phillip finished his meal, took his duffel bag, and made his way toward the door. A few seconds later, his beeper went off.

"I guess that's business calling, huh? Well, better go to your next appointment. You don't want to miss that," Isabelle said as Phillip made his way out the door.

In the morning, Isabelle would call the movers as she and Antonio left Phillip's apartment in Washington Heights to move to Shirley's house on Liberty Avenue in Queens, where Antonio would start his formal education. His street education would begin one day during his middle school years.

April 2002 | Eight years after Isabelle left Phillip, Antonio, who was a few months shy of his thirteenth birthday, was playing basketball at the local park with his classmates. His parents would divorce a few months after he left Washington Heights, which left Phillip the opportunity to see his son on the weekends.

His mother still did not feel comfortable trusting Phillip around her son, but she had no choice but to agree with the divorce proceedings that gave Phillip custody over the weekend. But on this particular weekend, Phillip called Isabelle and told her he had to cancel his weekend appointment with Antonio because he had "a few things to take care of." Isabelle rolled her eyes. Whenever Phillip reneged on an obligation, it meant that he was in trouble with the law, or his extracurricular activities had extended.

Antonio, however, was not too disappointed because he was looking for any excuse not to visit his father. It was not that Antonio did not love his father, but he had a secret feeling that his visits often put him in a bind. Phillip would rather be involved anywhere else than spending time with his son.

But when he was engaged, Phillip taught Antonio many skills early in life, including some martial arts tactics, how to take care of business in the streets, and how to handle a gun. He taught Antonio how to load and unload guns, and he taught him how to snap the barrel back into place tightly so the bullet would not stick whenever he shot the weapon. However, Phillip did not want his son holding or owning a gun under any circumstances until he was older and owned a gun license. Antonio never told Isabelle about Phillip teaching him how to use guns because he knew she would be mortified.

Attending I.S. 139 in Queens, Antonio hit his growth spurt a year later and had shot up to be just about six feet tall. He let his hair grow out so they could be dreaded by Aunt Shirley. They were short dreads, and Antonio was not too crazy about his hairstyle.

It's the year 2002, man. Why won't my mom let me braid my hair into some dope cornrows?

But his mother was on a tight budget and could barely afford to keep the bills paid with Shirley. She worked as a bank teller in Citi Bank, the largest bank in the borough, sometimes working long hours because one of her co-workers was recently laid off, and until they could find a replacement, she was pulling extra hours.

The park was about ten blocks from where Antonio lived, so he started walking home, sweat drenching his throwback Knicks jersey that he wore from playing in the park. Antonio was not the greatest ball player in the world, but with his height, kids never passed him up when they were picking players for pick-up games.

Antonio normally held his own. He was great around the rim, but his jump shot was weak. He had to work on his game. He was not very quick either. Two of his classmates, Jamal Samuels and Omar Keaton, would routinely blow past him during games for easy layups.

On his way back home, he saw two boys in a corner alley by a One Stop corner store. He had no idea what the boys were doing, but they were involved in a heated discussion. Both boys looked older than Antonio, and he remembered the words of his father. If you have no dealings with anyone, just keep walking.

But as he passed them, one of the boys called him.

"Aye yo, you wit' the dreads, come ova hea'."

Antonio's senses were in high alert at the time, and he was secretly shaken up. He had never seen the boy before, not even in school. He appeared to be about fifteen or sixteen years old and a few feet shorter than Antonio, but he was stocky. Antonio walked over to the alley where the boys were standing. Nervously looking around, he wanted to make sure the sidewalk was nearly empty, which in hindsight would be a negative factor should the boys decide to attack or mug him. But the boys had no such thoughts in mind.

"What's up, B? Yo, check it out. I gotta get a package dropped at this address. I would drop if off myself, but I gotta go to the opposite end of town, and I ain't gonna make both before it gets dark. Think you could drop this off fo' me?"

The boy held a medium sized package that resembled a white brick. Antonio knew right away what it was. Drugs.

Thoughts were reeling in his mind. What if I get caught? What if the buyer of this package sees me and decides to kill me? What if the package gets damaged?

While Antonio wallowed in his thoughts, the boy grew impatient. "C'mon, man, this ain't a math quiz. You down?"

Not wanting to give the boy any reason to start anything, Antonio reluctantly agreed to drop the package.

"Alright, so the address is 150 Highland Avenue, apartment 1C. A man named TK is supposed to meet you to pay for the package. Tell him Terrell sent you. The moment he pays you, meet me straight back here with the money, alright?"

"Yeah, I got you," Antonio said.

Terrell smiled, which relieved Antonio. "My boy. Alright put it in your bag so you can avoid Five-O," he instructed the young boy.

The other boy who was with Terrell lent his bike to Antonio so that he could arrive at the location to drop off the package. Luckily for Antonio, he was very coordinated, and riding bikes was natural to him. Arriving at the address in twenty minutes, he was surprised that the front apartment door was wide open. In a city that was full of gang activity, robbery, and burglaries, whoever owned this apartment had guts.

He soon found apartment 1C and knocked on the door, heart at his throat, praying that whoever opened would not shoot him dead. The door opened about two inches, and a voice bellowed from the inside: "Who the fuck are you? Never seen you round here before."

"Antonio. Um, Terrell sent me to deliver this to you," he whispered in hushed tones as he handed over the package. "TK, right?" he asked.

The man did not bother to answer him. A few seconds later, an envelope slipped out, filled with cash.

"Don't skim nothin' either. Make sure it gets to Tadarius straight up," he replied, and before Antonio could ask who Tadarius was, the man had already shut and locked the door.

Thrusting the envelope in his backpack, Antonio mounted the bike and made his way back to the alley where he met the boys. To his surprise, the alley was empty, and the sun had begun to dip in the sky. Antonio checked his watch. He should have been home hours ago. He knew he would get an earful from his mother and aunt, but he did not want to go home with the cash in his bag. Terrell insisted that he be handed the money to give to this Tadarius person, whoever he was.

After what seemed like thirty minutes of walking around and posting in the alleyway, Terrell came back alone, panting as if he had been running. "What up, man? You got the money?" he asked.

Antonio reached into his bag and handed the envelope to Terrell.

"Good lookin' out, B," he replied.

"No problem. TK said to make sure Tadarius got the money. Who the hell's Tadarius?" Antonio asked, stepping off the bike and handing it to Terrell.

"He's the big dawg—the OG who run shit around here. I'm wit' his crew. Ever heard of M.O.B.?"

"Nah, ain't never heard him, or them. Some kind of set or something?"

"We more than that, B. We family," Terrell replied, showing him the gang emblem tattooed on his forearm. "Yo, what we just did today, keep it on the DL, ight? Think you can meet me back here tomorrow?"

It may have been a rhetorical question, and Antonio could have refused the invitation, but the confirmation that Terrell was in a gang struck fear in Antonio. If he refused, he would probably end up on their hit list. Antonio knew better than to play around with his life.

"Yeah, I can meet you back here tomorrow."

"That's what's up. By the way, I be Terrell, but you already know that." Terrell was trying to diffuse the tension that he felt was rising within Antonio. "So, you like throwbacks, huh? I see you rockin' Sprewell. He nice, but I got me a Kobe throwback at da crib."

"Oh yeah, Kobe a beast. Him and Shaq are unstoppable. Think they'll three-peat this year?" Antonio asked.

"I don't know. They gotta get past Sacramento first. They got a helluva squad too," Terrell replied.

As the boys walked in the direction of Antonio's apartment, they began to develop a friendship and build camaraderie. Antonio would spend the next few weekends helping Terrell make drops and even sell on the other side of the alleyway.

One day, a kid with his hair half-braided and half-afro walked up to Antonio, who had pounds and grams of coke, weed, ecstasy, and other drugs in his possession. He even had a 9-millimeter gun that Terrell handed to him.

As soon as Antonio gave the price that Terrell set for the cost, the boy insisted that the price be dropped. Antonio refused. He did not want to cheat Terrell or Tadarius out of his money. Even though Antonio had never met the notorious gang leader, he was sure he would be punished if Tadarius did not get his quota for the products.

But the boy would not hear any of it. Without warning, he ripped one package of weed right out of Antonio's side pocket and broke out running along the sidewalk. Blaming himself for being wide open, Antonio furiously chased the boy across two blocks, unaware that he was being watched by a figure just a few blocks behind.

Antonio, filled with rage, surprisingly caught up with the boy as he entered under a bridge overpass. All he could think about was his life at that moment. If Antonio did not sell all his products, and if any of them were stolen, his own life would be at risk. He could not have that hanging over his head. He tackled the boy from behind and turned him around to demand back the package he stole. But to his surprise, the boy laughed.

"The fuck's so funny? Gimme the damn package!" Antonio demanded, drawing out his gun.

Suddenly, people started to appear out the shadows of the bridge overpass. Young men and women, wearing black and white throwback jerseys, shirts, and the same sneakers were everywhere. Fear gripped Antonio. The boy had purposely led him to a trap, and now he was outnumbered. Sure, he had a weapon, but he counted more than twenty people that had just appeared before him. His gun did not have that many bullets, and he knew he was in trouble.

Suddenly, a voice that Antonio recognized filled the entire overpass. "What'd I tell you, T? I told you my boy was down," Terrell piped excitedly, appearing from the opposite end of the bridge.

"Yeah, you weren't lyin' Terrell. Looks like we got a keeper."

The person who responded stepped under the light of the overpass so that Antonio could have a good look at him. With his arms and chest tatted, wearing a white tank top with gold chains around his neck, which gave him an aura of superiority, Antonio knew that he was finally facing Tadarius, the gang leader, at last.

"That was a test of loyalty right there, son, and you passed it. You was willing to put it down for the cause. I wish we had ten more like you, kid. Welcome to M.O.B."

CHAPTER 3

LOREE'S REBELLION AND DEMISE

His head beading with sweat and eyes squinting, Antonio gritted his teeth as the needle protruded into his skin. It had been a few months since his induction into M.O.B., and he was finally getting the gang emblem tatted on his forearm. Terrell, who accompanied him to the tattoo parlor, laughed when he saw Antonio grunt in pain. As hard as Antonio tried to conceal his pain, he could not hide the feeling every time the needle punctured his skin.

It was his first tattoo, which was being completed by Trez, a well-known tattoo artist and an informant to M.O.B. He was responsible for the various tattoos worn by Tadarius, and he had tatted each member of M.O.B. with their emblem, which was a picture of guns pointing at each with drops of blood and dollar bills.

Antonio, just a few weeks removed from his thirteenth birthday, was the youngest to get a tattoo, and he was sure once his mother noticed it, she wouldn't approve, and an argument would follow as soon as she glimpsed the artwork. But it was a sign of acceptance, a rite of passage into one of the most feared organizations in Queens. M.O.B. was far removed from the typical gang depictions that were normally portrayed on television or seen through people's perceptions of gangs.

Tadarius, realizing that his gang had kids who were under eighteen years of age, allowed them to go to school and live their lives just like anybody else. In fact, he insisted that they go to school because he had a vision of M.O.B. becoming an enterprise one day. In order to run an enterprise, he needed people with intelligence, accountants who knew how to manage money, and people who could forecast the financial climate of New York, New Jersey, Pennsylvania, and most of the tri-state area. He needed visionaries with him that would one day carry out his plan.

More importantly, Tadarius did not want to draw any negative attention to his gang, which was another reason why he wanted his underage members to go to school. If they constantly missed school, he knew the school would do background checks on them. Then they would notify the parents, and the breadcrumbs would lead back to him. He did not need any negative exposure to rattle his plans. Tadarius had plenty of members that were over eighteen, and those people had made a decision to forego college and run the streets to earn the family money, giving Tadarius a lion share of the proceeds.

After a few weeks of being a member of M.O.B., Antonio also realized that Tadarius had members all over New York, not just Queens. He had connections in Brooklyn, Bronx, Staten Island, and even in New Jersey. Those members were so covert that at one glance, one would have never guessed that they were members of M.O.B. When Tadarius and David were released from juvenile hall a few years earlier, they had spent the year recruiting members and had inducted well over sixty.

Tadarius sold them on the dream and a vision of M.O.B. being a business empire and booming with worth over millions of dollars. He realized what few others realized—that there was a demand for recreational drugs, especially in New York.

Preferences varied from depressants to cocaine, to weed, heroin, and other drugs. Tadarius had a connect bring the product from overseas, and he would pay the supplier while he, in turn, would resale the product and recoup the money from the sales. People always had a vice, and it was easy to earn money off them. That was the way Tadarius saw it.

While M.O.B. had grown in recruitment over the last year, Antonio made it a priority to acclimate himself with the local members of the gang. There was Terrell Washington, the boy who had recruited Antonio. He was only two years older than Antonio, and he attended Richmond Hill High School as sophomore, although he was in danger of being retained because he'd missed so many days of class, and it threatened to hold him back a grade.

But Terrell hated school and saw a future with M.O.B. He was one of the members that had completely bought into the vision that Tadarius shared with them, and it was not just a pit stop for him. Tadarius, although he loved Terrell's dedication, was always perturbed, however, upon finding out that Terrell often cut classes. But to Terrell, it did not matter. His father had passed, and he was raised by a single mother.

To complicate matters, Terrell was one of six children as well as the baby of the family, but the mother closed her eyes to all of her youngest son's wrongdoing and kept a close eye on her oldest sons and daughters. M.O.B. provided Terrell an escape from the crowded home environment and a chance to learn street economics under Tadarius.

There was Greg Dawkins, better known as G-Dawg, who was one of the older members of the gang. He was the one who pretended to be the druggie who stole the dime bag from Antonio during the initiation. He was the comic relief of the group.

Then there was Malik Jones, a large heavy-set man, who worked at various clubs as a bouncer. Whenever M.O.B. had closed-door meetings in apartment buildings and isolated locations, it was Malik's job to stand guard outside the door and alert the group of law enforcement. He also knew some of Tadarius's overseas contacts after having traveled to different countries during his earlier tenure as a club bouncer.

There was Terrance, who was the human map. He knew all the busy roadways in New York. He knew which block was hot, and he knew when the police were on the prowl. He was the strategist of the group, and he was also very skilled in gun play.

There was Xavier Furrows, the boy who provided Antonio his bike to make the run the very first day that Antonio met Terrell. He was four years older than Antonio and had dropped out of high school a few months earlier. His role was more mobile than the other members, as he would ride throughout town distributing and selling to his old neighborhood in South Jamaica as well as Queensbridge. He was planning on saving his portion of money to buy a new motorcycle.

There was Quincy Harvey, a boy just two months removed from prison, who also had connections in Staten Island and Long Island.

Then among other notable boys, there was David Anderson. As the second leader of M.O.B., he was the reinforcement within the gang. Anyone who stepped up against Tadarius would deal with him. David was large in stature as well, except that he was not burly like Malik, but he was muscular. He loved working out, and he had a special talent for football. He was a quarterback and could throw the football at great distances.

Whenever the crew was finished selling, some members would catch NFL football games on TV at David's apartment. David, who was raised by his grandmother, had a subtle streak of sensitivity that had clouded his judgment that would routinely annoy everyone in the group.

Then there was Tadarius, the top alpha leader of M.O.B. What started out as a vision for the young convict started to become a reality once he got in contact with his connects and began the brainchild that would become M.O.B. Tadarius was a fearless, ruthless leader, and although at times he had a laid-back demeanor, he was also known for becoming enraged when his plans fell through.

Tadarius was a no-nonsense person when it came to his supplies and his money. Anyone who threatened his long-term vision of turning M.O.B. into an empire was in immediate danger and in his eyes, should be eliminated. So far, Tadarius had not gotten on Antonio for anything, and the young boy wanted to keep it that way.

Terrell told Antonio the story of the last guy who got on Tadarius's bad side, and as Terrell often put it, "He took care of him." Antonio did not want to know what became of that guy, and he felt the less he knew, the better. If he followed Tadarius, then he knew he had to watch his manners and his tone around him.

Another aspect of Tadarius that made him different from other set leaders was his recruitment of women into the gang. There were young women, high school girls, and college girls who were apparently part of the gang that Antonio observed. There was Zeena Martin, a female just a couple of days over eighteen years old, who was loud and outspoken. She was the first to welcome Antonio into the gang although he would hardly call it a welcome.

"So, I see Tadarius is recruiting out the crib again," she had replied when introduced to Antonio.

But he did not take it as a dig. He only laughed. She was also a comic relief type of person.

Then there was 23-year-old Shaquana, who moonlighted as an exotic dancer in the Apple Kim's Gentlemen's Club in Queens. She was tall herself but beautiful. She often referred to herself as the Amazon because she felt she was a warrior in her own right. Frequently, she entertained the male members of M.O.B. with her hypnotizing hip gyrations, which would cause the men to throw dollar bills her way.

Then there was Fatima, a girl whom Antonio was familiar with personally because she lived in the same apartment building where he lived with his aunt and mother. She was more laid back, so much that she was considered one of the guys, and she could smoke a pound with the best of them. Antonio often found himself questioning if Fatima was really a girl because she had male tendencies.

There were Sophia, DeWanda, LaToya, CiCi, Monica, and Simone, who were not actually gangbangers, but they were known as correspondents. They covered for the gang and provided alibis for the gang in case an operation went haywire and law enforcement was on their tails. They were also street prostitutes who would gladly get down and dirty to do what they had to do to bring more revenue for themselves and for Tadarius.

But out of all those women, one of them stood out to Antonio. She was five foot seven, with soft brown skin, nice long legs, full lips, and jet-black hair that she combed to the side. She was the most stylish out of all the call girls in the gang and was notoriously the most promiscuous out of them all.

Her name was Loree McAfee. The rumor was that Loree, although she was underage at the time Antonio was added to the group, had slept with over fifteen of the gang members. She loved playing innocent even though Antonio observed that she was far from that. Although she was a self-proclaimed nymphomaniac, she seemed to be especially attached to David.

The two struck up a conversation one day, and from that day forward, they became inseparable. Loree and David would isolate themselves from gang activity frequently, going out on dates and watching drive in movies while fogging up David's car windows during those dates.

Normally, Tadarius did not mind David getting involved with other girls, but this one was different. Loree was outspoken and just as brash as he was, and she was starting to convince David to disassociate himself from M.O.B. and focus on his own life. That conversation vexed Tadarius to no end.

He hated when anyone interfered with his personal affairs, and at that moment, Loree made herself a target. M.O.B. could survive a few members leaving the family. It happened regularly. But David was Tadarius's right-hand man, and losing him could leave M.O.B. dangerously exposed to other rival gang attacks or law enforcement. Tadarius was determined not to let the situation arrive to that point.

One trait that Antonio found comical about Loree was how she continued to portray that innocent "girl next door" profile that she had been playing for so long. Unlike the other girls who were motherless or fatherless, she had both parents in the household, and she had a little sister.

At times, Antonio had seen Loree walk into the Green Acres Mall and other locations with her sister, and sometimes they would be accompanied by another girl, Shania Hillman, who was reportedly the daughter of some pastor in town. Antonio gathered as much intel about Loree, but he refused to dive deeper because he felt a certain way about church folk.

He couldn't put his finger on it, but he could not stand how fake they were, going to worship on Sunday when most of the same people would be in a club or other places during the week. In his mind, God did not really exist for men to see, and if He did, there would be no way the world would be filled with this level of violence.

What kind of God allowed families to be separated or innocent men and women to be killed in the streets? What kind of God kept men and women bound in their drug addictions? Going to church to worship a God that allowed all types of calamity in the world was a waste of time to him.

Loree did a great job of masking whom she really was—a freak who loved sex and was known to be an instigator of major drama.

Antonio had had only one encounter with Loree, which he reflected on while Trez put the finishing touches on his tattoo. A few days earlier, he, Simone, CiCi, and Terrell were hanging out in one of Tadarius's apartments at the corner of 101 Avenue and South Ozone Street. It was a rest day for the crew, and Tadarius and David had gone out of town to meet with a connect for shipment of new substances. Tadarius had various apartments scattered in Queens, where some were used as safe houses, and others were just hangout spots. At times, members would crash in one of Tadarius's apartments whenever they needed to rest or relax and have a smoke session.

Antonio's hair had grown an extra inch, and CiCi had offered to do his cornrows for him. Sitting on the floor between CiCi's legs and playing video games with Terrell, Antonio's hair was carefully being twisted and styled into neat cornrows.

A joint was being passed around the room, and Antonio had it in his hand. Taking a deep drag, he closed his eyes as he relaxed. It helped with his anxiety which, at times, could lead into full blown panic attacks. Luckily, he had not experienced such an episode in years.

Terrell and Antonio were playing Grand Theft Auto: Vice City on PlayStation 2, and while the group relaxed, they heard a sharp knock on the door. At first Antonio thought that Tadarius and David had returned from their business dealing. He looked around to make sure the room was clean. Tadarius did not tolerate any type of messes in any of his apartments. But Simone answered the door, and in walked Loree.

"Yo, I need to talk to David. Is he hea'?" she asked.

"Um, excuse you. You don't just come by asking for David. David will call you when he good and ready," Simone replied sharply.

Early on, Simone never trusted Loree, and she always felt that Loree was doing everything in her power to pry David away from M.O.B.

"Bitch, please. He waitin' on me, okay, boo? So, if you can please move yo' scary lookin' ass out my way, I'll wait for him."

Loree walked in, and Antonio and Terrell both instantly looked her way. "Can we help you?" Terrell asked, turning back to the game.

"Nah, I'm waiting for David. You can go about your business, lackey."

Upon hearing that, Terrell paused the game and looked her up and down. "Who you callin' a lackey?" he asked.

"Umm, you. Both of you, especially 'ole boy there gettin' his hair rebraided. Who you tryin' to be, Tadarius Jr.?"

"Hold up, you think you could just push up in here talkin' shit about boss man like that?"

"Look, ya could keep suckin' his dick if you want, but trust me, ya gon' find out the hard way that Tadarius ain't shit."

"You talk a lot of shit for a girl who be smokin' crackheads' dicks until she pass out," Antonio joked, causing everyone in the room to burst into laughter.

"How old is you again? Twelve? I got shoes older than you, boy," Loree bit back.

"I bet you do, wit' yo' outta date ass. I bet you got some Doc Martens in yo' closet somewhere," Antonio cracked.

Terrell and the girls laughed.

"Whatever. Terrell, if you see David, let him know I was lookin' for him." Loree left, closing the door behind her.

"Yo, what's up wit' that girl, man?" Antonio asked Terrell.

"I don't know all the facts, but from what I heard, Tadarius ain't feelin' Loree because she ain't givin' him no play, and David's been hittin' that for a minute. Word is, that's causin' some tension in the fam. Homeboy ain't been on the block in a minute, and wit' business slowin' down, boss man startin' to get tight. She better chill talkin' all mafioso and shit, or she gon' end up like that fool Theo."

Antonio sat up straight, having previously slouched his head. "Who's Theo?" he asked.

"Some fool who used to be cool wit' T. He ain't eva' been part of the fam, but he was our informant. Used to look out whenever we had to handle business and used to count the money. But one day, T found out that Theo was stealin' money from him. His ass didn't get away for long. Boss confronted the bastard and sliced him up, ole school boxcutter style. He ain't killed him right away. He let Theo out, but I don't think he made it back home. News reported him missing a few days later. Word on the street is that he bled out, and the homies threw his ass in the Hudson River. But you ain't heard it from me."

Antonio sat back without so much as a reply, and even while he sat there, the first seeds of doubt began to enter his mind. What had he gotten himself into? All members of M.O.B. were armed with some type of firearm, but they were only to use it when absolutely necessary, and Tadarius made it clear he did not want any street activity to be traced back to him.

But if Tadarius had truly murdered Theo and dumped his body in the river, would he be crazy enough to do away with anyone that disagreed with him? It just did not seem like Tadarius.

Little did Antonio know how prophetic Terrell had been and that one year later, Loree's lifeless body would be found on an isolated road, struck by two bullets, and the circumstances that surrounded Loree's death would be nothing short of a nightmare for Antonio.

CHAPTER 4

ANTONIO'S BREAKING POINT

"You're a real hero, son. What you did back there was pretty heroic. You're proof that real heroes don't wear capes. They do the right thing."

As he prepared to go to work a few days later, Edward adjusted his tie in front of his vanity mirror. It had been a few days since his one-night stand with Jackie, and although the night had been pleasurable, he did not see a future with her. His decision to end their brief relationship had nothing to do with her performance in bed, which he enjoyed thoroughly.

But it was their compatibility level. Edward just did not see eye to eye with Jackie at all. Even though it made him highly selective, there were a few traits about her that he found unattractive, including how possessive she was in bed. She had the audacity to tell Edward how she wanted to receive him, and she was adamant in having the pleasure she thought she was overdue for, but it rubbed Edward the wrong way because she came off as controlling. Edward liked being in control.

Another factor that was a little bit obscene was Jackie's fascination in anal play while having sex. At one point in bed, Jackie had Edward turn around, and while he laid there on his stomach, stark naked with his back and bottom exposed, she went underway with the fellatio play, and it turned Edward off almost immediately.

Overall, Jackie was outgoing and adventurous, but Edward just did not envision a future with her and figured that she would be better off with a man who shared her level of crazy.

Driving to work, he took the bridge that connected the Upper East Side to the route downtown, and he maneuvered his way around traffic.

"The family will always remember what you did for them."

The quotes from Edward's past replayed like a broken record, and if there was any memory that he would love to eradicate, it would be the memory of being a hero the day he testified for David Anderson in court while also betraying M.O.B. He helped exonerate an innocent man, but he did so at a terrible price.

A few days later after the trial, Edward found out that Tadarius and Terrell were apprehended following a shootout with police. Yet, at the time, Edward still did not feel safe because he knew Tadarius had contacts all over New York, and there was no doubt that the gang leader would seek revenge on him. This caused one of many panic attacks back in the day.

Even after going through the court system to change his name and starting over in a new school amidst different surroundings, Edward still never felt completely safe. Tadarius had operatives in all counties, and it would not be long until they found him and made him pay for betraying the family.

With the help of the lawyers and other people in the media, Edward was able to leave no trail behind for anyone to follow him, but he still could not shake off the feeling that he was always being watched and followed. He remembered immediately after giving his testimony how he asked to be unidentified, and he wanted to drop the hero moniker. Edward did not want to hear the term "hero."

What Edward discovered throughout his life was that heroes normally never lived long. "Hero" was a word that was synonymous with the word "martyr." Edward did not want to be a hero. Despite their accomplishments, their debt to society and the inspiration to others, none of those accolades meant a long and fruitful life by any stretch of the mind.

No, Edward was not focused on being a hero. He was focused on using the law to prevent anyone from experiencing the same trauma he went through at a young age. The world did not stop for heroes. There were still people that lived a practical life, and Edward would not trade it for anything else.

As he arrived at the firm, he prepared for a staff meeting with the lawyers. Then he had a desk full of cases to work on afterwards. As he began work, his mind wandered back to the time his life took a turn, where he thought his life would come to an end, and severing ties with one of New York's dangerous gangs. Everything changed in the year 2003.

September 2003 | It had been about a year since Antonio had joined M.O.B., and as the months passed by, he discovered that the rift between Tadarius and David had continued to grow. While Antonio, Terrell, Xavier, and other members of the family still ran packages and sold on the streets, it was hard not to see the relationship that Tadarius had with David had taken a turn for the worst. David was spending less time in M.O.B. and more time in school and football, which enraged Tadarius.

The gang leader knew that David had been exclusively dating Loree, and Loree had been doing quite a bit of talking. If anyone had the ability to bring down the drug empire that Tadarius built, it was Loree. She was slowly but surely influencing David away from Tadarius and the other members of M.O.B.

With David seemingly out of the picture, that left his position open, and Antonio was one of the boys that Tadarius looked at as David's replacement within M.O.B. He had grown a couple of inches taller, and he now attended Richmond Hill High School, where most of the other members of the street family went.

One day in September, Antonio and Terrell were out on the block near 141st and Lefferts Boulevard. Sales had begun to slow down as the sun began setting. Antonio knew police would be roaming the streets, and the sooner they abandoned the spot, the better. However, there was a different vibe that day, but Antonio could not put his finger on it.

It started when Terrance pulled up next to Terrell and Antonio at their spot. "Yo, boss man got work for ya'll. Let's go," he said, gesturing to the car.

Terrell and Antonio hopped in the back seat. "Yo, what work does T got for us?" Antonio asked.

"You know how we do, Tone. We don't talk about shit out in the open. You know how we do," Terrance repeated.

Antonio instantly kept his mouth shut. Out of all the members of the gang, with tattoos lining up his neck and his chest, Terrance was the most ruthless and one of the more feared members of M.O.B. If there was any enforcer that would be able to take over for David, it was Terrance.

They arrived at a familiar haunt, an old apartment building that was abandoned. Tadarius was not present, and rumor was that he was dealing with his Mexican connect in order to procure more drug supply, so Terrance was temporarily in charge, revealing that he had spoken with Tadarius before he left, and the boss had given him specific orders for a hit that he wanted carried out by Terrell and Antonio. Terrance reached into his back pocket and pulled out two guns and handed one to Terrell and the other to Antonio.

With his heart pounding, Antonio looked at the small firearm and checked the barrel. It was fully loaded, but Antonio was confused. Who were they going after?

"Ight, so check it. David's bitch opened her mouth too damn much, and Tadarius wants us to blast her."

What?

Antonio initially played off his initial shock, but he was starting to sweat profusely and often. It was well documented that Tadarius hated Loree, but what could she have done that would warrant her death?

But Antonio did not dare question Terrance or anyone else. He was a soldier that represented the family. He had to take care of business without hesitation or remorse.

"Right now, she's right outside that Wendy's on 158th and Parsons with some other chicks. Ya'll are gonna get her in the car, drive her someplace out on Brewer Road, and once ya get there, pow!" Terrance poorly imitated the sound of a gun going off while Terrell snickered.

Antonio remained silent although it was not uncommon of Antonio to carry a gun because whenever he was out in the streets, he needed to defend himself if he encountered anyone out of pocket or any strange characters. But this was a different situation. Now he was being asked to murder someone.

Sensing the doubt in his resolve, Terrance asked, "What up, Tone? You still down? You look like you bout to wet yourself."

"Nah, leave my nigga alone, T. He always got that constipated look on his face. We got you, B," Terrell replied, covering for Antonio.

"Ight, take the keys, and get to Hillside. Make sure she gets her ass in the car. Don't let that ho' get away," Terrance said, handing Terrell the keys.

Before long, Terrell and Antonio were in the car and on their way to get Loree. During the whole ride, Antonio started questioning his commitment to M.O.B.

I joined this set to make money sellin' a little and get my rep up, not to commit murder. This ain't me. I can't do this. What happens if we get caught by the police? How long am I gon' be locked up?

"What's up wit' you, Tone?" Terrell asked, cutting through the awkward silence. "You ain't scared, right?"

"Nah, I ain't scared, dawg. But why we gotta blast her though?" he asked.

"Shit, that's the way it is now. T's tryin' to build something out hea' and if anyone's threatening that, they gotta go," Terrell replied.

Antonio looked out the window at all the kids that were playing in the park without a care in the world, playing in the playground while the older kids were playing basketball or handball. At that very moment, Antonio felt trapped by the organization that he once revered and had ambitions of climbing up through its ranks. He had to find a way out of this at once.

"There she go," Terrell remarked, as they both saw Loree hanging out with two of her friends from school.

After parking in an illegal zone, they walked out of the car and made a beeline toward Loree. There were other kids in the restaurant, and one of the kids called out to Antonio, but at that moment, he didn't pay attention as he approached Loree.

When she saw the two boys approaching her, Loree rolled her eyes. "What ya want?" she snapped rudely.

Terrell didn't plan to beat around the bush or to conceal his intentions of being there. "Tadarius wants to meet wit' you somewhere, so get in the car," he replied.

"What? Get outta here! Fuck you and that bitch ass nigga Tadarius. He can kiss my ass!" Loree answered defiantly.

Antonio and Terrell both looked at each other and knew what they had to do next. When negotiation failed, they had to deploy a fear tactic. Both boys raised their shirts, revealing their guns as her friends shrieked in fear and left the area. Loree's eyes widened in shock as she saw that both boys were strapped.

"I ain't gon' say it again, Loree. Get yo' ass in the car," Terrell repeated.

Loree, still defiant as ever, rolled her eyes, but seeing that the boys were armed, she walked to the car. Never in her wildest imagination did she ever think the boys would dare harm her in public, and if all they wanted to do was to get her to Tadarius, they would not kill her.

If Tadarius was still upset about what she had done to his third leg while she was applying oral sex to him on a back end of some ridiculous bet, he needed to get over it and let it go.

"Where ya takin' me?" Loree asked, clearly irritated but clearly apprehensive.

"None of yo' got-damn business—that's where. Just sit there, and shut up." Terrell replied.

Loree turned to Antonio, who sat in the passenger seat next to Terrell. "I asked, where were ya takin' me?" she asked.

"I don't know, ight?" he answered.

"Ya two just don't get it. Do you? Why you lettin' yourselves be used by Tadarius? He don't give a damn about ya'll."

"You should've never said nothin. Shoulda' kept yo' mouth shut," Terrell replied.

As they drove down the busy expressway, Antonio felt his stomach churning, not from motion sickness, but from anxiety.

What the hell am I doing in this car? Why am I helping this fool commit murder? I might be a lot of things and might have made plenty of stupid decisions, but there has to be a line drawn somewhere.

Shaking his head, Antonio said, "Yo, let me out, man."

Terrell stared at Antonio incredulously. "What you say?" he asked.

"I said, let me the fuck out, nigga. I ain't stutter."

Terrell sharply turned a corner on 158th Street, three miles off Guy R. Brewer Road, and doubled parked next to a blue Sedan. "Where the hell you think you goin'?" he asked.

Antonio was not even sure where he was going. But he knew he was not going to prison. It would break the hearts of his mother and aunt, who were already questioning his activities after school and were concerned about his dress code, braided hairstyle, and his tattoos. Isabelle always thought that her son was going through a phase of teen angst and figured, at some point, he would outgrow it, but she had no idea that he was part of one of the largest gangs in the borough.

Antonio knew that to survive in the streets, he had to be tough and relentless, but this was where he drew the line. "Just let me out, man. I'm done wit' this shit," he replied.

"Nah, this shit ain't done wit' you. We got a job to do, so you betta' man up, and stop actin' like a pussy."

"Oh, I'm the pussy now?" Antonio asked sarcastically. "Yo, I ain't down wit' this, man. Unlock the door!"

At that moment Terrell reached for his side to pull out his gun, but Antonio anticipated the move and pulled his own weapon out with the equal amount of dexterity.

Loree held her breath in the backseat as both boys had their weapons pointed at each other. Antonio looked down the barrel of the gun pointed at his head and knew that at any moment Terrell could pull the trigger and blow his brains out in the car. But Antonio no longer cared. M.O.B. was clearly not the move for him, and he wanted no parts of it.

"I'm just as fast as you, homie. You wanna kill me? Go ahead. Watch them put yo' ass in county for life," Antonio said, hoping he could scare Terrell by having him face the prospect of going to prison for murder.

Fortunately, his gamble paid off. Unlocking the door, Terrell said, "Whatever, man. Get yo' bitch ass outta here. You was neva' down wit' the crew no ways."

Without another word, Antonio opened the door and exited but not before he glimpsed the back window and saw the look of horror and betrayal on Loree's eyes, a look that might have said, "Why did you leave me back here? You could have gotten me out, but you left me wit' this gangbanger."

Terrell then proceeded to punch the accelerator and speed away, leaving tire tracks on the asphalt.

Antonio's heart sank because he had the feeling that it was going to be the last time that he saw Loree McAfee alive. But at that moment, he had to save himself. He turned his back on the M.O.B. family, which was a grave mistake, and he knew that after Terrell killed Loree, he would be next on their list. He had to get back home quickly and preserve his family.

Taking a shortcut to return to his apartment building, he rushed in quickly and locked the door behind him. Isabelle and Shirley were having dinner in the kitchen when Antonio quickly passed them and headed to his room, locking the door.

"What's wrong with Antonio?" Shirley asked as Isabelle shrugged her shoulders and headed to the room.

"Antonio, what's going on? Is everything okay?" she asked.

"Yeah, Mom, everything's okay. Just had a bad day. That's all. I don't wanna talk about it right now."

Figuring that Antonio needed time, Isabelle left as Antonio stretched over his bed.

An innocent girl was going to get murdered, and he was sitting in his room doing nothing. He had to call the police and tip them off. But when he went to grab the receiver, he paused.

No, I can't call the cops. If I do, then they'll know it was me that snitched, and I'm as good as dead. Not only me but my family will probably get killed too.

Antonio recalled a critical warning issued by Tadarius to his clique one night. "You better not open your mouth and snitch on the family because if you do, you best guarantee I'm going to come after ya'll and put your fam on notice too."

It was virtually a threat that Tadarius would harm the informant and their families if they so much as peeped a word about M.O.B. activities. Taking the gun out of his pocket, Antonio looked it over, tracing his finger along the copper handle.

I ain't no killer. This doesn't even belong in my hands. Gotta get rid of this.

Antonio wrapped the gun in an old T-shirt, threw it in his wastebasket, and took the wastebasket to the dumpster behind the building.

Returning to his room, Antonio shut the door behind him. He was going to have to find an alternative route to get to school. He had to find a way to avoid Terrell and other members who went to Richmond Hill High School because if any of them saw him, word would get back to Tadarius, and he was going to do great harm to him.

CHAPTER 5

THE STAR WITNESS

The very next morning, the tragic story hit the news. A young woman was found on the side of a road bleeding to death from two gunshot wounds, and her life was hanging in the balance. Before the news anchorwoman provided any information, Antonio knew the woman was Loree McAfee.

Terrell completed the execution, and there was no doubt that he would alert Tadarius about Antonio's betrayal, and he would be their next target.

A wave of nausea overcame Antonio. He rushed to the bathroom and opened the toilet, where he retched and threw up for about three minutes before slumping to the side of the toilet. Sweating profusely, he flushed the toilet and ran to the sink and washed his face with cold water.

Upon hearing the retching noises, his aunt Shirley rushed to the bathroom. "Antonio, what's wrong? You sick?" she asked. Isabelle had left for work an hour before Antonio woke up, and Shirley did not have to work for another two hours.

"Aunt Shirley, I really messed up this time," Antonio replied, and while he worked his way to calm his heart through the anxiety attack, he revealed to Shirley his involvement in M.O.B., the year he spent dropping and delivering drugs to various streets around Queens, and his involvement in the kidnapping of Loree. He did not murder her, but he also did not prevent the inevitable.

Antonio knew Shirley would be all ears if he confessed, and sure enough, she listened to every word he Antonio explained to her.

After Antonio confessed, she shook her head. "Antonio, I'm happy you came to me to tell me the truth. But your behavior was foolish. How could you let yourself get caught up in all this?"

"I don't know, Aunt Shirley." Antonio replied. "At first, it was just doing jobs here and there and hanging out wit' people that I was cool with. I ain't eva think it was gonna get this far. Now Tadarius is gonna come after me. I know it."

"Listen, Antonio, you need to go to the police with this..." Shirley began, but Antonio shut her down immediately.

"Hell no. I'm not going to the police for nothing. Don't you know what happens out here if you snitch on someone as dangerous as Tadarius?"

"It can't be any worse than anyone identifying you in the scene of the crime. You got to go to the authorities with this, Antonio. Maybe you can get justice for that young woman."

"Aunt Shirley, I can't go to school today. I know Tadarius is gonna have his underclass crew in there lookin' for me, and I can't chance it. Can I stay home?" he asked.

Shirley lightly ran her hand through Antonio's braids, a look of deep sympathy in her face. "Okay, nephew. You can stay home today, but at some point, you're going to have to go back to school, at least until I can talk to your father and your uncle Keyshawn. I will ask if you can stay at his apartment in Brooklyn. You know, your younger half-brothers, Tony, Bruno, Steven, and Josh live there too. They go to a private school up there."

"Oh yeah, I remember Mom telling me that. She don't like to talk about my brothers a whole lot though."

Shirley rolled her eyes. "Who can blame her? Your father being who he was, sleeping around when he was younger. When she sees them, she's reminded of his infidelity most of the time. But they're still family, and we need to keep you safe."

"True, but I don't wanna put Uncle Keyshawn or my brothers in danger."

"Oh, trust me, them boys ain't gonna come nowhere near Keyshawn or Phillip. They ran the same circles, and they know how the streets work. But you must tell your father about your situation."

Antonio hung his head but agreed to tell his father. Deciding to stay home from school, Antonio called his father and reluctantly confessed his ordeal with M.O.B. Phillip was disappointed when he found out that his son had followed his footsteps and joined a street gang, but he instructed Antonio to lay low and not draw attention to himself until the police arrested Tadarius. Phillip knew if the victim died, a full investigation would be launched, and the evidence would lead back to Tadarius.

Phillip also lauded his son on his instinct in exiting the car because that would remove him from suspicion. As the day wore on, the local news revealed that Loree was in critical condition, and the family was bracing for the worst. For two days, Antonio lounged around the apartment, staying in, reading, or watching TV. When Isabelle had arrived home from work on the first night, they did not tell her that Antonio elected to stay home from school, and they did not reveal his activity with M.O.B.

But on the third day, which happened to be on a Friday, Antonio wore a durag to cover his braids, and he wore a black baseball cap with the brim covering his eyes. Wearing an old Yankees jersey over his shorts, he grabbed his book bag and took a longer route to get to school. He figured that if he took the back roads, he would not be spotted by anyone that knew Tadarius. For the first half of the day, everything went according to plan, aside from him having another panic attack that occurred while he was in class, and he had to immediately rush to the bathroom.

When school was over, Antonio snuck out through the back door, hoping to get home without harm, but those hopes were quickly dashed when he rounded the corner. To his horror, he saw a familiar boy riding a bike, holding a package in his hand.

Without warning, Antonio turned around and started to back away slowly to go to a nearby corner store until Xavier was out of sight, but he soon found out very quickly that Xavier was not the one to watch for.

Without warning, Antonio was struck in the back of his head by Malik's closed fist. Seeing stars, Antonio dropped to the ground.

"Grab that mark-ass nigga!" he heard a voice say.

Antonio's vision blurred from the blow to the back of his head, but he was not too groggy to realize that the voice came from Terrance.

Antonio felt two hands grab him and drag him over to South Ozone Park, just a block away. With every bit of strength that he had, Antonio struggled to fight his way out of their grasp, but another punch to the gut took the wind out of him, and he fell to the ground, gasping for air.

The park was empty as kids were still going home from school, but Tadarius knew it was the opportune time to give Antonio an ultimatum. With Malik and Terrance holding both of Antonio's arms, Tadarius walked over to Antonio and began punching him violently in the stomach, head, and chest.

After three minutes, Antonio, who was spitting blood from cuts in his mouth, was finally released. He dropped to the ground in intense pain and dizziness. Thankfully, he landed on the grass instead of the asphalt. The right side of his face swelled up from Tadarius's blows, and he had welts on his cheeks and bruises to his abdomen.

Out of the corner of his eye, Antonio saw Tadarius approaching him again, and he heard the unmistakable sound of bullets being loaded into a barrel. He heard the click as the barrel closed. Then Antonio closed his eyes.

This is it. I'm about to die here like a dog. No way out. Father, please forgive me for all the stupid shit I've done.

"You know, Tone. I invest a lot when I put my trust in ya 'lil niggas, and the one thing that pisses me off is when somebody doesn't do what the fuck I tell 'em to do."

Antonio's head started to clear up as Tadarius stood over him and pointed the gun at his head.

"If you don't listen to me, then you're no good to me. It's a waste of time and a waste of soldiers. I need soldiers in this family, and if you ain't ready to step up, then maybe I should eliminate yo' ass."

Antonio was never one to beg, but seeing his life flash before his eyes, he pleaded with Tadarius not to kill him.

"Okay, okay, my bad, man. Just please, don't shoot."

Antonio pleaded, and while doing so, he could hear Terrance and Malik laughing behind him. He felt a new level of hate towards them.

Tadarius lowered his gun. "You know, when Terrell came up to me and told me that you punked out, I couldn't believe it. You were on yo' way to the top of the fam, homeboy, and you blew it, all because you decided to turn into a pussy at the last minute. I had high hopes for you, man. With David gone, you could've easily taken his spot in the inner circle. Speakin' of David..." Tadarius reached into his pocket and took out an object wrapped in a white cloth.

Right away, Antonio knew it was a gun that had not been used. Tadarius had a weird habit of wrapping new guns in cloth.

"I'm gon' teach David a lesson. You still wanna prove that you down?"

Antonio closed his eyes and nodded. He was willing to do anything to keep a bullet from entering his head.

"Get to Richmond Hill High at 8:15 in the morning. Head to the weight room. David's in there working out, lifting weights, and what-not, with his juiced-up ass. Take this piece, and put it in his backpack in the locker room. Twelve's all over the block askin' people about Loree's murder, so we gotta help the police somehow—do our duty to society and shit," Tadarius laughed while his cronies laughed with him.

"Do this, and keep quiet, and ain't nothin' gon happen to you or your mother and aunt."

Through his swollen right eye, Antonio looked at Tadarius in shock. "Wait, how you know about…" he started to ask.

"C'mon, son, you think I go recruiting for young soldiers without finding out what they all about, their family history, where they lay their head? I keep tabs on all my peeps, ya know what I'm sayin'? You think Malik and Terrance found your bitch ass by accident? I got eyes everywhere, kid. There ain't nowhere you can go to get away from me, and if you punk out on this, I'll make sure I track yo' whole family down, and you gon' wish I pulled this trigger," Tadarius threatened. With that, he dropped the cloth-covered gun on the grass, and he walked away, flanked by Terrance and Malik.

Limping back home, Antonio knew that his aunt and mother were not home from work, so he walked into the bathroom and checked his cuts. He had some over his face and mouth. His right eye, although not completely swollen shut, did show signs of swelling.

Filling a Ziploc bag with ice from the tray in the freezer, he applied the ice over his eye to slow the swelling down while he began to devise a plan to get to Richmond Hill High School the next morning to plant the gun in David's book bag. For the rest of the evening, Antonio remained in his room, refusing to step out, even for dinner.

Shirley encouraged Isabelle to give Antonio some time on his own. Antonio refused to step out the room because he knew his mother would see his face and would immediately start asking questions. And he knew that his family would be targeted if Tadarius had the slightest suspicion that they were aware of his operation.

Early the next morning, Antonio woke up, and with his mother and aunt still asleep, he got dressed and placed the cloth-wrapped gun into his backpack and made his way over to the school. Normally there was a zero-tolerance police on bringing any weapons into the school, and with the school set in the midst of rough neighborhoods, the Board of Education suggested that the school invest in metal detectors to confiscate weapons.

Fortunately, they had not built any detectors yet, but with Loree's murder and the influence of public opinion, Antonio would not have been surprised if weapon detectors were built throughout the school within the next two years. But with the coast currently clear, he walked around the main entrance and opened the door to the gym and weight room. Normally, the janitor, Nate Plummer, opened the doors before 7 p.m. Rumor had it that he was usually shooting hoops in the school's basketball courts then.

Sneaking by the basketball court, Antonio saw that the gym was currently empty. Figuring that Nate was in his office, Antonio made his way over to the weight room, and sure enough, David was in there, lifting weights. Fear and doubt suddenly gripped Antonio.

What if he sees me slipping the gun into his bag? What if I do this and Tadarius still hurts my family? What if I get caught and go to jail?

But Antonio worked on pushing the pressure down and calming his irregular palpitations. Taking a deep breath, he snuck over to the football team's locker room. Unlike the main student one, the football team's locker room did not have any actual lockers or combination locks. It was designed to resemble a college or professional locker room where all the football players' belongings were placed in their own personal spaces with their player number listed on the top of their space.

Antonio spotted David's number 3 space and saw his bookbag. With caution and ease, Antonio unzipped the bookbag and placed the gun inside the smallest section, burying it under some smaller books and a pack of pens. Antonio knew that there was a possibility that David might open the bag and notice the gun during school, and if he did, it would be traced back to either himself or Terrell, who had dropped out of Richmond Hill High School a few days earlier. Antonio also knew that there were a couple of other students who were members of M.O.B. and a few female students were who associated with M.O.B.

Carefully zipping the bookbag, Antonio made his way out of the locker room and headed to go back outside. He had barely made it outside the school when the first few students started filing inside. Waiting for the bell to ring for homeroom, Antonio went inside the bathroom to wash his face. Staring at his reflection, he despised what he saw.

Gangbanger, thief, accessory to murder, and now infiltrator...

The wave of nausea that Antonio felt never left him that day, and he sat through his classes unable to focus on anything but the fact that he aided in framing an innocent person for murder.

Later that afternoon, the authorities entered the school during their investigation of Loree's death. With David as the prime suspect, the police searched his belongings and sure enough, the gun was found in his bookbag. He was arrested and booked for possession of a deadly weapon. Tadarius's plan had worked flawlessly, and with David in lock-up and nobody stepping forward, David was charged with the death of Loree McAfee.

But while David awaited his fate behind bars, Antonio was on his way to his uncle's home in Brooklyn. His mother all but threw a fit when she saw Antonio's face upon returning home. And with Shirley present, Antonio was forced to confess his involvement with M.O.B. and his recent confrontation that led to his physical assault.

A few days later while Antonio stayed with his uncle Keyshawn, someone knocked on the door while he was watching television.

Don't answer the door. It could be Tadarius, Malik, or Terrance, and they might be coming to finish what they started at the park.

But he heard another voice.

"Open up. This is the New York City Police Department."

Antonio felt his stomach churn.

Keyshawn stared at Antonio. "What the hell's the police doing at my house?" he asked. Opening the door, he saw a tall black man wearing a leather black jacket with a shirt and tie. "Can I help you?" Keyshawn asked.

"Yes sir, my name is Detective Isaac Sands. Is your nephew Antonio Franks around?" the man asked.

"Maybe, but what is this all about? My nephew ain't done nothin'," Keyshawn replied.

"All the same…I'd still like to ask him a few questions concerning his involvement with Loree McAfee."

"Antonio wouldn't have anything to do with that girl's murder," Keyshawn replied, folding his arms over his chest, denying the detective entry.

But Antonio knew he had to cooperate. "No, Uncle Keyshawn, let him come in," he said, and Detective Sands walked into the house.

"Mr. Antonio Franks, I presume? Detective Sands, NYPD. Please sit down." The detective sat in the kitchen across from Antonio. He seemed to be studying him intently.

"Well, let me cut to the chase. Loree McAfee was fatally shot on Guy R. Brewer Road on September 20th. I'm sure you're aware of that by now?"

Antonio shrugged. He planned to lie to Detective Sands and had no intention of telling him about M.O.B. or his part in Loree's murder. "Yeah, I heard about it on the news like everybody else," he replied, keeping a stoic expression.

"Well, a few days later, we arrested her ex-boyfriend David Anderson after a firearm was found in his bookbag, and witnesses stated that Loree and David had had some verbal and often physical altercations in the days leading up to her death. Was that something that you were aware of?" Detective Sands asked.

"I mean, yeah, they both go to my school, and I knew they've been goin' out for a minute, but I didn't know nothin' about their relationship," Antonio replied.

Detective Sands smirked for a moment. It was like trying to crack a code or figuring out a Rubik's Cube. He knew he was interrogating a gang member, and he knew how fiercely loyal they were about protecting their crews.

"Mr. Franks, how do you think I tracked you down today?" Detective Sands asked.

"Hell if I know. Maybe cuz I go to the same school that they do, but that don't mean I run wit' the same crew," Antonio replied.

"See, I think that you're lying to me right now. I think you run in the exact same circles David does. Tell me, do you know this man?" Detective Sands asked as he pulled out a photo that turned out to be an old mugshot of Tadarius. He watched Antonio intently, looking for a flinch or any sign of recognition.

"Nah, I don't know him."

"Listen, Antonio, Tadarius is a well-known gang leader for a crew named M.O.B. He's already wanted for several assault and battery cases as well as illegal drug distribution, money laundering, and fraud. I've known him and David for some time now, and my suspicion tells me that Tadarius was involved in Ms. McAfee's murder, but we need hard evidence to tie him down. Tell me, what happened to your face?" Detective Sands asked.

The detective noticed that Antonio was starting to get uncomfortable, and he was fidgeting in his chair. But Antonio was ready with his reply. "It was dodgeball day at P.E. four days ago. You know how rough we get playin' sports."

But Detective Sands knew that Antonio was lying. He let out a low whistle. "Somebody must've really beamed that dodgeball at you real hard, or you must've come in contact with a closed fist."

"Nah, I just got hit in the face a few times with a dodgeball, that's all. Go hard or go home, right?"

Keyshawn was beginning to get fed up with Detective Sands and his line of questioning. "Listen, detective, Antonio didn't have anything to do with what happened to that girl or that gang. Antonio ain't in no gang, so if that's all, I'd like to ask you to leave."

But Detective Sands was determined to get to the truth. "You know what I see across from me right now? I see a scared, confused, and hurt young man that is bound by some street code to stay loyal to a crew that don't give a shit about him. We spoke to witnesses at the restaurant where Loree was last seen accompanied by two young boys, one of them matching your description."

Keyshawn stared at Antonio, who was gritting his teeth. Small beads of sweat were forming on his head.

"Now, what I think happened is that two young boys kidnapped Loree on Tadarius's bidding and forced her into a car. One of the boys panicked, got cold feet, and bailed on his homeboy and left Loree in the hands of her killer. Now when Tadarius found out, I bet he wasn't too happy to hear that, huh? So he did a number on that boy's face, and the only reason that he didn't kill that boy is because he needed him for another job, or he didn't want to get his hands even more dirty than they already are. Let me know if I'm getting warm," Detective Sands reeled off.

Antonio knew that he was not being interrogated by some chump cop. Detective Sands was exceptional at using clues and logic to his advantage in solving unsolved crimes, and in this case, he was spot on.

"What I'm having a tough time figuring out is what did he need that boy for? What other job did he give the boy that helped him avoid a bullet to the temple? What did he have over that boy? Is it money? Threats to kill him and his family?"

As hard as he tried to conceal it, all pretense was gone, and tears rolled down Antonio's eyes.

Though he remained serious, Detective Sands smiled on the inside. Got him.

"He's dangerous, Detective. I don't wanna be next on his hit list, and I don't want my family in the mix."

"I understand, Antonio. I do. But now we have a situation where an innocent young man is in jail for a crime he didn't commit, and you, alone, may hold the keys to his release."

"I ain't sayin' shit, okay? I don't owe David nothing. I ain't even cool wit' him like that. Who gon' look out for me when Tadarius comes after my ass?" Antonio asked, unaware that he had implicated himself in his panicked state.

"Antonio, you got two choices here. Either you keep silent, and Tadarius tracks you down and eventually kills you because he has no use for you or just because he feels like it. Or, you can testify in court, help release David, and in turn we can offer you protection and keep you and your family safe."

Facing the two alternatives that he had, Antonio did not like his options. But he had to do everything he could to keep his family safe, and David should not have to rot in prison for a crime he did not commit.

Adjusting himself in his seat, Antonio told Detective Sands everything, from his initiation to M.O.B., to delivering and dropping off drugs for Tadarius. While Detective Sands was aware that Antonio had confessed to committing various crimes, but he promised he would work on getting them expunged in exchange for his testimony.

With Keyshawn at his side, Antonio reluctantly agreed to testify. A few days later in court, a few hours before the jurors would deliberate on the case, Antonio was called to the witness stand, where he took an oath and testified before the judge, while defense attorney Arthur Blaylock and prosecutor Dale Rosemond both interrogated the young man. Antonio's testimony was groundbreaking and helped swing the verdict.

At the end, David Anderson was pronounced innocent and would not go to prison. Antonio was the star witness, and there were no shortage of accolades from those that attended the courtroom session. But Antonio knew that the news would not get past Tadarius, and he knew he had a bull's-eye on his back. It was time for change.

CHAPTER 6

ON BECOMING EDWARD REED

After David was acquitted in court, he was placed under the witness protection program. Antonio and his family were placed under the same program because Tadarius and his members were not yet apprehended. They had successfully eluded law enforcement, which meant the lives of David and Antonio were still at risk as they were considered high value targets for the dangerous syndicate.

Antonio remained at his uncle's house in Brooklyn while his lawyer and caseworker began the process of transferring him out of Richmond Hill High School. With the area mostly populated by members of M.O.B. and its informants, Detective Sands felt that it was safer for Antonio to relocate and transfer to another school.

While he was initially crestfallen when he learned that he would have to leave the only area he knew around Lefferts and 101 Avenue, Antonio also knew that if he remained at Richmond Hill, he would pay dearly for his betrayal of M.O.B.— with his life. Therefore, staying the next few days at Brooklyn with his uncle and half-brothers was a change for the better for Antonio.

Antonio learned more about his brothers, and because he was the oldest out of them and for the unflattering fact that he was a former gangbanger, his brothers looked up to him. Antonio did not understand why.

There was Bruno, who was thirteen years old, and he was the fake tough-guy of the family. Antonio figured that Bruno was just trying to overcompensate for his skinny frame and small head.

Then there was Tony, who was twelve years of age. He was a chubby boy who was still growing out of his baby fat. He never met a meal that he did not like, and he had a strange, but hilarious, chuckle that would cause Antonio to double over into laughter.

Then, there were the fraternal twins Steven and Josh, age nine, an age where elementary school was still intriguing for them.

Phillip had been with Tony's mother, Bruno's mother, and Steven and Josh's mother in short periods of time. He was especially enamored with Steven and Josh's mother, Sydney, so much so that he decided to marry her in an impromptu wedding shortly after divorcing Isabelle. Phillip was also paying monthly child support for Bruno and Tony. In other words, he was quite dearly paying for his infidelity out of his pockets.

But due to the rising tension between Tony's mother Tiffany and Bruno's mother Ophelia, both women sent their sons to live with Phillip's brother, Keyshawn. The arrangement was set, and both Tony and Bruno remained with their uncle. Steven and Josh still lived with their mother, and although it was an awkward way to reunite with his siblings, Antonio was overjoyed that he wasn't facing this difficult time on his own.

With Antonio's school future in jeopardy, Isabelle, Antonio's caseworker Rick Fenton, and Attorney Arthur Blaylock sat down at the living room table to discuss school.

"Listen, Mrs. Franks, the best option right now is to enroll Antonio into a private school over here. It's the best way to keep a low profile and not mortgage his future," Rick said.

"I don't know, Rick. I can barely pay the admission fees for some of these schools, and even if he does enroll there, they aren't guaranteed to keep him safe. Plus, you'll be taking him away from his friends and many others," Isabelle protested.

"I hear you, Mrs. Franks, and believe me, if there were other alternatives, I would take advantage. But this is the safest route for now," Arthur chimed in.

Antonio sat behind the kitchen door, listening to the conversation. When he was young, he was always instructed not to eavesdrop, especially when it came to grown folk conversations, but if they were talking about him, he had every right to find out what would happen to him. With Keyshawn away at work and Tony and Bruno at school, Antonio was bored, and with nothing else to do, he decided to listen to the conversation.

"Listen, Antonio was in a terrible ordeal for the past year. This Tadarius character is extremely dangerous, and he's going to do whatever it takes to track Antonio down. This is the best-case scenario because M.O.B.'s membership doesn't really extend to this area. For all they know, Antonio might have just headed out of the state," Arthur said.

Before the adults commented further, they heard a knock at the door. Scrambling to act as if he was watching television, Antonio sprawled on the couch and started flipping channels. He would have answered the door, but the head chief of police, who had placed two units outside of Keyshawn's home, had advised Antonio never to answer the door, especially if he did not know who the visitor was. Isabelle answered the door, and in walked Detective Sands.

"Hello, Isabelle. Hey Antonio, what's up, man? Listen, I need to talk to you and your mother together, if that's okay," he said.

"Sure." Isabelle led Detective Sands to the kitchen, where he shook Rick's hand as well as Arthur's hand.

"Can I get you something to drink, detective?" Isabelle offered.

"Water would be good, thanks."

Isabelle went to the kitchen to get a bottle of water. As soon as she returned with the water, she took her seat.

"Alright, now that everyone's here, I have some news to break to ya'll. Tadarius Hill and Terrell Washington were apprehended yesterday at an old apartment, just past Merrick," Detective Sands revealed.

Antonio's heart skipped a beat. Had Tadarius, the mastermind gangster illusionist, who was known for evading law enforcement, really been captured? It seemed too good to be true.

"Are you serious?" Arthur asked.

"Yeah. I took about ten uniformed officers to the location, and we had David wear a wire since he led us to the location, and once David confronted Tadarius, all hell broke loose," Detective Sands explained, his voice starting to crack.

"What do you mean?" Isabelle asked.

"When I asked Tadarius to freeze, he opened fire on my squad, and we had no choice but to fire back. There must have been ten to fifteen rounds exchanged, and when the dust settled, there were two bodies on the floor. They were later identified as Terrance Dregs and Malik Jones, both members of M.O.B."

Antonio sat there, unsure of what to say. He still remembered how Terrance and Malik had grabbed him roughly and held him down while Tadarius beat him to a pulp, and although he hated Tadarius's henchmen, there was a stripe of sympathy. Their lives were cut short, all because they decided to follow a narcissistic madman who only saw his way or the highway.

Detective Sands turned to him. "So, Antonio, I guess that means you got nothing to worry about. There's no doubt Tadarius's lawyer will try to plead no contest for his client's involvement in the Loree McAfee murder, but he shot at law enforcement, and with his lengthy list of crimes, I don't see him getting anything short of life, and that may be without parole."

Antonio stood up. In retrospect, this should have been good news, but it provided little comfort. "With all due respect, detective, that don't mean a damn thing. Tadarius says he got eyes everywhere, and even if he locked up, he still got people on the outside. If they see me, I'm good as dead."

"I understand, son, but we cut the head off the snake now, and most likely, his remaining members are going to scatter across the borough. Since Tadarius was the major player in international drug imports and distribution, and the guys in the inner circle are either dead or in the wind, there's no way M.O.B. will function."

Seeing that his news still brought levels of doubt, Detective Sands decided to discuss alternative solutions. "Okay, if there are still members of M.O.B. out there, I'll continue searching after I get confessions from the men that are in custody."

"Detective, you have a better chance of hell freezing over than to get any type of confession from them. I already know Tadarius ain't gon' talk, and I know Terrell very well. He ain't gonna talk either cuz he too loyal to them. Plus, there are still others that you ain't caught yet. What about Xavier, E'Twan, T-Note, and his female informants?"

Detective Sands shook his head.

Antonio instantly knew that he did not have a clue who the other members were.

"We're gonna do our best, Antonio. That's all I can tell you. I have to work with the evidence that is provided to me, and if I can pull up the records of the other individuals that you named, then I will bring them in for questioning as well."

"So, what am I supposed to do in the meantime?" Antonio asked.

"Lay low for now. Your caseworker and lawyer are working on transferring you to a different school, and life goes on," Detective Sands answered.

"What if he were to change his name?" Arthur asked.

Antonio and Isabelle looked at him as if he were crazy.

Change my name? Nah, I'm good on that. I'm Antonio, and I've always been Antonio. That ain't gonna change.

Noticing the rising tension in the room, Arthur took the moment to explain his reasoning. "Hear me out for a moment. If Antonio changes his identity, he can start with a fresh slate—new school, new neighborhood—and even if there are members of M.O.B. that are still unaccounted for, they won't know it's him. Tell me, Antonio, how close were you to M.O.B.'s external members?"

Antonio took a moment to think. Outside of the people he dealt with in Queens, such as David, Terrell, Xavier, Malik, and Terrance, he did not build any type of rapport with any other member, which intensified his fears because anyone out in these streets could be a member of M.O.B. "I don't know too many guys outside of Queens."

"Do you still think he has to change his name? I still think it's too drastic of a change," Isabelle pointed out.

"I hate to say it, Mrs. Franks, but Arthur may be correct here. Even though Tadarius is in custody, we still have other members that are still out there, and if they identify Antonio, he's considered a high value target," Detective Sands replied. "Look, we all still know him as Antonio, but if we want to keep him safe, it's imperative that we take action immediately, at least until the remaining members of M.O.B. are apprehended."

Antonio looked at Detective Sands. He was unsure if changing his name would work, but he had to remain incognito for self-preservation. "Alright, I'll do it."

Three days later, Arthur Blaylock walked out of the Queens County courtroom accompanied by Antonio. He was holding legal documents in his hands that were signed and notarized, stating that Antonio Franks' new name was now Edward Reed.

"I don't know, Mr. Blaylock. Couldn't we have found a much better name than Edward? Sounds like a square-ass name to me."

"Come on, you could use it like a nickname. Ed, Eddie...you know there are so many ways you could shorten it. At least none of Tadarius's boys are looking for Edward Reed. Trust me, it's all gonna work out."

Antonio hoped that Arthur was right. It would not be long before Edward enrolled into the prestigious Montresor High School in Brooklyn,

New York, where he would continue his education. Oftentimes, he would wonder what became of the remaining ex-members of M.O.B.

CHAPTER 7

COACH OF THE YEAR

NOVEMBER 2017

As the two football teams lined up in the center of the field, Townsend Harris High School quarterback Pierce Bell held his hands in ready position at the snap. The defensive lineman corrected his stance and formation as the ball was snapped.

"Hike!" Pierce yelled as the ball found his hands. Backpedaling, he scanned the field, looking for pass options. The wide receiver, Troy James, was covered by the cornerback, and his tight end was draped with about three defensive linemen.

With both of his pass options taken away, Pierce decided to run the ball to the end zone. With incredible speed and amazing change of direction, Pierce was able to elude the pass rush, and with a few quick movements, he broke through the defensive line and ran as hard as he could to the end zone.

Defenders dropped in his wake in failed attempts to tackle him as Pierce veered towards the sidelines. His speed was met with his balance and endurance as he managed to stay infield without going out of bounds.

Out of the corner of his eye, he saw the cornerback, Kendrick Donaldson, approaching him, but the end zone was only a few yards away. As Kendrick prepared to barrel into Pierce, the wily quarterback tucked the football in his chest and dove to the end zone. A whistle blew, and the scrimmage referee raised both hands in the air, signaling a touchdown. Pierce got up as he was congratulated by his teammates on the incredible touchdown.

"Yeah, boy, that's the way to do it!"

"Let's go, son!"

"THS all day, baby!"

As he ran to his team on the sidelines, he was congratulated by Townsend Harris High School coach David Anderson.

"Good take, Pierce!" Coach Anderson exclaimed, patting his star quarterback on the shoulder. "Defense, I need you to be more aware out there! You guys are too busy ball watching, and in the meantime, Pierce has enough time to break through the line. If we want to continue improving from last season, we can't have that type of defense. Alright c'mon, everybody. Huddle up," he added as the team ran to huddle at the sidelines.

It was the last practice before the next game versus Lincoln High School, and Coach Anderson wanted to make sure that his team was prepared. It was the homecoming game, and there was plenty of hype surrounding the match. Only a year earlier, David Anderson was hired as Townsend Harris High School's football coach, and he had led the team on an amazing turnaround season. Townsend Harris had only won five games the previous season, which added to the history of football futility at the school.

But once David Anderson was hired, the school and the community experienced a football odyssey, becoming only the third school in district history to go from five wins to eleven wins—a six-game improvement. The school qualified to play for state but was eliminated in the second round of the playoffs. Nevertheless, Coach David Anderson was awarded the district's Coach of the Year by opposing coaches and the Public Schools Athletic League (PSAL).

With advanced college-style plays that allowed the quarterback more options on the field, Coach Anderson had successfully changed the culture of the school's football program. Upon arrival, he focused on a summer training camp and a meal plan that kept players healthy and conditioned. Although his methods were questioned earlier in his coaching stint, the criticism declined as Townsend Harris continued piling up win after win after win. So far in the new school year, Townsend Harris had won two games and had hoped to keep the momentum going as they prepared to host Lincoln High School for the homecoming game.

As well as Coach Anderson's football success was documented, he had no qualms in his personal life. Married to former beauty pageant contestant, Renee Watson, they shared three children together: Dennis, age eleven; Cree, age nine; and the youngest, Katrina, who was six. Living in a nice four-bedroom home in Flushing, New York, the Andersons had arrived at a point where they were comfortable, and David Anderson could not have asked for anything else. It was a far cry from where he had come from and the circumstances that he had escaped from.

Early in his life, David's parents had abandoned him and left him under the care of his grandmother. The early neglect from his parents had its consequences as David got into trouble early and often, associating himself with troublesome neighborhood kids and fighting whenever he could. David was known to have a short fuse, and when he became enraged, he was known to be violent. But being violent, alone, was not the reputation that David built.

He was the co-founder and chief enforcer for the dangerous street gang M.O.B. and its ruthless leader, Tadarius. He'd met Tadarius in juvenile hall, and since the chance meeting, Tadarius had convinced David to join him in creating and recruiting young men and women that would form the nucleus of the gang.

David and Tadarius ran 101 Avenue, Richmond Hill, Lefferts Boulevard, Liberty Avenue, South Ozone Park, and Van Wyck Expressway like they were a part of their own personal playground, selling and running drugs and weapons and controlling the gambling underworld. Oftentimes, they would run into opposing gangs, but the confrontations were few and far between, mostly because other sets feared Tadarius, who was rumored to be irrational, temperamental, and bordering on insanity.

At first, David shrugged those characteristics off as Tadarius being goal-driven, ambitious, and seeking ways to make money. He had seen and experienced firsthand the way the government would turn a blind eye towards the inner-city citizens, and Tadarius was offering houses, money, and free drugs to those boys and girls who grew up in broken homes.

But as time went by, David started to see the true nature of the man that he had once considered closer than a brother. Tadarius was self-possessive, aggressive, and murderous. David had witnessed Tadarius kill a man with a box cutter. The crime was very intricate, yet very well concealed, in that he was able to avoid any charges from the authorities.

David thought that he had no way out of the gang because he felt he had no other talents to contribute to society other than his big muscular frame and enforcer skills. But then he found football, and he enjoyed playing the quarterback position. After promising his grandmother that he would remain in school and improve his grades, David eventually tried out and made Richmond High School's varsity football team in his junior year of high school.

Although the school's football record was modest, David's incredible skills began to draw interest from colleges around the nation, and his interest in being a member of M.O.B. began to dwindle.

David was constantly M.I.A. during gang meetings, and Tadarius soon found out that football had begun to peak David's interest. Tadarius acted as if he supported David, but David knew that he was looking out for his own pockets. The hope was that David would play college ball, possibly win the Heisman Trophy, and go to the NFL on a multimillion-dollar contract, and Tadarius and the rest of the family would be financially set.

Tadarius, however, never foresaw David's interest in a girl that once ran as an informant of M.O.B., Loree McAfee. As she talked David out of the gang, Tadarius saw her as a threat, and with David supposedly whipped, he decided to make him pay by attempting to frame him for Loree's murder.

But David was exonerated, and he helped the police take down and arrest Tadarius. Although the police arrested Tadarius and placed David under witness protection, David insisted that the extra guard be removed. He did not fear any type of retribution.

Tadarius was behind bars, and he was going to remain there for the rest of his life.

David remained at Richmond Hill although he took his remaining courses online under the witness protection program and eventually graduated high school, but inexplicably, his football skills began to decline. Having been committed to Seton Hall his freshman season, David was red-shirted and did not see the field. Angered by the coach's decision to bench him, David left Seton Hall and played quarterback and tight end for LIU Post.

Previously, in high school there had been rumors that David was allegedly taking anabolic steroids, and although the allegations were never proven, Tadarius dangled the threat of exposing the truth to the public unless David stayed out of his way. David eventually stopped taking steroids and played the right way, but once his body lost the boost that it regularly received from the steroids, his game suffered, but David still felt that he had a shot at the NFL until a devastating knee injury in his senior year at LIU Post ended his NFL hopes.

After his collegiate career, David joined on the staff as a graduate assistant coach for LIU Post, where he gained experience, and he learned about the tactics and schemes of the offense and defense. He placed applications and his resume on the Internet for a head coaching position, and he was grateful when Townsend Harris called and brought him in for an interview.

By this time, he had already married his college sweetheart, Renee, and was building a stable home life. But David would often be haunted by the memories of Loree and his time with M.O.B. in addition to a much darker secret that he held from his family.

He was not the perfect parent, but he would be out of his mind to let his kids grow up without a strong father like he did. So, he was a strict disciplinarian in the household. Everyone had chores and responsibilities each day, and if they were not working other jobs, he expected his kids to get nothing short of A's and B's in their classes.

David made sure that his kids brought their progress reports to him every two weeks, and if any of them brought home a C grade point average, the individual would lose access to his or her smart phones, tablets, and gaming systems, along with access to social media for a week until he or she brought the grades back up. Some parents would say this type of discipline was harsh, but David did not care what anybody else thought.

Nobody knew what David had seen or witnessed early on in life, and if it were not for football, he knew he would have either died in the streets or in prison.

But he did not want football to be the saving grace for his children. He wanted them to excel in their studies to become scientists, engineers, doctors, or lawyers. He was pleased, however, that his children had taken interest in athletics.

Dennis was beginning to show promise as an athlete, excelling in both football and basketball. He also played for his middle school's lacrosse team.

Cree was an ascending gymnast whose spellbinding moves and acrobatic ability had people predicting an appearance in the Olympic Games.

Katrina loved to run track, and she was one of the fastest girls in her class when it came to field day.

But David always preached the same message: education first, then athletics. He knew athletes had a shelf life, and one day they may be unable to play sports, but education went a long way, and it would guarantee that they would not lose income and would begin building generational wealth. David himself earned his degree in sports management and one day had hopes of heading a major sports program, but he was content with being a coach.

"Okay, boys, good practice. Defense, I still need you guys to tighten up. Walker, Lebowski, Johnson, pick up after each other out there. I want us to be on point when we play Lincoln," David said.

After the players made their way to the locker room, David checked his cell phone for missed calls. Normally, his cell phone would be on silent because he hated any distractions during practice. Aside from two missed calls and a voice message from Renee, there were no other calls.

He received a news flash on his phone. A sixteen-year-old boy was taken into custody after robbing a corner store on 104th and Main Street. As he read the news, David rolled his eyes.

Nothing's ever gonna change around here. It's another generation of knuckleheads out here doing stupid stuff.

But the last sentence on the news article caught his eye. It stated that the suspect of the robbery may be connected to a local gang, and it was the latest in a string of robberies in the area.

As he got into his Ford Explorer, David could not wait to arrive home to have his wife's homemade pasta, linguini with alfredo sauce. He also could not wait to hug and kiss his children and check on their progress reports as usual.

As David slowed at a stoplight, he saw a virtual billboard advertising an R&B and gospel extravaganza show that was scheduled to take place at New York City's Radio Music Hall. There were many artists that were scheduled to perform that evening, but a certain artist headlined the event, and her celebrity headshot was broadcasted throughout the virtual screen. David couldn't help but notice how familiar the artist looked to a woman he knew in the past.

The smile, cheekbones, soft eyes, and straight black hair combed down to her shoulders—it was as if he were seeing a ghost. He was seeing Loree McAfee all over again. This girl had the traits that attracted him to her when they met at one of Tadarius's house parties in 2001.

The girl on the billboard was none other than Adia, the gospel artist who'd started her career singing R&B music but then changed to gospel after being underpaid and undervalued by her former record label.

She also happened to be Andrea McAfee, Loree's little sister who keenly felt the loss of her sister and used her influence, resources, and gifts to sponsor a non-profit organization that was established in Long Island, Queens, and Brooklyn. The organization was known as Stop Street Violence Immediately, or SSVI for short. It would sponsor many black-owned businesses and outdoor events during the summer, raising money for awareness and teaching programs. David had donated money to the organization, and he was pleased that people were taking the steps to put an end to the violence that permeated the streets.

He was astonished at how much Adia resembled her late sister. She virtually embodied her very image. David felt his heart sink. Although he was found innocent, he regretted not being there for Loree when she needed him. He felt even worse in knowing that before she died, she told him that he could be so much more than just a gang member and a drug dealer.

They loved each other, but their relationship was abusive as David confessed during the trial that he had violently laid hands-on Loree on more than one occasion. But he acknowledged that he had seen the error of his ways and had apologized to Loree. He felt that his aggression towards Loree may have also been a side effect of the steroids that he was taking during his high school years to enhance his strength, but he never confessed that in the courtroom. At that point in time, it could have ended his career, and he would have never continued playing through college.

Loree was a beautiful young woman that would never be replaced, and she was dead, partly because of him. But he was with Renee, and when they met in college, Renee represented the type of woman that David never thought he would find again since Loree. Renee was patient, ambitious, outgoing, sassy, but supportive, and she was a dedicated educator and mother to her children.

What really attracted David to Renee was her passion and her seductive lovemaking. He had been with other girls in the past, but there were two women that had insatiable sex drives, and they were Loree and Renee. Renee was extremely intense during sex, and David would be nothing short of satisfied at the end.

The only other woman to physically satisfy him to the point of exhaustion was Loree. Sometimes David would find himself so blissful to where he mistakenly said her name in bed. Chuckling to himself, David recalled a night years ago when they were in bed, and he accidentally blurted the wrong name.

"Mmm, that's it, Loree. Keep going," he whispered absentmindedly, and at that moment, Renee stopped pumping and grinding to their body rhythms.

"Wait, who's Loree?" she asked.

David closed his eyes, secretly beating himself up for making the crucial error. "Nobody, baby. It was nobody."

But the damage was done for the evening. The romantic mood had been compromised.

"Okay, David, get off me," Renee said, pushing him off.

"Baby, I'm sorry. Seriously, it was a mistake. I promise," David protested.

Renee rolled her eyes. They had just become exclusive for a few months, and he was already blurting out some other chick's name. Could she trust this man?

"I mean, David, you need to be up front wit' me here and now. Are you fuckin' somebody else?" she asked bluntly.

"Baby, no I ain't fuckin' nobody else."

"Then who the hell's Loree?"

Sighing, David sat on the end of the bed. He had promised himself that if he was fortunate to get involved in another serious relationship, he was not going to bring up his past with her. But he saw that he had no choice at that moment.

"Renee, look. Loree was a girl that I was seeing in high school. She was the last one that I truly fell in love wit'."

"So, if you love her so much, why don't you call her and do her then?" Renee asked, edgily.

"She's dead, Renee," David replied. It was clear that they were not going back to their blissful act of lovemaking, so he began to put his boxer shorts back on.

Renee, realizing that she had overreacted, softened her voice. "I'm sorry, David. I didn't know. How did she die?" Renee asked.

Inwardly cursing himself, David hated that he had to revisit a past that he had worked extremely hard to eradicate. But since Renee opened the door, he might as well guide her inside.

"She was shot to death by some guys that ain't got no lives of their own. She must have pissed off the wrong person, and he retaliated."

"That's terrible. But the way you described it, it's almost as if…"

Her voice trailed off, and David feared that Renee might have arrived at the conclusion that so many Queens residents had come to prior to his date in court.

"No, Renee, trust me I don't know who did it, and I sure as hell had nothing to do with it, if that's what you're thinking."

"What? No, I would never think that about you, David. You're the nicest man I've ever been with. I can't see you in that light."

She would be surprised if she knew who I was and what I did before she met me. But all that stays with me. She's never gonna know. I did a bang-up job covering myself about the tattoo.

When Renee had asked about the tattoo earlier in their relationship, David just explained it as a "relic of angry adolescence." He never explained the significance or the meaning of the gang tattoo. Renee, who had a few pieces of body art of her own, did not further question it.

As he arrived home from football practice, David could already smell the pasta and the alfredo sauce wafting through the dining room. Entering the kitchen, he saw Renee, accompanied by Cree and Katrina.

"Daddy!" Katrina yelled as she ran to hug her father.

"Hey, Tri-Tri! How's my cupcake? Helping Mommy cook dinner?" he asked, lifting her in the air and kissing her.

"Yup. And Cree and I boiled the water and poured the linguini, and I put in the salt and the pepper and spices."

"Stop lying, Tri. You didn't do all that. I did the spices. Always gotta tell the story," Cree remarked, hugging her father.

"Alright, did you guys receive progress reports from school today? I hope I see some great grades. Where's Dennis?" David asked, walking over to Renee, kissing her on the cheek.

"He's upstairs doing his homework. Probably got his headset in so he couldn't hear you come in. He was pretty quiet after he came back from school," Renee replied.

"Well, I'll go upstairs and see how's he doing." David said, as he went up the stairs to see his son.

CHAPTER 8

THE BIKE CIRCUIT CHAMPION

David knocked on Dennis's room door for two minutes, but he received no response. *That boy probably got his Beats headphones in. That's why he can't hear me.*

Rolling his eyes, he knocked again. "Dennis, open the door, son. This ain't your mama or your sisters, I promise." David knew that Dennis loved his privacy.

Although he'd just turned eleven, Dennis had started to display all the characteristics of early adolescence: a thirst for sports, interest in girls, and a penchant for violent action movies.

Finally, David took out his cell phone and called his son's number. Initially, David did not agree for his son to have a cell phone yet, but Renee insisted upon her son having a phone in the event of an emergency.

Answering after the third ring, Dennis said, "What's up, Dad?"

"I'd be doin' a whole lot better if I didn't have to call my son's number in my own house. How loud do you have that music on, boy? I've been out here knocking on your door for three minutes now."

"Oh, my bad," Dennis apologized before hanging up and unlocking his room door.

David stepped inside. A pungent odor of worn tennis shoes, dirty socks, and Axe body spray filled the room. Dennis was sitting at his lamp desk, which had different school textbooks sprawled everywhere.

"You know, son, you should really invest in a Glade plug-in or at least a can of Lysol."

"I would if I had an increase in allowance," Dennis laughed.

David usually gave his kids an allowance of five dollars after each week, and on progress report card weeks, if they maintained a straight A average, the amount would increase to ten dollars.

"Stop playin' me, Dennis. You know what it would take for me to give you an increase in allowance. But I see you're working your way towards it. How's school going?" he asked.

"Not bad. Mrs. Alvarez says I'm getting an A in geography, and everything else is going pretty good."

"That's what I like to hear. Now remember, the higher your grades are, the higher your allowance is."

David began to walk out the door when Dennis called him.

"Hey, Dad, can I ask you something?"

"Yeah, go ahead. What's on your mind?"

Dennis took his headphones off and put his pen down. "Well, there's this girl in my class. Her name is Xyla, and she keeps trying to talk to me even though I ain't tryin' to talk to her like that. I mean, I don't have a problem with her, but she always tryin' to start a conversation with me, and today at lunch she came to sit at my table where my other friends sit, and she kept butting in our conversation. I got so annoyed, and I told her to get lost. She tried to hide it, but I saw tears in her eyes, and she ran off. I feel kind of bad. Did I say something wrong?"

David looked at his son. *So, he's a ladies' man, just like his old man was in the past.*

Planning on giving his son the best advice possible, David shook his head. "Dennis, come on, man. I taught you better than that. When it comes to girls, there are certain ways that you speak to them. Sounds like this girl likes you, and that's why she's around you all the time. She can't have liked you for the way you smell."

"Funny, Dad. I see you got jokes. But if she likes me so much, how come she won't listen to me when I tell her to leave me alone?"

"Son, you got to understand that women are very persistent. When they see something they like, they just gotta have it, you know what I'm saying? Think about your mother and your sisters in the mall the other weekend. When they saw those designer shoes, they went crazy because it's a hot commodity. Maybe this girl doesn't want to see you get snatched up by any other girl."

"Yeah, but Dad, I ain't feelin' her like that. She needs to go bother other dudes. What can I do?"

David sat down at the foot of his son's bed. "Dennis, I will start by telling you this. You were wrong to yell at her. I know she was annoying you, but yelling at her in front of others embarrassed her. I didn't raise you to disrespect anyone. You want to treat people the same way that you wanna be treated."

"Even if she talks your ear off and cuts you off every time you're trying to talk to your boys?"

"No exception to the rule, son. You gotta apologize to Xyla tomorrow morning."

"Alright, Dad, I'll apologize to her. But have you ever met a girl like that when you were my age?"

Dennis had unknowingly asked a question that was not comfortable for David to discuss. He did not want to tell Dennis that at his age, he was still committing petty crimes and getting in trouble repeatedly.

At the age of eleven, David was trying to listen to his grandmother and stay away from the streets. Willamena Anderson was now deceased, but her impact on David's life was immense. She took him in when she didn't have to, and when he was wrongfully accused of murder, she was the only one who believed in his innocence before it was proven in court.

"Well, I did meet a girl like that Xyla. She used to talk my ear off every day, and she wouldn't leave me alone, not even when I was around my friends. Son, when I tell you that girl was a straight-talking machine, I kid you not. There were times I wish I had some Krazy Glue or something to keep her from talking so much."

Dennis laughed. "Man, she sounds worse than Xyla."

"Yo, you don't even know half of it. She followed me everywhere I went, tried to talk sports when she didn't know squat about it. I mean she mixed up her basketball teams and her football teams so many times, it was gettin' on my last nerves. She was really hopeless, son, trust and believe when I tell you this."

"So, how did you deal with that annoying girl?"

David looked around, like a naughty little schoolboy that was attempting not to get caught in wrongdoing.

"Well, son, you're not gonna believe this, but the most unbelievable thing that happened was that we ended up getting married."

Dennis's eyes widened in shock upon the realization that the annoying girl that David was referring to was his mother. "You mean...Mom?"

He started to ask, but David made a zipped-lip motion to his son. "Don't tell her I told you any of that, okay? Dinner's in ten minutes, kid."

Patting Dennis's head, he walked out of room, closing the door behind him. He had walked no more than three steps when he stopped dead in his tracks. Staring at him, arms crossed, was Renee.

David's heart sank nervously. How much of that did she hear?

But Renee smiled wryly. "Really, David? Talking machine? So that's what we're doing now?"

David smiled sheepishly. "Hey, nothing strengthens the bond of a father and son than talking about the mama behind her back. Besides, I was joking. You weren't that annoying, baby," he said, kissing her.

"I mean, okay, if you want to get technical about it, I was jockin' you a lil' bit when we met at LIU, but it worked, didn't it? I ended up getting my man in the end."

David raised his eyebrows as they kissed passionately. He loved Renee and his kids more than anything in the world. "That you did, baby. But I'm starving. Let me go set the table for dinner," he offered as he walked to the living room, placing the table mats on the table and setting up silverware for the family.

Later that evening in Jackson Heights, Paul Choy waited on his client. Checking his watch, he complained about his customer's poor timing. As a motorcycle seller, he wanted his clients to be on time and wanted all his money up front. Nothing angered Paul more than a cheap buyer.

Finally, his buyer arrived at his shop, riding in a blue 2016 Kawasaki motorcycle. Wearing a blue helmet that matched the color of his motorcycle, the man slowed his bike down, turned the engine off, and pushed the kickstand down to hold his motorcycle in place. Taking his helmet off, Xavier Furrows took his pick out of his side pocket and took his time styling his short afro back into shape.

Paul rolled his eyes. "C'mon, Xavier, I ain't got all night, man. You wanna trade your bike in, or not?"

Ignoring the storeowner, Xavier placed his pick back in his pocket.

"You better have something worth trading, bro, or this shit's done. I got a race tonight, and I need a bike that got some serious engine power. Show me what you got."

Paul walked through his lot with Xavier, showing him different motorcycle models, from the Suzuki and Harley Davidsons to the Yamahas. After examining the first couple of motorcycle, Xavier's eyes fell upon a silver-colored Triumph one.

"Oh, this is the one right hea'. I can definitely rock with this."

"The Triumph? You know this bike is about $500 more than your Kawasaki, right?"

Xavier looked at Paul, his eyes, gleaming. "I'll make a deal wit' you. You let me trade my baby wit' this, I'll race it, and once I win the money, I got you first thing in the morning."

Paul shook his head. "Hell no, Xavier. What you take me for?"

"I take you as a dude that knows a sure bet when he sees this. C'mon, you know how I get down. I'll have the money in hand by morning, word is bond."

"Xavier, you just got out like eight months ago. What if you're rusty?"

"Don't even sweat that, B. Bike racing's an acquired skill, no matter how long of a hiatus you take. You either know how to do it, or you don't. Plain and simple. So, we good?"

After thinking it over, Paul decided to take the bet. "Okay, fine. But your ass is on the clock as of right now. You better make good on your word, or I'm coming to collect."

Such a threat would have dismayed many, but Xavier was used to threats, and he showed no fear, even taking the moment to laugh at his seller's promise of retaliation.

"Man, I got you, Paul."

After exchanging motorcycles, Xavier was back out on the road, as he made his way onto the freeway. After ten minutes of riding the freeway, he finally arrived at his destination. Northern Boulevard, which was normally busy during the day, was virtually a ghost town after midnight, so it provided a lively venue for racing enthusiasts.

Motorcycle racing was against the law in New York, and any violators faced serious jail time. But there was a society of underground motorcycle riders that formed a racing circuit within Northern Boulevard. Closing off a two-mile stretch of road, bikers raced one another to win cash prizes. Many bikers formed teams, which were typically sponsored by larger companies and their affiliates.

There were motorcycle gangs that participated in these races that took place between midnight and four in the morning. The stretch of road had nothing but shops, bodegas, and businesses along the side of the road, and cars parallel parked alongside it.

Aside from the motorcycle gangs, there were individual bikers that challenged other bikers and earned reputation in the streets.

Xavier was in the category of individual riders who raced for extra money. There was no other life that suited him better. Born to a single mother in Queens, Xavier grew up without any type of male influence in his life. Known for acting out of character, he often got into fights whenever he was angered. He also rode the subway all throughout New York City, studying the city map and learning about streets, alleyways, and secluded locations.

By the age of fifteen, Xavier had moved out of his mother's home and stayed with a school friend named Etwann Victor, who was three years older but lived in an apartment just inside South Jamaica. Although he had a roommate, Xavier never had a dominant male influence, so there was no direction in his life.

But all that changed when he was introduced to Tadarius and M.O.B. Tadarius, who had just established his syndicate only months earlier, needed someone with knowledge of the city and zones who was ideal to sell spots for his dealers. Xavier was an integral part of the gang, and he was finally in a group where he was accepted and had a strong male presence that he respected.

Xavier was also an avid bike rider, and with his knowledge of the streets, he rode his bike while making drops to many clients. His efficiency paid off as M.O.B.'s seasonal revenue increased twofold after his induction into the gang. Just like many other members, Xavier was instructed to keep his mouth closed when he witnessed events happening within the gang, which was the case when he witnessed Tadarius slice a man with a box cutter for refusing to pay him what was owed.

Then there was the murder of David Anderson's girlfriend in which the public implicated David, but when he was found innocent, all fingers started to point at Tadarius. Xavier knew it was only a matter of time before Tadarius would be captured. When the news of the shootout between the police force and M.O.B. hit the news, Xavier, who was visiting family in New Jersey at the time, knew that the gang would fall apart without Tadarius's strong leadership. When Xavier returned to New York, the gang was virtually leaderless, and many of the members had moved out of state or renounced their membership.

Xavier then took an interest in riding motorcycles, and after getting his first Yamaha, he began to get involved in the world of underground motorcycle racing. Calling himself "Lone X," Xavier gained a reputation as a strong racer that was unbeatable, no matter how many bikers he raced.

One race in 2014 was stopped by police, and Xavier was arrested for participating in illegal races. He was charged and sent to jail for racing, but while he was in jail, he collaborated with the police and the city to confess to Tadarius's crimes. What was the worst that Tadarius could do to him? He was already locked up, and the way Xavier saw it, there was nobody else that would take the plea deal for less jail time.

So, Xavier confessed everything to the police, and it led to his release in the spring of 2017. Returning to the bike racing scene after being in jail for nearly two years, Xavier was back on the streets, but this time he was working a day job as a grocer in C-Town, but he moonlighted as a midnight rider because he lived in a tenement and had to pay rent, and the money he made as a grocer wasn't enough.

As Xavier arrived at Northern Boulevard, he stopped short of the small crowd that formed at the street corner, which also happened to be the starting line for the race.

Harry Dennitz, a well-known street promoter saw Xavier. "About time, Lone X. I was about to declare Crusher here the winner. Gotta learn to come on time."

"Gimme a break, Harry. I had to get me a bike that I could race on."

"I see. That Triumph's a real beauty. Let's see how fast she is."

The crowd, which was comprised of other bikers and race enthusiasts, gathered around the starting line.

Virgilio "Crusher" Manilli lined up at the opposite end of the starting line. Xavier measured his opponent, who was riding a Yamaha R10MAX. He'd heard about the Crusher in past races and had even seen some of his races, but he felt that nobody in Queens stood a chance against him in a bike race. Placing his helmet back on his head, Xavier revved his bike as the Crusher lined his.

Once both riders were confirmed to be exactly paralleled, a light-skinned black girl with brown curls and shapely hips stepped into the middle of the two, holding a white flag. Both riders waited until the girl waved the flag in a downward motion, signaling the green light.

Xavier and the Crusher sped off, speeding past street signs and business establishments and disregarding the traffic lights that were extended on green because of the late hour. The road was mostly flat terrain, but Xavier knew from previous races that there were two short hills approaching. The Crusher was currently ahead of him, and Xavier knew that if he did not speed up, he was in danger of losing the race.

The road veered. Virgilio leaned his bike slightly to the right, pushing his weight into balance to prevent himself from falling off. Xavier performed the same action on his bike, and when the bend straightened, he decided to take advantage of the opportunity to pull ahead on his opponent.

The Crusher had a reputation of applying speed pressure on his opponents by tapping the clutch, allowing them to gain a false sense of hope in the race before proceeding to dust them. But Xavier had been riding for years, and he knew a trick or two of his own. As he applied more acceleration to his bike, Xavier could see the crowd at a distance. He was almost at the finish line, but The Crusher was not ready to call it quits yet. He accelerated, and the tip of his bike barely led as the riders approached the final stretch. Xavier revved up his acceleration, and as both riders crossed the line, one of the spectators took a photo to determine the winner.

"Alright, folks, that was a hell of a race. It was so close that we had to get a photo finish. Both riders showed their stuff today, but only one of them is walking home wit' three G's in his pocket. Alejandro, what you got, dawg?" Harry asked as they looked at the photo.

"It was a tie," the Crusher said as he pushed his way through the crowd.

"A tie? Man, I whupped yo' ass all day, B," Xavier chuckled as the Crusher stepped up to him.

Virgilio stood about an inch taller than Xavier, but Xavier didn't back down, staring his opponent back in the face. "Better back up off me, or you gon' need the three G's to take care of yo' medical bills," Xavier replied. He did not care which sect the Crusher came from. All that he cared about was the fact that he was whining about the finish of the race.

After a few minutes of checking the photo, Harry said, "Alright, guys, it was a close one, but the winner of tonight's race by a slim margin is Lone X!"

The crowd cheered and yelled. The Crusher spat on the side of the road in anger. After Harry gave Xavier the money, Virgilio approached him again, and Xavier braced himself. Fights rarely broke out in underground racing, and when they did, they were normally in response to someone losing the race.

But the Crusher held his hand out graciously, and Xavier shook it. "Good race, man. But I want a rematch though. We definitely gonna have to set that up."

"Respect, son. Anytime, anywhere. You know where to find me, bro," Xavier replied confidently.

With the money firmly in hand, Xavier was pleased that he was finally able to pay Paul the rest of his money. But while he got back onto his bike, the girl who had started the race approached him. Xavier had seen her in other races but had never approached her. He normally wanted to race and collect his winnings so he could return to his apartment and catch a few hours of sleep before waking up to go to work.

"Nice race. What's your name?" she asked.

Xavier smiled. "You heard Harry. They call me Lone X," he replied.

But the girl shook her head. "Nah, I mean, what's yo' real name?"

Xavier never liked to share his real name with anybody because he did not trust the crowd that attended the races. Any of them could be undercover law enforcement or covert strategists for other bike gangs who studied opponents before upcoming races. Xavier also did not share his real name for fear of being identified as a former member of M.O.B. He had worked endlessly to erase that part of his existence.

He wanted to be known as Lone X, the bad-ass racer who loved everything fast, from fast bikes to fast women.

"My real name's Xavier. What's yo' name, sweetie?"

"Nakea, but everyone calls me KeKe," she replied.

"That's what's up. You need a lift back to yo' place?" Xavier asked.

Smiling sexily, Keke walked behind him, mounted the back of his motorcycle, and wrapped her polished fingernails around his waist. "Yeah, but I thought we could stop by yo' place first."

Oh yeah. She sounds like she's ready. Guess it's gonna be a long day at work in the morning cuz it's gonna be a good night.

As Keke clutched him as hard as she could, Xavier pushed the kickstand up and made his way back to his apartment with both prizes.

CHAPTER 9

ANDREA'S BIG NEWS

DECEMBER 2017

Inside the booth at Omega Studios, a young woman prepared herself to sing a playback of a song she had previously recorded. With her headsets firmly on her ears and the music intro beginning, she immediately gathered herself internally and focused her heart on the words that she wrote from her heart:

Even though I never got the chance to say goodbye/There are days I see you in the corner of my eye/A spiritual feeling that I can't shake or break/Trying to keep afloat in this emotional lake/Fearing that I'll only envision you in my deepest dreams/All while still figuring out what it all means.

The sound technician, Rodney Grady, worked on managing the treble and pace while producer Yandy Mitchell managed the playback and controlled the song takes. Both were intent on making sure their artist had the best music out for radio play and sales.

Having worked in Omega Studios over the past five years, 26-year-old Andrea McAfee was enjoying a steady stint in the gospel music industry. Over the years, she had released four EPs with more than eight songs nominated for Best Gospel Song at the Grammy Awards. Her success, however, did not arrive overnight.

When she began recording, she sang and toured as Adia, the pop and R&B songstress who was releasing music for Metro Records. Her fame was instant. Wherever she toured, Adia had adoring fans in every state, and she was featured in different interviews, talk shows, and magazines. Her popularity soared to greater heights when she started publicly dating labelmate and Metro Records resident rapper De'Von Franklin. He helped raise her profile and helped elevate her career in ways she could not have imagined.

Then the dream turned into a nightmare. After discovering that Metro Records had cheated her out of thousands of dollars and amidst poor record promotion and dwindling sales, Andrea felt isolated and unwanted at the record label where she had cultivated so much success since the age of seventeen.

Matters got worse when she discovered that De'Von was cheating on her with another woman, which resulted in a very public and nasty breakup. It was the straw that broke the camel's back. It was not long before Andrea left Metro Records and upon a referral from a late friend that she signed with Omega Studios.

It was the best decision because Andrea felt free to make her own music. Omega Studios, which was a Christian-based label, kept its end of the bargain with her contract, and Andrea enjoyed success. Although it paled in comparison to her previous success as Adia, Andrea was still overjoyed because she had finally made music that she enjoyed without any studio drama.

Many music critics questioned her decision to leave Metro Records, and they predicted that it was career suicide and that she would fall off the charts. But Andrea proved them wrong with her debut album on Omega entitled "My Own Words." The EP had tracks that made the top ten in gospel music and to Andrea's surprise, top twenty in the R&B music charts.

It was vindication and proof that people still listened to Adia, no matter what music genre she decided to sing. Work and talent always shined in the forefront, and God was at the center of it all.

Despite her success, Andrea always stayed close to home. She loved signing autographs for her fans, and she was always called by various pastors and religious leaders to lead their choirs on Sunday mornings. Andrea was obliged, and she always brought the house down whenever she arrived at a church.

But she enjoyed singing at the church where she grew up, The Rock of Jacob Baptist Church on 101 Avenue, because there was a family feeling whenever she sang there. Andrea enjoyed talking to the pastor of the church, Mike Hillman, and his wife, Robyn. She loved the conversations she had with her former Sunday School teacher, best friend, and surrogate sister, Shania McClain, along with her husband, Trevor, and their five-year-old daughter, Loree, who was named after Andrea's late sister and Shania's best friend.

For every blessing that Andrea has received, there were days that she felt alone. She longed to tell her sister about her success, but she could not because her sister was no longer with the living. Although it had been almost fifteen years since her sister's untimely death, Andrea often found herself crying as though she had just died recently. The grief was still fresh, and the best way Andrea expressed it was through her music.

Andrea recalled how intense her grief was, to the point where she visited a grief counselor and psychologist, Dr. Jan Ralwinski. She had taken the time to talk Andrea through her grief and depression and for the most part, her sessions with Andrea helped greatly. Andrea also relied on her music and her faith to get her through the pain. There were days where she would hear Loree speak to her, but she would tell nobody but Dr. Ralwinski about those conversations because everyone else would have thought she was losing her mind.

Unfortunately, her busy schedule prevented her from seeing Dr. Ralwinski, but they managed to keep in touch when she was not performing or touring. With a gospel-fest tour coming up later in the month, Andrea wanted to make sure she laid down more tracks for her upcoming EP, "My Source."

It was Saturday afternoon, and after finishing the song, Andrea stepped out the booth and listened to the playback. She loved her engineers and producers because they always brought their A-game when they came to work.

"Nice vocals...we don't even need the treble to augment it," Andrea pointed out.

"Yeah, we could cut it the way it is. Spectacular, just like always," Yandy said.

Andrea grabbed her sweater and bag from the back room. "Cool, so I'm gonna take off. I'll see you guys on Monday."

"Leaving so soon?" Yandy asked, laughing.

"Of course, you know how I do. I gotta rest these vocal cords for tomorrow. A hoarse voice ain't good for nobody during Sunday morning church service," Andrea replied, laughing.

As she made her way to the parking deck to her car, somebody stepped out from a corner, covering her eyes with two hands, putting her on high alert.

"Whoa, who...?" she started to ask before the mystery person revealed himself.

"Guess who?" he asked playfully.

Upon recognizing the voice, Andrea laughed. Quentin Stevens laughed as well as he unshielded Andrea's eyes.

"Quentin, you play too much, boy!" she snapped playfully as she tapped his shoulders.

Quentin and Andrea had both attended Richmond Hill High School, even attending prom together.

But their careers had taken them down different paths. While Andrea had toured the states as Adia, Quentin was studying engineering at Morehouse College in Atlanta, Georgia. After earning his B.A. in IT engineering, he had moved back to New York and worked for different computer software companies.

Over the years, Quentin and Andrea had reunited and had begun seeing each other more often. With Quentin's soft brown eyes, broad shoulders, warm smile, and clean-cut hairstyle, it did not take long for Andrea to fall head over heels for him. They soon began dating exclusively, and it was the best time for Andrea because she had longed for reliable companionship, one that was not based on money and status.

Quentin was a hardworking man who had his own career and path and was just as ambitious as Andrea was about her music. Andrea would often laugh about the early days when Quentin was still wearing glasses and had a skinny frame and was, for the most part, socially awkward, but he'd still mustered up the courage to ask her to the prom. It was a decision that Andrea never regretted because Quentin was easy to talk to, and she felt she could tell him anything.

After Quentin went to college and his physical appearance changed for the better, it only added to Andrea's desire for him, but she also kept her eyes open because Quentin was attracting other women, and she knew there were women out there who would love to destroy her happiness. But Quentin showed no signs of wavering in their relationship.

"You know I had to surprise my lady," he replied, handing her a dozen long-stemmed roses.

"Aww, Q, you shouldn't have! These are beautiful! But what are you doing here? You almost never come to see me at the studio."

"I know...I just wanted to surprise you. Come on. I'mma take you somewhere," Quentin started to guide Andrea to his car.

"Q, my car's over there though," Andrea started to protest, but Quentin told her not to worry.

"It'll still be here when you get back. I wanna take you somewhere. I'll drop you back to your ride. I promise."

After a thirty-minute ride through Manhattan, Quentin parked across the street from a familiar location where tourists and New Yorkers alike were walking in vast numbers.

"Central Park? What are we doing here in Central Park?"

Quentin smiled. "Patience, Andrea. Or should I call you by your performer name?" he teased, knowing that Andrea had a pet peeve about being called Adia in public settings when she wasn't performing.

"Uh, uh. Boy, you gave me flowers and all, but don't get smacked up now," she warned, laughing.

"Aight, aight, I'm just playin', baby. Okay, we're almost there," he said, leading her to the Met Cantor Rooftop and Garden dining.

It was a restaurant that had tables on the roof, giving the diners a view of the New York skyline and an overview of Central Park. One of the tables was adorned with candles, and the plates and utensils had been set out with the menus. Two bottles of Merlot were on the table. It was an extremely romantic setting, and Andrea could hardly believe that Quentin would go to extreme lengths for her.

"Oh my God, Q, this looks amazing! But this couldn't have been cheap. I know this must've cost a grip."

"Baby, when it comes to you, money is no object," Quentin replied before kissing her.

Pulling out her chair, Quentin gestured Andrea to sit, and after he took his own seat, they picked up the menu. She had half-hoped that she would make it through the lunch without being recognized, but there was no such luck as four young men and women rushed to the artist.

"Hey, Adia, can I have your autograph?"

"Will you take a selfie with us?"

"We love your music! We're your biggest fans!"

After posing for selfies with her fans and signing napkins and papers, Andrea turned to Quentin, who smiled at her.

Three years dating, and he still has to sit through all of that, and yet he never complains. That's what I love about him.

"Sorry about that. So, do you know what you want?" she asked as she turned the menu.

"Baby, you never have to be sorry for that. I know how you do. You big time, so you're gonna have fans."

"Yeah, it's cool and all, but they're not you. Through all the times we went out, you never treated me like an artist or someone makin' bank. You treat me like Andrea."

"Well, that's who you are. That's who you were when I first met you at Richmond Hill—even back then, when I was wearing my Urkel frames and my buttoned-up shirts with my pocket protectors and two pens tucked in, wearing my high-water jeans," he laughed.

"Boy, you wasn't that big of a nerd. Now you stretchin'."

"Maybe a little bit."

As they laughed, Andrea looked around. Although it was slightly chilly, the weather was still great for outside dining.

"Anyway, that cooked salmon with asparagus looks good. What you having?" Andrea looked and ordered the chicken linguini pasta with brioche biscuit on the side.

After the waiter brought the food out, the young couple ate and enjoyed each other's company. Due to their work schedules, Andrea and Quentin felt that they never had enough time to go out as frequently as they did when they first began dating.

"So, you'll be going on a tour in the next couple of weeks?" Quentin asked.

"Yeah, we got thirty dates and thirty cities across the U.S. I'll be touring with some real giants of gospel music. You know Kirk Franklin, Canton Jones, Kierra Sheard...I can't wait for it," Andrea replied.

"That's what's up. You're gonna kill it in every city you go to. You know, back then when you were still singing R&B, my boys and I would play some of your tracks during HBCU kickbacks."

"Really? So, your college friends was down wit' Adia?" Andrea asked.

"Oh, all day, especially when them co-eds from Spelman came through. Then we got our slow dance on."

Andrea raised an eyebrow, which made Quentin nervous because he knew that Andrea only made that face to express suspicion.

"Okay, Mr. Don Juan, exactly how many co-eds did you cozy up to with my music?" she asked, laughing.

"Trust me, not too many of them. Two, maybe three, girls at most," he replied.

"Mmhmm, right. Your sure it wasn't two or three hundred girls? I know how these females be sweating you down south."

"Nah, I ain't had juice like that. That was my roommate at the time: Dean. I was social at times, but most of the time, I kept to myself. I ain't have too many friends down in the A. Speaking of which, what happened to your friends, you know, the ones that rolled wit' you in high school?"

"Well, after she graduated college with a degree in Organizational Leadership, Vanessa started a non-profit organization for underage rape victims. I peep her on Facebook and Instagram from time to time, but we don't talk as much as we used to before. Then Sean is, well Sean. After playing college ball for a couple of years, he worked as a grad assistant at his school. I still talk to him from time to time."

"I remember when ya'll did everything together, even going to prom. Remember who Sean brought to the prom?" Quentin asked.

"Oh, you mean Lashondra? The girl that got around with every dude? Yeah, and I remember Vanessa going with that jerk Jimmy from the football team," Andrea recalled smiling.

"Prom nearly sucked for me because my friend was almost raped that night. But you helped prevent it."

"You mean we helped prevent it. We both know that if you weren't there, Jimmy would've bum rushed me and called it an accident."

"That's what I liked about you, even back then. You risked yourself for me and my friend when you didn't have to."

"Yeah, but I wish I was there when that bastard Slam got to her at the party. I remember you told me what went down that night. No one should ever have to go through that."

Andrea rolled her eyes when the name was mentioned. Slam was from De'Von's neighborhood. He had infiltrated Metro Records files, stealing millions from the company. He also posed as De'Von's friend and a key member of his entourage in order to gain his trust. Andrea found out that he was nothing more than an opportunistic rat who used his friend to gain a reputation.

She also recalled the day that it blew up in Slam's face when she confronted him about the crime. He was arrested and charged with assault, wire fraud, and embezzlement.

"I still feel like Vanessa blames me for what went down that night."

Reaching over and holding her hand, Quentin said, "Look, Andrea, you can't blame yourself for what happened to Vanessa. I'm sure one day she will see that, and you two can patch things up."

Andrea secretly hoped the same, but she doubted if Vanessa wanted to hear from her anymore. After ten minutes, Andrea placed her fork down.

"Wow, I ate a lot today, Q. I don't know if I could take another bite."

"Aww, really? But you gotta make room for dessert though."

Quentin gestured to the waiter, who made his way to the kitchen. After two minutes, the waiter walked out with a medium red velvet cake with icing on the top. What took place next, even Andrea could not have foreseen it. When the cake was placed between them, Andrea noticed that it had a message written in red icing.

The message read,

"ANDREA MCAFEE WILL YOU MARRY ME?"

The next thing Andrea knew, Quentin was getting down on one knee, and in his hand, he held a diamond ring. Whether it was orchestrated or not, the song "For The Lover In You" by Shalamar started playing on the music speakers. The other patrons and restaurant attendees looked on, waiting for an answer while Quentin remained on one knee.

"Andrea McAfee, ever since I was in high school, I've had eyes for nobody else but you. I know you dealt with a lot of tragedy in your life, and I can't hope to fill the void that was left by your older sister, but I would like to build with you, cry with you, learn from you, travel with you, and just be more than just a mere partner. I want to share the rest of my life with you. So, with that all said, will you marry me?"

With one hand placed over her mouth in shock, Andrea tried to remain calm while various emotions coursed through her. Tears fell out of her eyes as she stared at the gleam of the ring.

"So, what did you say?" Shania asked excitedly when Andrea told her the news the next day at her house after church.

"What do you think I said, Nia? Of course, I said yes!" Andrea exclaimed, holding up her hand while proudly displaying the ring as both women squealed, unable to contain their emotions.

This got the attention of Shania's husband, Trevor McClain, who had previously gone upstairs to change clothes upon returning from service. "Whoa, what are you ladies screaming about?" he asked.

"Quentin asked Andrea to marry him yesterday, and Andrea said yes!" Shania explained excitedly.

"Wow, congratulations, Andrea! I remember you introduced me to Quentin a few months ago. He's good people. Why he agreed to marry you, I don't know," he joked.

"Shut up, bighead. Nia, just for that, you need to put Trevor on timeout at night, if you know what I'm sayin'."

"Nah, you don't get to decide that, superstar. I'm the man 'round here," he boasted proudly.

"Oh Lord, boy, don't you ever get tired of strokin' your own ego?" Andrea asked.

"Tired? Girl, he's just gettin' started, trust me," Shania chimed in.

"Baby, you know how I get down. You spoiled me," Trevor replied, sheepishly.

"Mmhmm, well keep acting brand new, and I might have to take my girl's advice to leave you on red," Shania warned.

"And that's a fact, Jack," Andrea added, laughing.

"You know what, I see it's Jump on Brothas Day today, so I'll leave you two to it. Congrats again, sis. Baby, I just received a text, and the club wants me to come in cuz they're short a couple employees. I'll see you later," Trevor said as he headed out the door.

"Club? On a Sunday?" Andrea asked Shania.

"Yeah, didn't I tell you? Trevor manages a Boys and Girls Club in South Queens now. Ever since he stopped playing basketball, he's been looking for opportunities to give back to the community and work with these kids. God knows they need it these days, what with all these dropouts and steady rise in crime and gangs re-forming again."

Andrea shook her head without commenting immediately, and Shania instantly regretted bringing back painful memories of Loree's murder.

"I'm sorry, Andrea...I shouldn't have mentioned gangs. That was over the line."

"No, it's completely fine," Andrea reassured Shania. "I still struggle with it even to this day, but with prayer, meditation, singing, and performing, I'm learning to cope with it."

"I feel you. Sometimes I still can't believe she's gone. Seems like yesterday, we were back at my parent's house, and she's going through my closet, jacking my clothes, and we'd have little fashion shows. Mind you, most of the clothes she was wearing, my father would never approve."

Andrea laughed. "To keep it a buck, I used to do the same thing to her. I would raid her closet, take her shoes and earrings, and Loree would come back, and no matter how hard I tried putting her stuff back in its place, she would somehow figure out that I'd been snooping in her room."

Shania playfully narrowed her eyes at Andrea. "See, I knew it was a learned behavior."

Andrea laughed. When she was not recording at Omega Studios or touring, she enjoyed visiting Shania's house, and in more ways than one, Shania had become her sister.

"Speaking of which, where is little Loree?" she asked, looking around for Shania and Trevor's daughter, Loree Emiline.

"Oh, she's sleeping over at a friend's house. I gotta tell you, your goddaughter is becoming more and more opinionated every day. She's five going on thirty. Girl, I had to check her the other day for snapping on me at the department store because I didn't buy a hair bow that she liked."

Andrea laughed. "If she gets out of hand, just tell her you'll call Auntie Drea, and she'll set her straight."

"Believe me, she'll start actin' right once I mention that Auntie Drea is coming. She lights up whenever you come around."

"She's a sweetheart, Nia. So, about the wedding, I wanted to ask you something. Will you be the maid of honor?" Andrea asked.

She hesitated to ask because when Shania appointed her to be the maid of honor at her own wedding, Andrea was unable to attend the wedding, and her absence reportedly crushed Shania. She nearly did not walk down the aisle, but thankfully, she proceeded with the wedding. Andrea blamed herself for letting Shania down and vowed to strengthen their bond to make amends, no matter how long it took.

Fortunately, Shania forgave Andrea, and it was only right that Shania helped her walk down the aisle in her wedding nuptials.

"Andrea, I would love to be your maid of honor at your wedding. There's no other person I would rather stand next to than my sister," Shania said, hugging her.

"Thanks, Nia. So, after the tour, we'll start planning for the wedding. We're projecting it to take place in the fall of 2019," Andrea said.

"Girl, there is no time to waste. We need to start looking for your wedding dress, then finding venues for the marriage. I'll hook you up with my homegirl Alice. She was our wedding planner, and she was amazing."

"Well, I was hoping we could do at the Rock of Jacob Baptist Church," Shania said and stared at a shocked Andrea.

"Really? Even after the falling out between our fathers?" Andrea asked, referring to the last argument that took place between Pastor Mike Hillman and Amos McAfee in the pastor's office.

Amos had been convinced that David had slain his daughter, and he had asked Pastor Mike to testify against David, but Pastor Mike had refused. As a result, Amos had walked away from the Rock of Jacob Baptist Church and had never returned.

"Don't worry about him, Shania. I'll talk to him. At some point, they'll have to make peace with the past," Andrea reassured, but in her heart, she knew it was going take a lot of convincing to persuade Amos to step foot back in his old church.

CHAPTER 10

THE REUNION OF
"HEISMAN" AND "TONE"

Lincoln High School's tight end, Bobby Wilson broke through the defensive line with less than two minutes on the clock in their football game against Townsend Harris High School. With unmatched strength and speed, he ran as fast and as hard he could, leaving a trail of defenders behind him.

"C'mon, guys, get him!" David bellowed from the sidelines, but it was to no avail.

Bobby Wilson saw nothing but green ahead of him, and he grinned at David as he strolled to the end zone.

The touchdown put Lincoln High School up 23-17 as time began to run out for Townsend Harris. After completing the field goal kick for the extra point, Lincoln was up 24-17.

David was beside himself. His team had led throughout the game, holding Lincoln to three points through two quarters, and he thought that the game was already decided, but Lincoln emerged from the locker room a completely different team.

They took advantage of blown coverages defensively and scored two times within the span of ten minutes to tie the game at 17-17 apiece. David took a sigh of relief and thought the momentum would swing his way, but Bobby dashed those hopes after he scored, and David was forced to call timeout to help the offensive coordinator design a sure-fire way to score.

They attempted to send the game to overtime, but the opportunity never arrived as Pierce Bell over passed the ball twice, resulting in a second down. Then on the third down, Lincoln's pass rush defense got the better of him, tackling him hard before he had the chance to pass the ball. Suddenly, it was 4th and 1st and the Lincoln players started to celebrate as Townsend Harris fans groaned in disappointment. David shook his head angrily. Nobody wanted this game more than he did, and he hated being in a position where he had to endure a tough loss, especially in a game that he felt they should have won.

As the clock winded down, the stands, which were largely filled with Townsend Harris supporters, began to file out of the field, disappointed. As the clock hit zero, and the final horn went off, the players from both teams headed into the locker room. David now faced the disappointing task of addressing his dejected players and coordinators, whose schemes were thwarted by Lincoln High School. The homecoming game was David's chance to make a huge statement against a ranked team, and nobody hated losing on that stage like him.

Walking back into the locker room, David slammed the locker room door angrily. I'm definitely going to need a drink after today. Maybe a drink and good pool game would cheer me up.

On Friday nights after a hard day of coaching, David would often head to Cue Ball Bar in Bayside, New York. It was a bit of a distance for him to travel, but he needed to blow some steam off after a loss to the rival school. A pool game and some extra ends would lift his spirits.

After calling his wife to tell her where he would be, David stepped into the bar. His favorite bartender, Jason, was behind the bar, and after he was done serving another customer, David stepped right up to the bar.

"What's up, Joe? Lemme get my usual."

Immediately, Jason picked up on the coach's mood. "Uh oh, I know that look. Them boys got beat tonight?" he asked.

"Yeah, man. The most frustrating part is that we had that game too. But we made too many mistakes down the stretch, and we couldn't hang on. We lost 24-17."

"Damn that sucks," Jason replied. "But that Lincoln team is one of the best in the state. They got weapons for days on that squad. I'm sure you did your best."

As David sipped his beer, he looked at the other side of the bar where the pool tables were set up, and to his dismay, a small crowd was gathered around the pool area. As a pastime, David enjoyed playing pool, and he had gained quite a reputation for being the "Billiards Boss." But as good as he was, he never drew a crowd with his play and yet, a crowd was covering his favorite table, Lucky Lucy as he'd coined it.

"Yo, Jason, what's going on?"

"Oh, we had this new cat breeze in earlier today. Businessman, by the looks of it. He's been dominating everybody and takin' money. Rumor says he bettin' about twenty a ball."

David stared in Jason in disbelief. Twenty dollars a ball? This guy's been robbing half of New York. Let's see him play someone as good as he is.

David walked to the pool tables. There were three set up, and one of them was empty, which would have benefitted David, but David wanted to learn more about the man who was dominating at his table. The man, on the other hand, had finished beating Clay Morgan in pool. Clay sulked off, having lost an excess of $200.

As David approached Lucky Lucy, he saw the man, who had his sleeves rolled up and was wearing gray slacks.

"Okay, I'm getting bored with all these pretenders. Where the real pool players at?" the man challenged.

"I'll take you on," David replied.

The man stared David up and down, and although he was taller than David, David had more muscle than his opponent. Taking a mental note of the fact in case the meeting turned violent, David took his favorite stick as the stranger racked the balls.

"So how much you want to play for?" the man asked.

"Well, I don't play for money like that. I was just hoping for just a friendly game," David replied.

The crowd, which had started dispersing, left the two men at the table. The man looked at David. Up until this big guy had appeared, he had been winning every pool game, picking up some cash along the way.

Edward Reed had changed his routine. When he was in the mood for drinks and pool games, the Cue Ball Bar offered that escape for him. He ditched his normal bar in the Upper East Side and made his way to Bayside to play pool while seeing if he could earn a few bucks on the side. The cases kept him busy during the day, and he needed to blow off some steam.

"Alright, I guess I already made too much money off you brothas. Might as well give you a break. Besides, I don't know how I'd feel about myself taking money away from a Board of Education staff member. Ya' need the money more than I do," he chuckled.

David did not find the statement funny at all. Sure, he was not making six figures as a coach, but he loved his job all the same. "You pretty cocky for a man who just breezed up in here lookin' like he dressed up for BET's Sunday's Best."

Once all the balls were placed in the triangle, Edward placed the white one carefully in the center as he prepared to break. After a couple of minutes, the game got underway. Edward watched the man closely. There was something familiar about this staff worker that he played with, but he could not put his finger on it.

"Here's a free lesson. Yellow ball, corner pocket," said David.

Edward watched as David sank the yellow ball into the corner pocket. "Lucky shot, bro," Edward remarked as his opponent prepared to shoot again.

"Red ball, side pocket." But David missed the side pocket, and now it was Edward who stepped up to the table.

"So what did you call this table again?" Edward asked. "Lucky Lucy? Looks like I'm getting' lucky with Lucy tonight. Green striped ball, corner pocket, B."

Sure enough, the striped green ball found its way into the corner pocket.

"You're pretty good at this game, son. What's yo' name?" David asked.

For a moment, Edward hesitated. Should he introduce himself to David Anderson? The main reason he feared returning to Queens was for this very reason: running into a former gangbanger. Edward now realized he was speaking to a man who was once considered more dangerous than Tadarius himself.

"They call me Eddie. What about you?"

David laughed. "David Anderson, man. What was with the long silence? Cat got yo' tongue?"

"Nah, nothin' like that. I can't believe I'm talkin' to David Anderson, former quarterback at Richmond High School back in '03."

David's interest piqued because, aside from his friends and other classmates, there were not too many people that remembered his exploits on the field.

"Yeah. How do you know about that? You must've went to Richmond Hill, right?"

"Something like that. I know that you were accused of a crime you didn't commit. The shooting of that high school girl, right?"

David starting tugging at his shirt collar, out of either nervousness or room temperature. "Yeah, but I don't like to bring that up though. Brings too many bad memories."

"But before you were gonna be locked up, you had a star witness in court that day, and his testifying proved your innocence. So, you weren't locked up," Edward continued.

"Look, man, are you gonna keep bringing up my past, or are we gonna play pool?" David asked impatiently.

The next words that followed widened David's eyes and put him on high alert, for he hadn't heard the words in years, but it was the nefarious slogan that had defined their set.

"I don't play about my ends or my riches. Cuz all I want is the money..." Edward started, and sure enough David finished the statement for him. "...and the bitches."

Edward rolled his shirtsleeve up and showed David the gang tattoo.

David was thrown aback when he saw the emblem. "Hold up, you rolled wit' M.O.B. too?"

"Yeah, but I know you. You was Tadarius's homeboy. Until he tried to frame you, and he jacked me up pretty good too."

Fed up with the guessing games, David decided to confront the man who seemed to know too much information. "Okay, who are you? I don't remember seeing you at all back in da day. I'm sure I would've remembered an Eddie who was in M.O.B."

"But you do remember Antonio Franks, right?" Edward asked.

"Antonio Franks? Yeah, I think so. He was the only cat that stood up for me in court, he helped me clear my name and exposed Tadarius for the slick jackass that he really was. I never saw him again after that though. I never got a chance to thank him."

"You're welcome, Heisman," Edward replied.

David looked at Edward again. Only members of M.O.B. called me Heisman. Then as the realization of who David was speaking with at that moment dawned on him, Edward smiled.

"Is that you, Tone?" David asked.

"In the flesh, homie."

Taken aback by the reunion, both men embraced and dapped each other.

"What's up, man? Long time, no see, bro. What's good wit' you?" David asked.

"I've been good, man...no complaints. Just busy working and playing after work, you feel me?"

"No doubt. Yo, I can't believe it's you, dawg. Last I heard, you was in the witness protection program after the trial. Then word on the street was that you went ghost. Nobody saw you again. Now you just walkin' up in hea' like nothin' changed."

"Technically, I did go ghost. Well, Antonio went ghost. After I got my name changed, I transferred out of Richmond Hill."

"Word? And what happened after that?" David asked.

"Went to Montresor Prep, up in Brooklyn. I felt like I was an alien up there, son. Mostly white kids, white teachers, people lookin' at you like you finna' do something wrong, you know what it is. Nothing like Richmond Hill. So, what about you?"

"Shit, with Tadarius out the way and M.O.B. breaking up, I finished high school, went to Seton Hall...that didn't go very well. Then I played at LIU Post for three years. I was close to making it to the league, son. Then I blew my knee out that last year."

"Damn, that sucks. We all knew you was going pro one day."

David shrugged his shoulders. There was a moment in his life where he regretted not going to the NFL, but he never dwelled on what could have been. He was content with his life, and he did not have to answer to anyone.

"Everything happens for a reason, bro. But on the real, son, I ain't realize that you had a peanut head. You look mad different without them cornrows, dawg."

"Yeah. Part of the new identity. Besides, you don't see a lot of cats with cornrows on their heads these days anymore."

As the two men chatted, they continued playing pool, and to his surprise, David found out that he was no match for Edward Reed. He was thoroughly dominating the pool game throughout the evening.

As they racked the balls for a rematch, David asked, "So, whose idea was it to change your name?"

"The lead detective in that case suggested it, along with my lawyer. Detective Sands, I think was his name. Funny thing is, I ain't seen him again since the whole thing went down."

"Yeah, he don't stay out hea' no more. Heard that he moved down to Atlanta, Georgia. I guess they pay him better down there or something."

"How do you know he moved down there?" Edward asked.

"We still keep in touch from time to time. He likes to hit me up to see how I'm doing. Detective Sands was good people. I just wish my hardheaded ass listened to him earlier."

"You and me both, kid. Tadarius played us all, using us to make his ends while we take the heat."

"So, what you doing these days, Tone? Or should I call you Edward?" David laughed.

"So far, you the only one here who knows me by Tone, so you can call me what you want. But I'm a lawyer now. Been practicing for four years after college. I work in a firm in the city."

David shook his head, laughing. "Damn. Never thought I'd see the day where a member of M.O.B. is out here workin' for the man."

"It ain't a big deal, dawg. It's boring as hell cuz I only get traffic citations and small misdemeanor violations a majority of my day. Ain't nothing glamorous about what I do."

"So, why work that job then?"

Edward took his shot at a solid blue ball, sinking it into the corner pocket. "I wanna make a difference out here, man. How many times in history do you see black men get a foot in their ass, and most of the time the government ain't gonna do a damn thing about it. I'm just using the law against them. People are always looking for a defender of the law."

"Yeah, I guess, but it don't matter what you do or who you accomplish it with, ain't nothing gonna change the urban filth out here. You still got unpaved roads in some areas, schools underpaid, and kids dropping out to sell in the streets. Ain't nothin' changed from when we ran the streets."

Edward could not bring himself to agree with David. He still held hope that he could invoke a change in the community, no matter how bleak it looked. Improvements were made recently to stem the flow of violence in the area, but in the last few weeks, there had been an uptick in store robberies and car jackings, reminiscent of the earlier generation.

"So, what's been up with you lately, other than being a football coach?"

"Well, I've coached Townsend Harris for two years, got voted Coach of the Year last year. I got a wife and three kids. My oldest is eleven, and my youngest one is about to be seven years of age."

Edward smiled. He always felt that out of all the members of M.O.B., David would be the one to have a family. Life in the streets always had a contract for its players, and the game was never done with them, but David appeared to be completely done, especially if he had started a family. Edward envisioned David and Loree being a family because both had ambitions beyond the gang.

"Dennis, my son, is currently excelling in football, basketball, and track. I'm trying my hardest to steer him towards football. Maybe one day, he'll have the career that I never had."

"Well, it's all up to what he wants to do. But can he throw that football like his old man?" Edward asked.

"Well, we're still working on his spiral. But it's coming along. So, does the lawyer have a girl?" David asked.

"Nah. Nobody special. I mean, I've messed with a few women, but ain't nothin serious right now. I guess I'mma be a playa for life."

"You know, I always thought that you and shorty that used to roll wit' us would get down. What was her name again?"

"You mean Cici? I mean she was cool, but we neva' kicked it like that."

"What? All those times, she used to be all up in you, messin' wit' your cornrows back in the day, I thought for sho' both of ya were gettin' it in."

"I could have messed with that if I wanted, but she was the homie. Not that I never imagined hittin' it if I could, but for all I know, Tadarius could've been messin' wit' her too."

David shook his head upon mention of his old friend. "Wouldn't surprise me if he did tap that. But is it true what they're sayin' about him possibly getting out of prison?" he asked.

There were rumors circulating around town that Tadarius was being paroled and was eligible for early release. His lawyers had been working feverishly to turn the case into an assault against him by the New York City Police Department upon his arrest. Originally his sentence had been life without parole, but his lawyers managed to reduce the sentence to twenty years, and having already served fifteen years, he was up for early parole.

When the news first aired, Edward's heart almost stopped. It could not be true. There was no way that Tadarius would be let out of prison early. Edward knew that his first order of business would be to re-establish M.O.B., and then he would promptly go after those who had caused his imprisonment, which included David and himself, thus the whole reason for his anonymity.

"Being in the courts all week, you hear little rumors here and there, and someone lets slip some valuable information. But yeah, I heard that Tadarius might be released any day now, and if they're releasing him early, they'll probably release Terrell."

"Yeah, but I ain't about to sweat all that. I mean, we don't really know if they gon' get outta jail, and even if they do, they ain't gonna recognize us anyway. I mean, we don't look like our high school selves anymore. Some of us still got our hair," David joked, jabbing at Edward's bald fade haircut.

"You still got jokes, Heisman," Edward said as he helped David rack up the pool table.

Later that evening at the Radisson Motel in Rosedale New York, Xavier walked into one of the hotel suites, accompanied by his female companion. Following a win in the midnight bike circuit over Clutch, a well-known biker, Xavier had started a conversation with a light skin black woman with long red hair, short denim shorts, and a pink parka. When Xavier had asked her name, she'd identified herself as "Bunny."

Whether it was her real name or not, it made no difference to Xavier. It was going to be another night of wild, mind-blowing sex.

These women really love champs. And Bunny is fine as hell. I'm about to give her this steel and lay her ass out.

With a bottle of Hennessey, a tray, and a dime bag of weed, Xavier was ready to go. Bunny wasted no time pushing him to the bed, pulling his shirt and pants off in the process.

As she kissed him ravenously, he began pulling off her parka, but she stopped him. "Hold up, baby. I got a surprise for you. Don't move. I'm about to have you whipped," she said, walking into the bathroom with her designer bag, all while making sure she gave him a show on the way there.

Xavier searched his pocket, frantically looking for a condom. I know I got one more rubber on me. I ain't tryin' to get any of these hoes knocked up. Note to self: Get some more rubbers. Can't be caught short out here.

Xavier's reputation of being one of the best bikers in New York preceded his reputation as being one of the biggest gigolos in New York. His testosterone level matched the extreme mileage of the bikes that he rode during his races: adrenaline filled, fast, and no quick stops. He could keep it up and going all night long. Then when he was done, he would pay for the girls' ride, maybe treat 'em to a breakfast or lunch, depending on the time, take their number as if he would call them, and go his separate way.

He would never give them a second thought, and why should he? More than half of these women were not looking for a long-term relationship. They just want to get their rocks off in a one-night stand as most men did, and as long as they got theirs, it was okay.

Xavier saw no harm in how he lived. He remembered how Tadarius would always entertain himself with at least three women at one time, and all of them were willing participants in their sex escapades.

When Bunny emerged from the bathroom, she was wearing a short leather skirt that exposed her buttocks and a black leather thong. She completed the set with a black leather bra, and her long red hair was tied in a ponytail. She had two pairs of handcuffs and a black leather whip.

Normally, Xavier was not a fan of the female dominatrix look, but Bunny's look was turning him on, and having already downed a few shots of Hennessey, he was ready to have fun.

"Damn, baby, I knew you was a freak at the race, but I ain' know you was that much of a freak."

Bunny smiled. "Well, you're so good at being bad, I felt like tonight you needed to be punished," she replied, cracking the whip for emphasis.

With his erection on full display, Xavier kissed Bunny throughout her chest as she worked on handcuffing him to the bedpost. Both of his hands were in cuffs, and lying spread eagle on the bed, Xavier was eagerly anticipating his "punishment."

But to his surprise, Bunny was not finished. She pulled out a black leather blindfold and proceeded to cover his eyes.

"Yo, Bunny, I don't really know about this blindfold shit."

"Don't worry, baby, this just adds to the whole effect. You don't like to role play?"

"I'm cool with role playing, but I'd like to see what I'm doing. Otherwise, what's the point of doing it at all?" Xavier's senses heightened, but he was not fully alert, partly due to his inebriation, which was what Bunny was counting on.

"C'mon, Lone X, I thought you was spontaneous and wanted to have fun. I mean, if you ain't down wit' this, then I could go."

Xavier's pride suddenly kicked in. He was not going to let his fears ruin what promised to be an eventful evening. "Nah, nah, I'm good. Just do yo' thing, baby girl."

Playing soft R&B music on her phone, she mounted Xavier and began to grind her body on him. While the music played, Xavier heard the unmistakable sound of unzipping, and he assumed that Bunny was removing her leather dominatrix costume.

But the zipping sound came from a bag that held an assortment of knives. Picking out the sharpest one, the predator leaned forward until she was close to the ear of her unsuspecting prey. "Oh, by the way, Tadarius says hi."

It would be the last words Xavier would hear before his throat was unceremoniously slit in half.

CHAPTER 11

TERRELL'S UNEXPECTED VISITOR

FEBRUARY 2019

Waking up just before six a.m., Terrell Washington rolled back the sheets in his single-bed cell. Dropping down to the floor, he proceeded to do one hundred push-ups. It was part of his daily habit whenever he woke up in the morning.

He was forced to develop habits, partly because it kept him sane at the Queensboro County Prison. After completing the pushups, he walked over to the edge of his bed. His bed was raised about fourteen inches above the floor, which allowed him to thrust his legs under it. Holding onto the ends of the bed, while lying on his back, he did one hundred pull-ups.

As he worked on his exercise, his mind often wandered back to the life-altering event that led to his arrest back in October 2003, a time when the world around him had crumbled. It started with the death of Loree McAfee.

Tadarius had given the order to have Loree killed, and he had selected Terrell and his friend and protégé Antonio to carry out the execution. But Antonio panicked and left Terrell in the car with Loree.

After Loree's murder, the town grieved, and the police worked overtime to find a suspect. Terrell, who felt deeply dedicated to M.O.B. and the cause of defending family and the streets, felt that Loree had what was coming to her.

Tadarius then devised a genius move to frame his former right-hand man David for the crime. David had left the gang behind, which meant he was a liability to Tadarius and the remaining members of the crew.

The rumors of David's physical abuse of Loree only raised suspicions about his involvement in her murder. But Tadarius had a contingency plan. If framing David did not work, Terrell had to take the fall and admit guilt for Loree's murder. Tadarius confided the details to Terrell not long after David was arrested.

Terrell had to stay loyal to the family, no matter how painful it was or how innocent he was. He did not have too long to agree to be the fall guy because, through an unspecified source, he learned that while David was tried in court, his former associate Antonio name-dropped him in court and implicated him for the murder. He found out in the worst way though, after going through one of the deadliest shootouts in the history of Queens.

David had confronted his old gang after being exonerated. Terrell thought David was out of his mind to reappear so boldly. Just when they were about to send him six feet under, they were suddenly surrounded by the police force. David was wired, and he led the police to their location.

What transpired next was an exchange of gunfire between the police and the members of M.O.B.

Terrell had to watch in horror as Terrance and Malik, two boys who had become brothers to him, were brutally gunned down. Terrell could still see Malik's eyes, still open as he lay still in a pool of his own blood. It was an image that he still saw in his dreams, and he could not shake the visions. Terrell was nearly killed that night as well, but a bullet only grazed his knee, and his leader was shot in the leg.

After they surrendered to police, Terrell and Tadarius were taken to Jamaica Hospital for medical attention before being booked at the Queens County Jail. Terrell remembered the lethal look in Tadarius's eyes when he rode in the police squad car with him. Both boys were treated at the hospital, and they were on the way to jail. Terrell had known that the police would catch up to them, but that did not stop him from swearing revenge on those that betrayed him.

"Stick to the plan." Referring to the plan of Terrell taking the blame for the murder, Tadarius's words to Terrell were chilling, but it was what he said next that made Terrell believe that he was not done.

"They ain't gonna hold me for long, and once I'm out, I want David and Antonio's asses. I'm gon' get them for what they did to Malik and Terrance. That's a promise. Both of them dead."

Terrell had seen Tadarius threaten other people before, but this was serious. Terrell knew that with the vast connections Tadarius had in the city, he would find a way to be paroled.

Terrell's situation was vastly different. He had to take the fall for the murder of Loree even though he had not pulled the trigger. It was his duty to ride for the crew all day, and there were no exceptions about it at any point.

He knew who the true murderer was, but he kept his mouth shut, and when Tadarius and Terrell were finally tried in court, the deliberation barely took an hour. When the verdict came out, both Terrell and Tadarius were sentenced to life without parole, although a few years later, his lawyer managed to lower the sentence to twenty years with the possibility of parole. He learned that Tadarius received the same deal.

The main reason the initial sentence was overturned was due to the insufficient evidence at the scene and the autopsy report that was released. A detailed analysis of Loree's corpse showed that the bullets that ended her life had come from a Beretta handgun, and the gun that was confiscated from Terrell at the time of his arrest was a Glock. Both guns had different bullet sizes, which meant that there was undeniably a third suspect in the crime, one that pulled the trigger.

When Terrell was asked if anyone was in the car with him, he maintained the same account that he was in the car by himself, and he was responsible for Loree's murder.

Two days earlier, Terrell was visited by a lawyer and was informed that he was working diligently with the parole board, and he was close to being released from prison due to insufficient evidence tying him to the murder. When the news went out, there were mixed reactions from the public.

Even the police shootout that took place back in 2003 was considered excessive force, and the officers involved were reprimanded, fired, or transferred. An argument was made that the boys fired back in self-defense after police fired first, and the story quickly gained traction.

Terrell was transferred to Queensboro County Prison in 2012, and he had been waiting for an opportunity to get out of prison ever since.

After finishing his pull-ups, the guard called his block as the men headed for the showers. Then breakfast was served at the facility cafeteria, and afterwards, the daily duties were assigned to the inmates. Terrell, who once was assigned to outside yard work, had switched with a fellow inmate and was now working at the facility office, filing paperwork and organizing shelves.

Later during the day, as Terrell was filing the last of the facility files, he was called by a guard. "Washington, you got a visitor. Let's go."

Accompanying the officer to the visitor center, Terrell looked at the other side of the glass and picked up the phone. A woman sat across from him, wearing all business attire and what appeared to be a thick weave or wig, topped off with designer sunglasses. Terrell initially questioned her identity. But what he did not complain about was the woman's legs. She had a nice set of legs and very toned curves, and as he sat across from her, separated by only glass, he felt himself pitch a tent. They both picked up the phone.

"Well, it's not every day I get a visit from a beautiful lady such as yourself. To whom do I owe this visit to?" he asked.

"Don't worry about me. I'm the one who'll be asking the questions around here," she replied sharply, taking Terrell aback.

Typically, in his heyday, he was accustomed to women showing him respect, and if he was lucky that day, showing him much more. But this lady was having none of it, and she displayed an arrogant and rude attitude as if he was the last person she wanted to talk to.

"Remember the girl that you shot back in '03? What kind of gun did you use to kill her?" she asked.

"I don't know. I can't even remember anymore. It might have been a Beretta or some shit like that. I don't even know why I'm tellin' you this. You ain't my lawyer."

"And you ain't worth my damn time, but I'm asking you this information because I want to know you ain't lyin' your way out of jail."

Terrell laughed, but he'd noticed that the woman seemed triggered whenever he showed any level of poise during her line of questioning.

"Who else was in the car with you that day?" she asked.

"Well, Antonio's punk ass was in the car with me at first, but he couldn't roll wit' the big dawgs, so he rolled on out of there."

Now it was the woman's turn to chuckle. She knew that she was in the presence of a dangerous ex-gangmember who looked as if he was strong enough to break through the glass and choke the life out of her, but she did not fear him.

"Big dawgs? That's what ya call yourselves? Lemme tell you something, all of you gang members are nothin' but murderers and a waste of space. So, you're gonna tell me what I want to know now."

"You think I sweat you? Let me tell you something, lil' lady, you don't know T like I do, okay? Trust and believe he ain't gon' be locked up for long, and when he gets up out these chains, he's gon' be runnin' shit like he never left."

"Yeah, well keep dreaming. I'm gonna fight the parole board's decision to release you. Long as I'm alive, I'mma make sure both of ya never get outside these bars. Go run and tell dat."

Terrell snickered under his breath. It was all that he could do to keep from laughing. The woman spent half of her life in the entertainment industry, and she had the gall to come to the facility and make threats? It was comical.

"You know what? You just like your damn sister. She never knew when to mind her fuckin' business, and when she stuck her head where it shouldn't have been, her ass had it coming."

With her cover now blown, there was no need for pretense, as Andrea took her sunglasses off. "You don't know my sister, okay? I will do whatever it takes to make the person responsible for her death pay for it, and if I find out that you had something to do with it, and they let you out, being locked up is gon' be the least of your worries."

Terrell, still snickering under his breath, stared Andrea down for a few moments. Damn, she grew up to be fine. She ain't that annoying lil' tag-along sister that Loree had to pry off her at times. But she way out of her league if she think she gon' stop what's in motion right now.

"Check this out, Andrea, or should I call you Adia? I'm confused. Anyway, after you get off this little soapbox of yours, why don't we hook up sometime? I think you need a man that's gon' pipe you on the regular cuz you all in your feelings right now."

Andrea looked at Terrell in clear disgust. "First off, I'm engaged, you sick bastard, and secondly, even if I was single, I wouldn't give you the time of day. Now, look me straight in the eyes, and tell me now. Did you kill my sister?"

But Terrell did not feel pressured or threatened to answer to Andrea and continued to dance around the questions, which infuriated her. "I'm wondering, how'd you even find me?"

"I got my ways. Don't worry about it. Just answer the question."

But Terrell only danced more, even taking the chance to shoot his shot at the recording artist. "If I say no, baby, you wanna go to the back room real quick? You fine as fuck, and it'd be a shame to let you go without getting some. Yo' man obviously ain't givin' it to you right, and you on one. Just give me five minutes. That's all I need."

Andrea rolled her eyes. This was not going anywhere. Slamming the phone back onto the receiver, she got up and turned to walk out of the facility.

"You'll have to forgive me. It's been a long time," Terrell continued, laughing derisively as Andrea stared at him with disgust one final time before leaving the room.

Later that day, Edward was in his office working with Mrs. Hannah Brenner, a divorced woman who was filing a lawsuit with Infancia, a small company that sold products for infants, including strollers, baby seats, mobiles, cribs, and other miscellaneous items. Mrs. Brenner's infant son, Todd, was lying in his crib one day while Mrs. Brenner was cleaning the kitchen. She periodically checked on Todd every five minutes because she had reservations about leaving him unattended.

While she was busy working, she heard a loud sound from the room. Alarmed and panicked, Mrs. Brenner ran to her son's room and was met immediately by the sound of her son crying. The crib, which had been built sturdily, was missing one of its legs, and when Mrs. Brenner assessed the damage, she saw that the crib leg had snapped in two as if it was made out of dry sticks. She understood that accidents happened, but her son's life was in peril.

Fortunately, Todd was only startled by the crib breaking off, but Mrs. Brenner was extremely upset and had called Infancia to report the incident. She expected them to refund her, increase her warranty, or pay for repairs. But the customer care representative for Infancia was rude to Mrs. Brenner, and she was informed that Infancia would not increase her warranty or give her any credit for damages.

They offered to replace her product, but Mrs. Brenner refused the proposition for replacement. After declining her credit inquiry, she decided to file a lawsuit against the company, and she called Schorr Law Group to promptly file the suit.

Edward had been examining the case and decided to take the case. Mrs. Brenner asked him what her options were.

"Mrs. Brenner, after further investigation, I do see that you have a plausible case here. Infancia did place a warning on the box during assembly, warning that if the crib was mounted incorrectly, injury or death was possible."

"But I was not the one that assembled the crib. Infancia sent people to put the crib together, and I thought they did a good job until the crib leg broke," Mrs. Brenner protested.

"Yes, I do see what you are saying, but I also think that suing them in state court might not be the right move in this situation because they could combat it with their warning and their terms. But we can explore trying to collect damages by sending them to civil court. Now maybe if we can have them sign a settlement for $2,000, that might be the best step for us right now."

There was silence on the phone, and Edward knew that Mrs. Brenner was exploring her options. "Okay, that sounds feasible. I will definitely mull it over, and I will call you back tomorrow with my answer."

"Sounds good, Mrs. Brenner. Thanks for calling, and we'll discuss it again tomorrow."

Hanging up the phone, Edward leaned back in his chair. Checking his watch, he saw that it was about six p.m. As he began to gather his belongings to put them in his briefcase, he received a call from his receptionist, Jenny Mote.

"Hello, Mr. Reed, I have a David Anderson on Line 2. Should I pass him to you?"

Remembering that he had provided his number to David when they reunited at the pool hall, Edward allowed the call to be transferred to his extension. "Yeah, what's up, bro? Before you tell me anything, hit me up on my cell. All calls are being monitored on this line."

"Bet," David replied before hanging up.

A few seconds later, Edward felt his cell phone vibrate. "Talk to me," he replied.

"Man, you straight turned into Mr. Company Man these days now, huh?" David laughed.

"Yo, whatever, man. What you hitting me up for, Heisman? You in some type of legal trouble? I told you about all that bettin' down at the pool hall."

"Nah, it ain't that, Tone. Did you check the local news?"

"No, I didn't. Why?"

"Yo, if you can, go to Channel 3, Tone. They're talking about it right now."

Searching for the remote to turn on his office television mounted near the ceiling, Edward turned the television on and flipped to Channel 3, with David still on the line.

The news anchors were already underway reporting the breaking news. A 32-year-old man, who was later identified as Xavier Furrows, was reportedly stabbed to death in a hotel. According to coroners at the scene, apart from the superficial stab wounds, the murderer had slit Xavier's throat so deep, severing his carotid artery in the process, nearly decapitating his head. The crime scene resembled a bloody warzone with blood splatter everywhere.

According to the witnesses and the hotel guests, Xavier had entered the hotel in the early morning, accompanied by a female companion, when he was last seen alive. Xavier was popular around the area, especially with people who were involved in the late-night bike circuit.

But Edward remembered Xavier as the boy who was with Terrell the first time they met back in 2002. It was Xavier who had lent Edward his bike to make his first drug run. But Edward also remembered how Xavier indirectly sold him out to Tadarius, as he remembered the day he was brutally beaten as Malik and Terrance held him. Xavier was in the vicinity, and Edward was almost sure that he followed him into the store that day and tipped the gang leader off about his whereabouts.

There was yet a part of Edward that felt a level of sympathy towards Xavier. He did not deserve this untimely death.

But the other part of Edward, as cruel as it was, rejoiced that the snitch finally got what was coming to him. The grisly details of the murder made him shudder, but street justice was undefeated.

"Damn, I ain't think anyone was gonna take Zay out like that," he told David.

"Me too. You know, I was the one that recruited him back in '01. I got him caught up in that shit, and now he's dead."

"Look, man, let's wait till all the evidence comes out. We don't know if this was an M.O.B. hit or not. He probably owed a bookie some money and didn't pay up. It's obvious that whoever he was with was foul to begin with, so we can't be drawing no conclusions."

Edward did his best to convince David that Xavier's death was a fluke, but he had his own reservations. Was it possible that Tadarius was behind Xavier's death? He is still in prison, but there is speculation that insufficient evidence could lead to his release soon. Is Tadarius cleaning house, and if so, what did Xavier do to piss him off?

After ending the call with David, Edward turned the television off and resumed packing his materials into his briefcase. He needed a drink, so he decided to stop by the Diamond Bar for one. An hour later, he stepped out of the bar with Mia Haranata, an exotic petite woman who was born in the Philippines but grew up in Washington Heights.

As usual, Edward had brought Mia a drink and had enjoyed conversing with her. She was a professional choreographer who worked for different theater companies and choreographed various music artists. Mia was three years younger than Edward, but the two hit it off, and it was not long before both ended up back at Edward's apartment. Just like Jackie and the other women before her, Mia was not looking for a long-term relationship. She just wanted to have a good time.

Edward began kissing her as if he would never get another chance to be amorously infatuated with another woman, and when Mia stripped her small skirt off, he wasted no time diving into her headfirst as she laughed in pleasure.

"You like that, baby?" she asked seductively as she arched her back and rubbed her breasts behind her bra.

"I love it, baby!" Edward replied with exhilarating enthusiasm.

While they kissed, Mia mounted Edward on top of his bed, then took both of his hands and threw them over his head. Working slowly but intricately, Mia began using the sheets to tie Edward's hands to the bedpost.

Suddenly, Edward's anxiety was heightened. Aw, hell no! No, no, no. Something is wrong here. This is exactly how the police found Xavier. I don't know this girl too well. Xavier's killer is still at large, and for all I know, she might have been the one who did him in. She might be tying me up now, and the next thing I know, she's carving me up like a turkey on Thanksgiving.

Edward started to get visions of Mia tying his hands to render him defenseless while she looked to end his life. "Hold, up, Mia, what you doing?" he asked alarmingly.

"Nothing, baby, just a little foreplay. Are you okay?" she asked.

"Yeah, I'm good, but can we ease up on the foreplay and the hand-tying stuff please? I'm just not feelin' that today," Edward explained.

He did not want to appear buck broken or weak, but he could not allow what happened to Xavier to happen to him, under any circumstances.

Fortunately, Mia seemed to understand. "Alright, I'm sorry, Eddie. When we met at the bar, I took you to be the adventurous type," she said disappointingly as she untied the sheets from his wrists.

"Usually, I am, but I just want to take it easy for tonight, ya' know?"

Mia did not question it any further and continued kissing Edward, but through her kisses, Edward knew that Mia was turned off by his lack of aggression.

"Mia, listen, I think we should chill out tonight. Maybe we get down another time?"

Although Mia's heart was no longer in their passionate lovemaking, she was still disappointed that he decided to cut it off. "Eddie, is it me? I thought you liked me."

Rubbing his face, Edward could not believe what had transpired. The fear of being murdered in the same method as Xavier had ruined his evening.

"Mia, it ain't you, okay? It's me. I just got a lot on my mind right now, and on any other day, I would've been puttin' it on you, believe me. Look, if it's okay, I can drive you home," he offered, but the damage was done.

Mia rolled her eyes, got up, and started dressing. "Don't bother. If you're not into me, just say so. I'll just call an Uber, okay? Why don't you stay here and work on your issues?"

Grabbing her purse and her shoes, Mia stormed out the apartment, shutting the door behind her. Edward buried his face in his hands.

Damn, I can't believe I just did that.

CHAPTER 12

TONY'S NEW GIRL

As he watched the Uber pick Mia up at the end of the block from his bedroom window, Edward thought about the events that had led up to Mia's departure. Xavier's death had shaken him to the core and triggered his anxiety at the worst possible time.

Having suffered through panic attacks since he was eleven years of age, Edward had repeatedly gone to the doctor, but in his opinion, they offered little to no help. The only resolution they offered was Expiderol, an over-the-counter pill that decreased high blood pressure. Edward hated Expiderol because it came with some slight side effects that included change of mood, drowsiness, and at times nausea.

There was another unofficial treatment for his anxiety: marijuana. Ever since Edward was in M.O.B., he was a habitual smoker of weed, and the THC component helped calm his nerves. But after Edward left the gang and transferred out of Richmond Hill, he had had to find new creative locations to smoke. He was not allowed to smoke at Montresor School, so whenever school was over, he would enter a subway station, where he would meet with his old friend, Reese Groves.

Reese used to live in the same apartment where Edward lived with his mother and aunt in Queens, but he had moved out. Reese worked in sanitation during the day, but he moonlighted as a drug dealer, selling inside subways, the port authority, and other locations that kept him hidden from the cops.

Edward would routinely buy a dimebag from Reese and roll up on his way home. Then when Edward moved down to North Carolina to attend college at North Carolina A&T, he discovered ways of coping with his anxiety that did not include smoking marijuana.

One method was yoga, which was introduced to him by a girl name Anesha Favors. The breathing exercises and the subtle movements of yoga helped relax him even more than marijuana ever would. The open area made the environment more serene, but as soon as Edward returned to New York and the daily bustle of the city, the yoga was replaced with marijuana as he headed down to the subway station and bought from Reese, who still sold in the station.

There were times when Edward alternated between yoga and smoking marijuana. Looking in his drawer, he found a thin bag that held a miniscule amount of weed. Rolling up, he took his lighter and began puffing. After a few drags, he started to feel relaxed, and he calmed his heart down long enough to make his next move. Picking up the phone, he decided to call his stepbrother, Tony.

"Hey, Tony, what's up? What you doing next Saturday?"

"Big Ed, what's good wit' you, homie? I've been coolin' it, you know. I ain't got plans during the day next Saturday morning, but I gotta take my girl out next Saturday night though."

"Uh-oh. Who's the new victim this time?" Edward laughed.

If there was anything that he knew about Tony, he was a womanizer, and he dated and broke the hearts of many women in his life, not too different from Edward himself. Edward never figured out why he and Tony dated different girls throughout the years. Maybe they picked up the trait from their father.

"Shut up, Eddie. Ain't no victim. I met this girl at Revel Club last week. I'm tellin' you, son, she bad."

"Word? So, she a freak, huh? I know you like 'em that way."

"I like 'em in all different shapes, sizes, and colors, big bro. You know me. So, what time you comin' through?"

"I should be there around eleven, if that's cool wit' you."

Since graduating college at Fordham University, Tony was the owner of three Associated Grocery Stores, and he oversaw many of the operations at the stores. Just like Edward, he was active at the gym, building muscles and endurance.

"Yeah, cool eleven's okay. My girl should be back from work. She works overnight at the mall, so when she arrives, I can introduce ya'll."

After hanging up the phone, Edward took a deep breath. A visit to his brother's house was exactly what he needed to clear his mind.

"So, let me get this straight. You had ole girl in yo' crib. She was ready to go, you were ready to go, and you punked out because she tied yo' hands? What the hell happened to you?" Tony asked Edward on Saturday morning as he gave his guest a hot cup of coffee.

"I don't know, bro. I just panicked. That never happened to me before. Usually, when I get any female in that type of position, I close the deal. But that night was different. What if she was the one that did Xavier?"

"I mean, we don't know that. I know some of these women wild as hell, but to kill someone that way? Takes a woman who out of her damn mind to do some crazy shit like that. All the same, I'd watch my kitchen knives if I were you," Tony replied.

Edward glared at him.

"What? I'm just playin' wit' you, dawg. Look, I know what'll make you feel better. Lemme show you that new spot up in Flatbush. It'll take yo' mind off the whole Xavier thing."

Edward shook his head. Maybe Tony was right. He needed a change of scenery—a new place to visit, just to clear his head. Just when he was pondering it over, he heard a knock at Tony's front door.

Living in a sublet leased house with tenants next door, Tony went downstairs and opened the front door. After a few minutes, Tony re-emerged back upstairs, followed by a beautiful, brown skinned, voluptuous young lady. Her hear was braided into neat rows, and she was wearing designer boots, while sporting a Louis Vuitton handbag.

"Yo, Ed, I want to introduce you to Tina Leigh. Tina, this is my older, yet very confused stepbrother, Edward Reed."

"C'mon, son, what kind of an intro is that? Making me look bad in front of the lady...anyway, it's nice to meet you," Edward shook Tina's hand.

"Likewise. Tony's told me so much about you and his other brothers. I hear you're an attorney, right?" she asked.

Edward could not shake off how beautiful the woman was. Tony surely hit the jackpot with this one.

He better hold onto her because she seem like the type of lady that would drop any dude that doesn't have their stuff together.

"Yeah, I work for the Schorr Law Group near the Upper East Side in Manhattan."

"Which means he workin' for the man, baby. I've told that boy a million times to open up his own practice, and does he listen to me? Nope."

Edward stared at Tony with an exasperated expression. He hated being embarrassed in front of strangers, but he tried to play it off. "Well, Tony knows that these things take time and money. Eventually, I'll open up my own practice, but I need the resources to get that done."

"Well, I bet you make a lot of money now. Speaking of which, I don't know if Tony mentioned it, but I've been looking for an attorney. I feel like I'm being short-changed by my manager at the mall. He says he's paying me my full salary, but I know that greedy man's been shaving from my pay rate. He won't 'fess up to it though, so I'm going to have to see if I have a legal matter in my hands."

"Say no more. I got your back. Whenever you can, send me your paperwork with the hire date, job description, and pay rate, and I'll see what I can do."

Tina hugged Edward. "Thank you so much," she said.

"Well, don't thank me yet. I don't know what Tony told you, but my services ain't free. He may be family, but I got bills to pay too," Edward warned.

"Which is perfectly fine with me. Here's my IG and Facebook profile. Just message me the invoice, and I got you," Tina said, exchanging social media information with Edward.

He looked at Tony. "You see that right there, Tony? This is called a business transaction. Maybe one day you'll know how this works, instead of expecting free family favors," he mocked.

"Shut the hell up, Ed. You think you funny?"

"Actually, yeah I do. By the way, you talked to Bruno yet?"

"Nah, I ain't chopped it up with him in weeks. You know him...since he got that new job in Manhattan, guess he ain't got time for family no more."

Bruno was Edward and Tony's other stepbrother, who also stayed with their uncle. He had attended Georgetown and upon graduating, he became a city tour guide, working in Manhattan on buses that picked up tourists from out of town and giving them a taste of the city, including the sights and sounds of Manhattan, the landmarks, and the national parks.

Bruno was somewhat more straight-laced than his other brothers, even as a kid, achieving all A's from elementary school all the way through high school.

"Well, maybe when he has a chance to chill from his other job, he'll drop a line or a text."

"Yeah, I won't hold my breath. So, what's up, Mr. Fancy Lawyer? You gonna let us take you out tonight? There's a dope spot that just opened on Roosevelt and 3rd. You gotta let me hook you up."

"Nah, I'm good. You and Tina have fun. Besides, I got a lot of cases to catch up on before Monday, so I'm probably gonna be working all day tomorrow, which sucks cuz Sunday is usually a rest day for me."

"Man, forget all that. We going out tonight. Ain't that right, baby?" he asked Tina, who smiled in agreement.

Edward thought it over. *Maybe a night out will clear my head.*

Upon her return from a successful holiday tour, Andrea McAfee arrived at her house in Laurelton, New York. She saw Quentin's car in the driveway, which indicated that he was home, but he was most likely sleeping, preparing for his next work shift. Kicking off the shoes from her weary feet, she walked upstairs and sure enough, she heard low, steady breathing, and she could see Quentin sleeping peacefully under the sheets.

As she watched him sleep, Andrea smiled, slowly stroking his hair. She still could not believe that she would be marrying him in seven months. September could not arrive soon enough. Quentin may not flash jewelry or have what people call the "it" look, but she never wanted him to be anyone but himself.

Being in the music industry, Andrea was all too familiar with the pressures of fitting a certain public image, going out with rap's biggest superstar at the time and all the glamour that came with it. Unfortunately, she learned that everything that glittered was not gold, and money did not guarantee a happy relationship or a fulfilled life. She felt so hollow after breaking things off with De'Von, and she never thought she would be involved in another relationship again, until she reunited with Quentin.

The two had remained friends after he escorted her to her senior prom, and he went down to Georgia to attend Morehouse College. But after he graduated and moved back to New York, the friendship blossomed into a budding relationship. Quentin was there to dry her tears whenever they fell and was there to calm her down whenever she got angry. He taught Andrea how to love again, and their relationship remained strong. What Andrea admired the most about Quentin was that he never pushed her for sex or intimacy.

They were both transparent to each other in their relationship; neither one of them were virgins. Andrea had dated De'Von on her rise to stardom, and Quentin had a girl down in Georgia who he was briefly involved with while he attended college, but they had called it quits before Quentin moved back north. As a result, both Andrea and Quentin were starting over, and it was a fresh beginning for them.

After the tour, Andrea made a quick stop at Queensboro County Prison, where her sister's suspected killer, Terrell Washington, was held. She had heard news that Terrell and her sister's other suspected killer, Tadarius Hill, would be eligible for early release from prison, in part due to insufficient evidence tying them to the murder. The testimony that David Anderson and the young gangbanger Antonio gave were circumstantial at best.

As for the police shootout that occurred after David's trial, the police were accused of firing first, and Tadarius's lawyer was able to successfully paint the picture of a black man who was unfairly targeted by the police, conveniently leaving out the gritty facts that Tadarius had sold and trafficked drugs and has instigated assaults and illegally carried weapons. So, with the new information coming to light, Tadarius's release was all but eminent, and this enraged Andrea.

So, these two sick bastards are gonna get away with murdering my sister, and there ain't gonna get no repercussions?

She was determined to find out herself, and after meeting with Terrell, her anger and fury resurfaced. Terrell seemed so smug about what he had done, and he did not fear retaliation. Andrea remembered facing them as a little girl as they were tried and convicted for what was then life without parole for their part in Loree's murder along with shooting at police enforcement.

Terrell seemed as nonchalant as he was back in 2003 when he had the gall to tell Andrea that he was not the one who pulled the trigger. If Terrell was telling the truth, he would not reveal who really shot Loree because it went against his code. Gang members were taught to keep quiet and not sell anyone out, but Andrea was determined to uncover the truth.

Stroking Quentin's hair softly, she smiled serenely. She could not wait to share her life with this man, and while she felt overjoyed, she also felt a wave of sadness because her sister was not there to experience her happiness.

Feeling Andrea's hand on his head, Quentin stirred slightly. "You back in town, baby?" he asked.

"Yeah, I'm back, baby. I'm sorry to wake you, but you look so cute sleeping."

Quentin laughed with his eyes still closed. "I'm probably dreaming about you," he replied.

"Probably? Boy, you better be dreaming about me and not some other woman," Andrea replied, laughing.

"Come on, Drea, you know me better than that. You the only one I got eyes for, and don't ever forget that," Quentin took Andrea's hand and kissed it.

He could scarcely believe that he was going to marry the woman of his dreams. If someone had traveled back in time and told Quentin in high school that he would marry Andrea, let alone date her, he would have thought the time traveler was out of his mind. Quentin was not the most popular student at Richmond Hill. In fact, people had teased him for being a nerd, and the glasses he wore back in those days did not help matters.

Andrea was the girl that he often daydreamed about dating, but then he would snap back to reality. He thought there was no chance that she would ever go out with him until one day in class he gathered the courage to ask her to the senior prom. To his surprise, she accepted his invitation, and although her friends were not too excited about Andrea dating him, she never cared what people thought.

"So how was the tour, baby?" he asked.

"Oh, it was amazing, baby, but by the time we got to Detroit, I was ready to go home. I was so burnt out. But I never thought I'd share the stage with Kierra Sheard or Tye Tribbett. It was like a dream that I never wanted to wake up from. But I'm happy to finally be home," she replied, kissing him.

"Well, since you're obviously asking, my time at home was great. Just went to work and came straight back—no barring, no boozing, just came straight back to the crib."

"Sounds interesting. Maybe I can stay home during the next tour so I can enjoy your company."

Turning on the television, the couple settled next to one another as the news came on the screen. What the newscasters reported next completely rocked Andrea to her core. They reported that Tadarius Hill was going to be paroled from prison, and his release date was unconfirmed.

"No!" Andrea yelled at the screen.

Quentin, who knew about Loree's murder and the men accused of the crime, attempted to calm his fiancée down. "Drea, relax!"

"How could I relax? They just let a murderer go free, and I'm supposed to accept that? Oh, they got another thing coming," Andrea threatened as she angrily got up out of bed and walked over to the front door, slamming it with her fist.

"Baby, baby, calm down. We can't be rash here. I know what that sick lowlife did to your family, but please take it easy."

But Andrea could see nothing but red. Her visit to Terrell all went for naught, and now the main conspirator around her sister's death was released. She decided not to keep it a secret from Quentin.

"Okay, baby, I smell a setup here. I'm about to tell you something, but before I do, promise me you won't get mad."

Why is Andrea suddenly acting paranoid? She must need more rest than I thought.

"Okay, I won't get mad. What's up?"

Andrea took a deep breath. "Okay, so on my way back home, I stopped by Queensboro County Prison. That's where Terrell was locked up. I had to get the truth out of him. But that little worm didn't tell me squat."

"Wait, you what? Andrea you went to the prison and spoke with the dude without letting me know first?"

"I just thought that if I went, I could show him that I wasn't afraid of him. I told him that I would make sure that he stayed in jail."

Quentin stood up. He was not angry, but he was disappointed. "Baby, what were you thinking? You can't put yourself out there like that, okay? If he did kill your sister, who's to say that you won't be his next target if he gets out?"

"Quentin, I just had to find out for myself. Obviously, they're not talking to the cops, and they're so confident that they can get away with it. I just wanted to scare them into telling me the truth."

Quentin shook his head. Clearly, he disagreed with Andrea's decision to visit Terrell. "Drea, I may not look like it, but I grew up in these streets, okay? These cats don't fear nothing, and if you put yourself in harm's way, I won't be able to forgive myself. You've got to let the police handle this."

Andrea rolled her eyes. He can't possibly believe that the police are going to do anything about it.

"Yeah, well the police ain't doing enough, and now these guys are about to be set free? It just doesn't make any sense. I've gotta fight this, if not for me, then for Loree. I'm gonna find out the truth."

Andrea excused herself to go to the bathroom, leaving Quentin bewildered at the edge of the bed.

That following Saturday night, Tony, Tina, and Edward made their way over to Live Central Club on Roosevelt. After showing their ID to the bouncer, they stepped into the club. Tony and Tina were wearing their usual clothes, T-shirts and skinny jeans, although in Tina's case, she had her T-shirt tied just above her belly button. The music was live with underground rap artists and club promoters, and people were talking, dancing, smoking from hookah pipes, and drinking endless amounts of alcohol.

Edward, wearing only a polo shirt with khakis and Jordans, did not waste time going to the bar. The club scene was not for him, as he had done all his clubbing in his college years and early twenties. He enjoyed a quiet night at the bar, watching a game on television as opposed to the loud club environment.

Tony, sensing his brother's tightness, attempted to ease his tension. "C'mon, Eddie, you need to relax, son. You lookin' mad suspect up in here like you the po-po. Walk around man, find yourself a lady out here, and make sure she ain't got no handcuffs to tie you up," he laughed.

"Ha, ha, very funny, Tony. You know, I only came here with you to back you up. Make sure yo' girl ain't stealin' your wallet and dippin' out," Edward replied furtively when Tina turned to greet some friends.

"Chill, bro, she ain't triflin' like dat. At least she knows how to have fun, which is more than I can say for you. So, work yo' magic, and go to that bar, and get you some."

Leaving his brother, Tony left to mingle with friends. Edward started to make his way toward the bar when he suddenly stopped in his tracks.

He was sitting in the bar, laughing it up without a care in the world. Surrounded by women and two other burly men that stood on each side as if they were his bodyguards, the man got up to raise a bottle of beer in action to toast his newfound freedom.

With the man's arms, neck, and chest now covered in tattoos, Edward also saw that he was no longer skinny in frame. There was no doubt that he had put on muscle during his time in prison. Backing away slowly, Edward made for the exit as Tadarius Hill celebrated his release from prison.

CHAPTER 13

FREE AT LAST

APRIL 1996

Before he was the head honcho for Queens' most dangerous gang, he was struggling to survive in the streets. With his father dead, his mother experienced an unexpected disability, and she could no longer work. Having developed painful foot sclerosis, Faye Hill had to rely on disability checks, government assistance, and food stamps just to keep her and her son's head above water. He had no siblings although he had cousins and friends that lived throughout the tri-state area.

But Tadarius Hill was not one to ask for any handouts.

He refused to allow anyone to feel any type of sympathy towards him. Not expecting any sympathy from anyone had given Tadarius an icy indifference to anyone that crossed his path. There was no sympathy for him when his father was shot at point blank range in the head, so why should he feel any remorse for others? If there was anything that his father's death taught him, it was the very classic lesson to never trust anybody.

Tadarius kept his circle extremely small and kept to himself. He was a very smart student in school and one of the best artists in the state. Back in elementary school, he won an art contest by submitting a detailed drawing of an old Martin Luther King Jr. portrait. The art committee had never seen such intricacy in a drawing, and Tadarius was given a coupon to some restaurant and $200. When he got into high school, he focused on art appreciation but lost interest in other classes, and cutting classes became a regular for him.

Then the streets beckoned to him. Living in a housing project in South Jamaica, New York, Tadarius learned of a local gang called the Black Dices. They resided in the area, wearing black, white, and silver Raider colors. The Black Dices constantly warred with another gang known as the Pandillas, a local Hispanic syndicate. What started out as a war of words between factions soon escalated into brawls and casualties.

Over two weeks, members of the Pandillas and the Black Dices would appear in the obituary, and the streets would be littered with blood and chalk outlines of where those members breathed their last breath. The police had more than often interfered with the warring gangs, but his had not eased the tension. Despite the danger posed by joining, Tadarius was inspired by the prospect of joining the Black Dices. The members flashed nice jewelry, rode in nice cars, and always had girls by the handful.

The leader of the Black Dices called himself Smoke, and he was the most feared individual in the borough. Smoke was a dangerous gang leader and was rumored to have killed three opposing gang members over a matter of money. Nobody knew if there was any truth to the rumors, but the folklore was enough to strike fear in people's hearts.

The goal of Tadarius was to break through and join their ranks. One day, Tadarius was at a Met Store grocery chain on 157th and Jamaica Avenue. He was talking to one of the store associates that he previously met, a girl named Alicia, who happened to go to Hillcrest High School. Having been to the store on more than one occasion, Tadarius saw that it was the right time to strike a conversation with her.

"Are you seriously thinking about dropping out of school?" Alicia asked him when Tadarius explained his plans to her.

"Shorty, I'mma keep it real with you. I ain't gonna get nowhere in life with knowing who invented electricity or learning the Pythagorean

Theorem. I plan on doing something with my talent. I'm finna go to art school. Check this out," he said, pulling one of his detailed drawings out of his pocket. It was a detailed drawing of the cartoon character Bugs Bunny and Tweety Bird.

Alicia, clearly impressed said, "Wow, these are so good, Tadarius! Yeah, you should definitely go to school for the arts. Who knows, maybe your stuff will end up at the Brooklyn Museum one day."

"I hope so. What's up wit' you these days? So, you still wit' what's his name?" he asked.

Alicia laughed, rolling her eyes. "His name's Ulysses, and yeah, we're still going out. Why do you wanna know?" she asked teasingly.

"Because I think yo' boy don't deserve you, to be honest. When was the last time he took you to a bowling alley? Or to Coney Island?"

"Tadarius, he's busy most of the time. He works part time at the One Stop corner store in 103rd. He makes time for me when he can."

"Baby, I would make more time for you than he would."

Alicia giggled. She was three years older than Tadarius, but the boy was a charmer, and he knew how to sweet-talk himself out of anything. But the charming schemer was not sweet talking her for nothing.

Alicia was only one of two associates working at the time, and while Tadarius kept Alicia distracted, Tadarius's friend Terrance made his way through different aisles, taking food and drinks, candy bars, and a lighter, and stuffing them into his pockets. Terrance worked slowly so he would not draw attention to himself.

The other store associate, Clark, was the cashier at the front of the store and was reading a magazine, completely unaware of the shoplifting that was going on under his watch. While keeping Alicia occupied, Tadarius looked out of the corner of his eye and saw that Terrance beckoned to him from the next aisle over. Tadarius continued to sweet talk Alicia for two minutes, and then he made his way over to the register.

While Tadarius walked up to the register to pay for a few of his items, Terrance casually walked out of the store as if he hadn't bought anything.

Clark rang Tadarius up, and after a few minutes, he walked out of the store. Meeting two blocks later, Tadarius turned to Terrance, looking around to make sure nobody was watching them or had any air of suspicion.

"What you got, T?"

With a huge grin, Terrance turned his pockets out of his baggy jeans and revealed a huge variety of stolen goods, candy, and two soda pop bottles.

"They should call me Sticky Fingers, like the rapper," he chuckled as they drank their sodas and partook in the stolen goods.

"So, you still tryin' to get into the Dices?"

"No doubt, but Smoke ain't gave me a look at all, and I live right down the block from that fool. He probably don't think I'm serious about this shit."

"Man, I wouldn't even sweat that. Cats that roll wit' Smoke don't live too long out hea' anyways. Your cousins still rollin' wit' the Bloods off 32nd?" Terrance asked.

Tadarius hated when anybody brought up his gang member cousins. He did not trust anyone with that type of privy information. But Terrance had been his best friend for over seven years, and he trusted him with it.

"Yeah, they still roll wit' 'em. But I ain't interested in rollin' wit' the Bloods either. I ain't tryin' to draw too much attention out here. What if I was to make my own outfit?" he asked.

Many people would've thought Tadarius was talking about clothes, but Terrance knew his friend, and he knew Tadarius was talking about forming his own gang. "That would be dope if you had yo' own set. But everyone else is gonna see it as a sign of war. You ain't got the money or the rep to start yo' own."

But Tadarius was determined to start his own organization. He had an epiphany a few weeks ago about what he wanted his gang to look like, but Terrance was right. He would need respect, a title, and some capital.

"My cousin who works wit' the Bloods has a connect to all the major players around here. Everyone is gonna make money out here, but I want to do something that's gon' strike fear in everyone. I'm sick of goin' in stores and stealing small shit when in six years later, I could be running the show."

"What'd you have in mind?" Terrance asked.

Taking a drawing out of his pocket, Tadarius showed Terrance the early drawing of the gang sign, which showed dollar bills, drops of blood, and guns pointed at one another.

"Oh okay, T, I see you. Dope pic. But what's gonna be the name of your set?" Terrance asked.

Just let me worry about it, Terrance. I'll come up with a name soon.

A few weeks later, Tadarius's petty crimes caught up to him as he was caught shoplifting. Terrance was apprehended but would be released after two days. Tadarius would spend the next few years in and out of juvenile hall, and it seemed that he would be locked up for good. But when he met David Anderson and was released, Tadarius, David and Terrance were the founding members and cornerstones of M.O.B.

October 2003 | The apartment building lobby at Merrick Boulevard resembled a mini war zone in the aftermath of the shootout between M.O.B. and law enforcement. Tadarius, Terrell, and a female accomplice named Sophia were all apprehended at the scene. Tadarius and Terrell were both shot in the leg, and Sophia, although shaken up, was unharmed. The paramedics were called, and Tadarius and Terrell were prepped to be taken to the hospital to get their wounds treated before they were booked.

As they made their way over to the ambulance, Tadarius walked by two body bags, which held the bodies of Malik Jones and Terrance Dregs. The bag zipped all the way up to only their necks, so Tadarius was able to identify his deceased friends. A tear rolled down his cheek, and immediately his mind was possessed with thoughts of revenge.

David's gonna pay for this shit. He betrayed the family, and now because of him, Terrance and Malik are dead. It's not over. I'm gonna find a way to get him.

Having known Terrance since elementary school, it was as if Tadarius had lost a brother.

They knew the risks of running with Tadarius, but they never snitched and were loyal soldiers up until the end. Tadarius had tried his best to run his drug operation discreetly without bringing attention to himself or drawing contact with the police. His cousin, James "Pooh" Clarence, who resided in the Bronx and had gang ties to the Bloods and the Dices, always told him that in order to run the street game, it must be ran with intelligence, power, and control.

Pooh had always looked out for his cousin, especially early in his life when he always found himself in juvenile hall. But this time was different. He was going to be tried as an adult and sentenced to general population prison, unless they deemed him an absolute threat to society, in which case they would send him to a maximum-security facility. Tadarius didn't see a way out of his situation.

He lost his cool under fire, and the emotion of seeing his so-called "brother" work with the police against him was more than he could take. He shot at law enforcement, and when anybody shot at police, it was a one-way ticket to life in prison. Tadarius's theory would be proven days later when he and Terrell stood trial for their retaliation against the police. The prosecutor also placed a second charge on Tadarius and Terrell for their involvement in the shooting death of Loree McAfee.

The public defender, who was assigned by the state, had done a poor job of proving their innocence. In the end, the public defender inadvertently dropped another name that was key towards their conviction: Antonio Franks. By the end of the trial, when the verdict was read to them, Tadarius knew what the sentence would be. Tadarius Hill and Terrell Washington were sentenced to life in jail without parole.

Just like that, Tadarius's business in the streets came to a screeching halt, and he knew that once he got out, he would have to start at ground zero.

Throughout the years, Terrell and Tadarius were both transferred to other correctional facilities, and while Tadarius was in prison, the other inmates who were much older decided to test his mettle.

Jeffery Toomes, better known as "Jawbone," casually walked to Tadarius's table one day during lunch. He picked up the nickname because during his tenure at the prison, he tended to get into fights, and he broke more than a fair share of jawbones during those skirmishes. After his eighth fight, the other inmates decided to give him the nickname, and it had stuck with him ever since.

"What's up, folk? Heard you was on a set on the outs. What yo' name?" he asked.

Tadarius was sitting with the other inmates in his cell block, and while he heard Jawbone addressing him, he ignored the man. Jawbone grew irritated because if there was one pet peeve that he had, it was being ignored.

"Aye, I'm talkin' to you, nigga," he said, angrily grabbing Tadarius's shoulder.

Tadarius hated being grabbed from behind, and he took Jawbone's wrist and twisted his arm behind his back. The other inmates backed up, and the guards started to make their way over to the tables.

"You wanna know who the fuck I am? You betta keep yo' hands to yourself cuz the next time you grab me like that, I'mma break yo' goddamn wrist, you feel me?"

Jawbone was screaming in pain as his arm was twisted at an unnatural angle behind his back. "Ight, man, I got you."

"Hey, what's goin' on over there? You let him go right now!" one of the guards shouted, reaching for his baton, threatening to beat Tadarius within an inch of his life.

Tadarius then let him go, and from that day forward, Jawbone never bothered Tadarius again, and over the years, Tadarius built a reputation as the inmate that nobody wanted to fight because of his quick temper and gang connection. Over the next few days, Tadarius began communicating with his lawyer, Perry Wilcox, who was introduced to him by Pooh. He had defended Pooh on many occasions, and when he found out about his cousin, he decided the best option was to send Mr. Wilcox to open a case for him.

At first, Tadarius didn't trust Mr. Wilcox because he felt that everyone involved with the law was against him, and it didn't matter what side they were on, the prosecution or the defense. But Mr. Wilcox impressed Tadarius with his diligence and doggedness to prove that Tadarius was framed and railroaded in the Loree McAfee murder case, and the testimony that was given by David Anderson was inadmissible, so he chalked it up to be an emotional rant.

The two boys were in a rift over a girl, which happened frequently, and according to Mr. Wilcox, David was infuriated that Loree had been sexually involved with Tadarius, and as a result, he decided to use the testimony to frame Tadarius as being the mastermind for the murder. The firearm that was used to murder Loree was never officially recovered. The gun found in David's backpack was devoid of any fingerprints and did not implicate neither David nor Tadarius.

As for Antonio's testimony, Mr. Wilcox thoroughly studied Antonio's background. His father was a member of the Shower Posse in the '70s and '80s and was implicated on drugs and sex trafficking charges, so Antonio grew up in an unstable house. While he admitted to being a member of M.O.B., his testimony that would eventually sway the jurors' decision did not hold any weight in Tadarius's conviction because there was still no way to tie him to the crime.

Tadarius used his prison time to continue drawing various art pieces and also went to the prison library and read various book genres, autobiographies, instructional books on bombs and explosives, and books of weaponry. He also read The Art of War, a book that drew his attention because he felt as if he himself was in war, and he was fighting for his freedom.

Mr. Wilcox also addressed the night of the infamous shootout between M.O.B. and police officers. A testimony retrieved from Terrell stated that the police opened fire on the young men first, and the gang fired back in self-defense. Tadarius confirmed the testimony of his former associate and stated that the police were sent out there to terrorize them and the community.

Detective Isaac Sands could not be reached to provide a statement, so the police that were involved in the shootout were found in contempt for not Mirandizing the suspects upon arresting them. With the errors that the police made upon the scene, grouped with insufficient evidence tying Tadarius to the murder of Loree McAfee, Mr. Wilcox was certain that the courts would not deny an appeal for early release.

But there was one factor missing.

Tadarius had been implicated of murdering Theo Brunsen in 2002, but there was no evidence that he murdered the man. However, Tadarius found out that Xavier took a plea deal for an early release if he confessed that Tadarius killed Theo. However, there was no evidence tying Tadarius to that case, and with all the facts in hand, Mr. Wilcox made his most recent appeal for early release for his client in November 2018. This time, instead of denying his appeal, the parole board was forced to thoroughly review his case, and after further deliberation, they decided to approve his appeal for an early release.

Mr. Wilcox made his way to the Queensboro County Prison to tell his client the good news. As Tadarius made his way into the visitor's room, he lazily picked up the phone while facing Mr. Wilcox through the transparent glass.

"What's up, Perry? Why you so happy all of a sudden?" he asked.

"Get ready to pack up, T, cuz we outta here soon," Mr. Wilcox replied.

"Hold up, the parole board accepted the appeal? They overturned it?"

"That's right, man. C'mon, it's me. You know I wasn't gon' let you rot in here. Now we got to get everything ready cuz Pooh's waitin' on you."

A few weeks later, Tadarius stepped out of the facility. Taking a breath of fresh air, he looked at his surroundings.

Damn. Freedom never smelled so good.

Pooh had brought him a change of clothes so Tadarius could rid himself of the prison garments. After changing, Tadarius walked to the parking lot, where Pooh was waiting for him in his black Mustang.

"What up, son?" Pooh greeted as he dapped his cousin.

"What up? Yo, I gotta give it to you, dawg. You came up in the clutch, man. You and Mr. Wilcox bailed my ass out."

"Of course, B. We family. That's what we do. So, shorty already got the room set up for you. You can stay as long as you want till you get back on yo' feet."

"Appreciate that, man." Tadarius looked out the window as Pooh drove the highway. He saw buildings pass by, and he took it all in again. "I was thinking, man. I gotta get me another hustle. But what job's gonna want to hire me with my background?" he asked.

"Nah, don't even worry about that for now. We'll get you something. But the real question is, what's gon' happen to M.O.B.?"

"I don't know, man. Word is that everyone split after the whole shit went down at Merrick. But I still got some fam out there holdin' it down. I don't know if it's a good idea to recruit now. They gon' try to throw my ass back in the pen."

Pooh looked at Tadarius. "Are you givin' up on me, cuz? That don't sound like the Tadarius I know. Anyway, word on the street is that slim caught up wit' snitchin' ass Xavier. Tied him up on that hotel bed and slit that nigga's windpipe while he was blindfolded. He never knew what hit him."

Tadarius laughed. Xavier finally got his for snitching on the family, and he ended up on the six o'clock news. "Well, that's one down, and now we got two more to go," he said grimly.

"Well, I got intel on David Anderson. He's out there coaching football for a high school, and he got a whole family, livin' that Brady life, but Antonio's gone. He in the wind cuz ain't nobody seen him in years."

Tadarius stared out the window. David was next on his hit list, and he would make sure he found Antonio. He had to be out there somewhere, and if he was, his date with dust would not be too far away.

CHAPTER 14

REUNITING WITH LATOYA

MAY 2002

On a partially cloudy Saturday morning, the high school track and field athletes convened at Richmond Hill High School, which was the host school for the event. Students from Jamaica High School, August Martin High School, and Bayside High School filled the stands to observe the day's track and field events. Loree McAfee and her friend LaToya Richardson paid at the gate and entered the field.

Although Loree was due back at the safehouse where M.O.B. normally met, she was not going to miss her girl's track meet. She had been friends with Shania Hillman since freshman year, and although the two girls were vastly different, they bonded immediately.

Loree was an outgoing girl, an enticing female who was already fully developed, and she drew attention of most boys at Richmond Hill while Shania was best described as more introverted, and she was never one to flaunt her beauty just for show. But there were parts of Loree that she wished she knew more about, and the more she tried digging, the more her friend pulled away.

Shania heard the rumors about Loree being a "hood chick that got around," and while Shania always believed those rumors were false, she couldn't help but notice how secretive Loree seemed to be at times: the moments where she would cut their lunch breaks short because she had a "prior engagement" or when she did not attend church on some Sundays because she was not up to it. But despite how distant she seemed to be, Shania and Loree were best friends, and Shania would take a bullet to the heart for her at any time.

It was more than what she could say about LaToya. She lived in the same neighborhood as Loree, and they had been friends before she met Shania. If Shania doubted the lewd rumors about Loree, those doubts did not exist for LaToya. She was extremely promiscuous in ways that Shania could not imagine, wearing short skirts and blouses that she would tie just above her belly button, showing midriff. She was also no stranger to the extremely short dresses that accentuated her curves.

If the rumors were true that Loree had been intimately involved with over seven boys at Richmond Hill, then LaToya may have been intimate with fourteen boys. Although Loree attempted to integrate their friendship on several occasions, LaToya and Shania never quite saw eye to eye and soon, she gave up trying to force them to be friends and figured that the two girls would eventually warm to one another.

"Damn, Loree, do we really have to be here today? T is waiting for us back at the spot," LaToya protested.

Loree rolled her eyes. "Well, Tadarius can wait a lil' longer. I'm here to watch my girl Nia bust some ass today."

Sitting at the Richmond Hill cheering section, Loree and LaToya greeted many of their classmates, and before long, it was time for the 200-meter race, which was one of Shania's events. Shania normally competed in the 100-meter race, the 200-meter race, and the 400-meter relay. Loree started cheering as Shania stepped up to the starting line, accompanied by track athletes from the other respective schools.

With her hair tied back in a ponytail, and her eyes squinted in concentration, Shania prepared herself, waiting for the official to blow the whistle.

"Hey, girl! You got this! Show 'em what time it is!" Loree yelled excitedly over the brief silence.

Shania looked towards the stands for a split second. When she saw Loree, she smiled and waved at her briefly before going serious again. She had a race to win. As soon as the whistle blew, Shania sprinted in her lane and ran in long beautiful strides. But she was trailing Natasha Corley, the track star from August Martin. Natasha was two lanes over, and she was able to get a good lead ahead of her competitors, but Shania remembered the words of her track coach.

It's all about pace and control. Eventually, during the race, they'll all come back to you. Just pick your time to put on the jets, and you got them.

Shania felt that Natasha had a false start, and in starting quickly, she felt that she could gain some ground over everyone. But Shania practiced leg exercises endlessly, and she felt she had more stamina to finish the race. Sure enough, Natasha appeared in the corner of her left eye. It was only a second later that Natasha realized that Shania was neck and neck with her.

I got her. She's going down. Speed up, Shania. You got this.

Shania was able to pull ahead of Natasha slightly as they crossed the finish line. The students of Richmond Hill exploded in loud cheers as they stood up and cheered their track star. Taking a deep breath, Shania pumped her fist in victory. Afterwards, she walked up to Natasha and shook her hand as well as the other athletes' in sportsmanship. Shania was not arrogant in victory, for she knew Natasha could have won the race, but by the grace of God, she kept pushing.

As the day wore on, the host school also won the relay events and the long jump. Richmond Hill completely ran the table that day, and when it was over, Loree rushed from the stands and ran to hug Shania.

"Girl, you straight dusted their asses! That's how we do at Richmond Hill, you feel me?" She yelled out loud for the other school's students to hear as they filed out of the field.

"Appreciate it, girl. In twenty minutes, the team's heading over to Wendy's for lunch. You wanna come? LaToya, you can join us if you want," Shania said as she wiped away her sweat with a towel.

Loree started to reply that she would love to join Shania to eat, but LaToya quickly cut her off. "Nah, Loree and I got plans later. Ain't that right, Loree?" she asked, raising an eyebrow.

The latter hesitated while Shania looked at her, waiting for a reply.

"Yeah, LaToya's right. I gotta be somewhere in a few minutes, but we'll chop it up later tonight, okay? I'll call you," she replied as LaToya guided her away from the school, leaving Shania bewildered as she headed to the locker room to shower and change.

Walking two blocks, they waited at a bus stop on their way to the secret safe house where the members of M.O.B. met.

Sitting in the bus, LaToya turned to Loree. "Your girl dominated today. I'll give her that. But I still don't know how you can roll wit' her though. She too goody-good for me."

Loree laughed. "Now you know you wrong for that. Leave my girl alone. She ain't bout that life, but she stay down," she replied.

"She need to join the fam though if she really down. I mean she yo' girl, right? You'll keep an eye out for her. T always lookin' for new girls."

"Hell no. I'mma keep Nia as far away from Tadarius as much as possible. To keep it a hundred, I don't even like workin' wit' that fool. The only reason I'm still there is cuz my folks need the extra ends."

LaToya wrapped her arm around her friend. She knew if Loree had no other options, she would stay loyal to the family.

"You see what I'm saying? Gotta take care of them and Andrea too. How's my lil' princess doing, anyway?" LaToya asked.

"She's fine. Just doing what other eleven-year-olds are doing, I guess: listening to Destiny's Child, Alicia Keys, and Britney Spears on her CD player and trippin' about boys. She's startin' to develop in other places too, by the way. My mama is talking about shopping for her first bra."

LaToya laughed. "It's 'bout that time, huh? She'll be sixteen before we know it, and it won't be long till T sets his eyes on her."

Loree glared at LaToya. She did not want Andrea to have anything to do with Tadarius or M.O.B. Andrea and Mr. and Mrs. McAfee had no idea what Loree was doing in her spare time, and she would like to keep her activities a well-concealed secret.

"No, I don't want Drea doing what we do. She's still a lil' girl. She got plenty of time not to get caught up in the game like us. She don't need to be involved."

"Loree, get real. You act like what we do is God-awful, but it's all empowerment to me. We're using what we got to make men do what we want. Society's always tellin' us what's right and what's wrong all the time, but the world ain't black and white. You got the haves and the have-nots. You got folks out here that's literally rollin' in money while the rest of us got to scrap for ours."

"Yeah, but what's empowering about a gun clappin' gangsta tellin' you what to do with yo' body and how to use it? It just sounds like another form of slavery to me."

LaToya just shrugged her shoulders as the bus rolled on. Finally, they arrived at their stop, and both girls got off the bus and walked a few more blocks down Farmers Boulevard until they reached the apartment building. Three boys were at the front entrance, and Loree recognized them as Xavier, Malik, and E-Note.

"What's up, baby? When you gon' give me some?" E-Note asked Loree slyly.

"I'll give you some on the quarter past never. Now get out my way," she replied, pushing her way past them as she entered the building.

Walking towards apartment 1001C, she knocked twice, once, and twice again as a confirmation that one of their members had returned. Simone opened the door, and when Loree and LaToya walked in, they were greeted by the other members. Terrell and Antonio were playing video games while trash talking, as usual.

CiCi and Cory, who were cousins, were playing music on a stereo while drinking wine coolers and beers. Standing in a corner with his hands in his pockets was David Anderson. He was smoking a joint and looking out the window, eyes red and hazed.

Smiling and batting her eyelashes, Loree approached him. "Hey, you, what's goin' on?" she asked.

"What's up, shorty? I'm chillin' waiting for T. He workin' some deal with his distributors," he replied.

Loree pulled the joint out of his mouth. "Betta be careful, Heisman. You don't wanna fail some random drug test at school, and they bench you for the next game." She then proceeded to put the joint in her mouth. Taking a long drag of the marijuana smoke, she blew a large smoke cloud.

"Okay, I see you, Loree. You can handle this black kush?"

"Boy, I can handle anything you give me," Loree replied seductively.

Taking a drag from his joint, David laughed. "You know what's scary? I actually believe it."

As they continued flirting, the door opened, and Tadarius walked in. The music stopped playing, and Terrell and Antonio paused the video game.

"What's up, fam? Please don't stop what you doin'. I need to holla at my ladies right quick. Got a mission for ya'll."

Following Tadarius into one of the bedrooms, Loree, LaToya, CiCi, and Simone closed the door behind them.

"Aight, check it. So, the reason I'm late is because our regular supply distributor is actin' an ass right now. He playin' hardball, so I'mma play him right back. I need you ladies to go over to the cat's house, and convince him to lower the price on the product."

"And how exactly are we supposed to do that?" Loree asked, while LaToya flashed her a look that said, "Bitch, shut yo' mouth. You know what he wants us to do."

"Do what you do best, ho'. Give him something he ain't ever gon' forget so that he can drop his prices."

Loree knew exactly what he meant. Sex the man out of his mind, so that he can budge on his price.

But Loree was tired of doing Tadarius's dirty work. She knew being an escort wasn't a permanent gig, but she was tired of giving sexual favors to strangers for the sake of a few bucks.

Sensing her doubt, Tadarius walked over to Loree, an icy, indifferent expression on his face. "You got something to say?" he asked.

Loree was about to protest, but LaToya beat her to it. "Nah, she good, T. Matter fact, me and her are gon' go and get that deal done. Just wait for our call."

"Aight. Keep me posted after the shit's done."

Walking out of the room, LaToya and Loree went to the other room to check the closet for their assortment of clothes, wigs, and heels.

After getting dressed, Loree sighed as she walked out. I'm about to go down on another stranger. I gotta get out of this life.

March 2019 | After re-examining her living room wooden floor, Andrea went to the bathroom to clean the sink. Everything had to be perfect. She expected a visit from an old friend whom, until recently, she had not heard from in years. The last time Andrea spoke with LaToya Richardson, she was only twelve years old, and she had just dealt with the worst loss of her life. It was during the gut-wrenching moment during the funeral that LaToya approached her and comforted her for what seemed like hours.

LaToya was somewhat of a third older sister to Andrea, only trailing behind Loree and Shania. When LaToya and Loree were in middle school, Andrea recalled her tendency to follow them around wherever they went.

If Loree and LaToya were going to the mall, Andrea would attempt to accompany them. If they were going to get their hair and their nails done at the salon, Andrea was not too far behind. Loree eventually grew weary of Andrea constantly mimicking her and Latoya, but to Andrea, she looked up to them.

When Loree was ex-communicated by a popular group of girls known as the Black Barbies in Richmond Hill High School, LaToya was the one that comforted her and reminded her that she didn't need a clique to define who she was. Then Loree befriended Shania, and on more than one occasion, Loree attempted to spark a friendship between LaToya and Shania, but the spark eventually fizzled.

It was pretty evident that LaToya resented Shania for no reason other than the fact that she was a straight-A student, ran track and field for Richmond Hill, and her father, a former Richmond Hill football standout, was the pastor at nearby Rock of Jacob Baptist Church, which gave Shania the appearance of a stuck-up princess who had everything handed to her.

LaToya, on the other hand, grew up in a single-parent household. Her mother raised her, but they did not have a healthy relationship. Her mom constantly abused her physically and mentally, and LaToya searched for any good reason to escape and get out of her mother's apartment, often slumming with other friends at their houses, but there was no other girl's home that she frequently stayed at more than Loree's place.

Loree's family lived in a two-room apartment at the time, and although both her parents worked, they struggled at times to pay all the bills. Loree thought about getting a job to help her family, but LaToya showed her another way to get money: seduce men, and if the opportunity presented itself, be intimate with them, and lay down with them. LaToya knew older men would pay money to sleep with her, and because Loree was well developed beyond her years, it was easy to pose as an older woman to get what she wanted.

The women worked for various pimps, hustlers, and gang leaders before they crossed paths with Tadarius Hill. After Loree's funeral, LaToya and her mother moved out of the apartment, and Andrea never saw them again until one day her phone vibrated, and there was a strange number on her cell phone's caller ID when she was leaving the studio.

Who's this?

Few people had Andrea's phone number. Normally, all her calls went to her booking agent, Roy Havers. Thinking that it was just a scam call, Andrea picked up. "Hello?"

"Hello, am I speaking to Andrea, or Adia?" a woman's voice asked.

Andrea rolled her eyes, unsure if the woman was serious or joking around. But Andrea was not a big fan of surprises. "Depends. Who is this?"

The woman on the other end laughed.

"Don't tell me that you already forgot me, Drea. It's me, LaToya."

Andrea's eyes widened in shock as realization dawned on her. She had not heard that name in more than fifteen years. "Oh my God, LaToya? Are you serious? Girl, it's been forever! How you been? How'd you know my number?" she asked.

"How else? I went by your spot and ran into your mama. She was shocked too, and I asked about you, so she gave me your number."

"Mom. I should've known. Girl, it's been too long! Are you back in New York?"

"Yeah, girl, I've been back for about five months."

"Five months, and you just now calling me? Shame on you," Andrea laughed.

"I know, I know...cut me some slack, girl. You know I had to get re-acclimated to the New York state of mind. Feels like I been gone forever."

"Speaking of which, where have you been? I ain't seen you since Loree's homegoing service."

"Well, I enlisted in the U.S. Army. My mama withdrew me from Richmond Hill after everything went down that year, and I finished my diploma program online at Jamaica High. After that, I enlisted. I was stationed everywhere you could think of—Georgia, Texas, Cali, Washington. They even had me in Japan for a couple years."

Andrea shook her head. It certainly explained LaToya's disappearance after high school, but there were so many blanks that were left unfilled.

"I mean, you never told me that you was gon' bounce."

"Don't worry about that. None of my friends knew I was gonna leave. Mom made me keep it quiet."

"Wow. So how's Army life?"

"Well, it was great. It gave me opportunities and benefits that I never thought I'd have. Plus, it kept me on the straight and narrow for a good minute. Mama got tired of me runnin' the streets."

"Shoot, girl, we got tired of you running the streets. I remember that was all you and ReRe were doing back in the day. My mama would get so pissed, and when ya came back, ya would sweet-talk her and Daddy."

"Yup. Then we would head up to the room and blast Aaliyah on the CD stereo for hours and dance like we wanted to be her. Looks like one of us finally made it happen."

"Girl, believe me, it ain't all sunshine and rainbows in the industry. I'll tell you about that later. I gotta hang up. You know how New York is wit' the 'hands-free' policy. Can't even place a 911 call in your car these days anymore. You should come by my place so we can catch up some more."

"Okay, cool. How does Saturday sound?"

"That's perfect. I ain't really workin' that day anyway, so please come through, or I'mma have to hunt you down," Andrea laughed. It was the most pleasant call she had ever experienced in years.

So that Saturday, Andrea stayed home to clean the kitchen and bathrooms and wax the floors. As she finished, she wiped the sweat from her brow, took a shower, and waited for LaToya to arrive. With Quentin gone at work, it gave Andrea some time to catch up with her old friend. Suddenly, the doorbell rang. Bursting with excitement, Andrea answered the door, hugging LaToya before closing it behind her.

Looking around, LaToya admired the house. "Alright, I see you, Andrea. Livin' large up in this piece. Got the real silverware, not them cheap-ass silverware and definitely not them plastic sporks."

"Ay, ay, don't diss them sporks now. They saved our butts on more than one occasion."

"Damn, girl, I see you dropped the little cornrows and hair beads. Now you done graduated on gettin' your jawn slayed," LaToya laughed.

"You know I had to do it, girl," Andrea replied.

Latoya then looked down and saw the gleaming reflection of the diamond that was on Andrea's finger. "And is that what I think it is?"

"Yeah, it is. I'm gettin' married to the love of my life, Quentin Stevens."

LaToya raised an eyebrow. "That's his name? Sounds like a square, if you ask me. I figured you was into them bad boys, the type of dudes yo' sista would try to holla at, like the rapper that you was wit' at the album release party, De'Von. What happened to that?"

"Ugh, girl, don't get me started. It just didn't work out between us. We're too different. But we're still friends, and he's moved on. He's got a wife and son now, and he does a lot of production work these days, so he's not in the public eye as much."

"What about yo' home girl that used to tag along with you whenever Loree and I would be getting our shine on? I remember ya used to have matching braids."

Andrea lowered her gaze. "Yeah, if you're talking about Vanessa, we used to be tight, but since she went away to college, we kinda lost touch over the years. I've tried reaching out, but she hasn't returned my calls. I guess she's been too busy. Life goes on, you know."

Andrea knew deep down inside that was not all that caused Vanessa to alienate herself from Andrea. She had caused a rift early on in her career between her and Vanessa, and after Vanessa was brutally raped at an event that Andrea invited her to, she felt that Andrea neglected her and had since kept her distance.

"Anyway, girl, since I'm back in town and shit, we might as well paint the town red. We goin' out tonight, a lil' dancing and singing. Who knows, maybe I can treat people to a free Adia concert."

But Andrea shook her head. She had reservations about going clubbing. "Nah, not anymore, Toya. I ain't into the whole club scene anymore. I'mma have to pass on that."

"Girl, what you talkin' about?" LaToya stared at Andrea as though she was sick.

Turning to face the window, Andrea said, "LaToya, I don't know where you've been the last six years, but I don't do R&B music anymore. I'm a gospel artist now, and there are certain venues that I don't frequent in as much anymore, including the clubs."

"C'mon, Drea, it ain't that serious. Everything's on me tonight, and I won't try to push no man up on you. I won't even pressure you to drink or smoke no hookah pipes there. I'll handle all that for you," she laughed.

Sharing her laughter, Andrea thought about appearing at the club. Stepping in clubs had been difficult because she could never walk inside without envisioning the horror that Vanessa went through when she was raped at a promotion event that took place in the club. People drank, smoked, danced, and had a good time to erase their troubles of the week, unbeknownst that there were moments where trouble was just around the corner. But Andrea did not want to disappoint her friend.

"Okay fine, LaToya. I'll go out with you tonight. But then that's it, okay?"

LaToya slapped Andrea back hard, causing her to jump forward out of place. "That's my girl!"

CHAPTER 15

CHRIS POPE

That following Saturday at the Cue Ball Bar, Edward and David met up again for several games of pool, but from the onset of the first game, David saw that Edward was clearly distracted. He missed easy pocket shots that he normally sank with his eyes closed, and he scratched the cue ball twice.

Edward had so many thoughts running through his mind that he accidentally bumped into a teenage boy at the entrance of the bar. The boy was hanging out with a group of older friends, who were drinking and playing cards. The boy took exception to being bumped abruptly and looked back at Edward, his eyebrow raised. But Edward paid him no mind as he made his way over to the bar and ordered his usual beer.

David was already waiting for him at the pool tables. They were three games in, and David knew that Edward's mind was not right. So, he decided to break the ice.

"Yo, man, you straight? That's yo' second scratch tonight, man. You lucky we ain't playin' for no money."

But Edward did not reply to him. He only racked up all the balls in the triangle and prepared to break for their third game. The image of

Tadarius, sitting completely relaxed at the club the previous Saturday bothered him...it was his smug face and the way he celebrated with his associates. Edward could still feel the blows that Tadarius landed to his face as a teenager, and he saw the gun pointed at his head all over again. It was a memory that he could not shake loose, and it affected his concentration on the pool game.

"C'mon, man, for real, tell me what's up?" David insisted.

"I saw him," Edward replied abruptly.

David looked at Edward, puzzled. "Saw who, Ed? What you talkin' about?"

"Tadarius, man. I saw him last Saturday. My brother and his girl took me to some new club, and I walk in there, and when I walked over to the bar, I see him laughing and pouring up bottles."

David shook his head. "No way, bro. Look, Tadarius is locked up, and he ain't goin' nowhere. That stupid man shot at law enforcement and was behind Loree's murder. Ain't no way he gettin' out."

"I'm tellin' you right now, son. Tadarius is out here in them streets, and as long as he's out there, we ain't safe. He knows we dimed him out, and you can best believe he's gonna come after us."

"Okay, hold up, kid. Are you sure you didn't see another man that probably looks like him?"

"Look, I know it sounds crazy, but I know what I saw."

"And you sure it was him?"

"Look, bro, I know what I saw. Tadarius was in the club, and he was throwin' them drinks down like he ain't worried about nothin."

David looked at his friend. *Maybe Ed needs some help or something.*

"It was him, B. It's not a face that you'd forget. When I saw him, I had to get up out of there. I didn't even let my brother know that I was leaving the club early. I just bounced."

"Okay, okay, so let's just say hypothetically that it was him. He ain't lookin' for you, man. All the gang stuff, that's ole history, man."

"Didn't matter. I had to get up out of there before he saw me."

"Why? You scared that he gon' blast you right there in the club with all them people? Look, I know T better than anybody, and one thing I know is that he's vindictive, not stupid," David pointed out.

"Look, Heisman, you got a lot to lose. You got a family and a career—two things that you took from him when you helped lock him up. If I were you, I'd lay low for a while," Edward warned.

But David shrugged as he put his stick down and took a swig of his beer. "Yo, I'd fight the devil himself when it comes to my family, best believe that, so anytime T wants to settle things with me, I ain't running."

Although Edward applauded David's confidence and bravery, he could not help but sense a streak of arrogance in him. Edward knew that Tadarius always had means of getting his targets, and he would not put it past the convicted gang leader to use spies to track their movements and plan his revenge.

"All I'm sayin' is to keep yo' guard up, man. Tadarius is dangerous, and I don't give a damn how long he's been out. I'm keepin' my head on a swivel. You think Xavier's death was an accident?"

As the men continued talking, suddenly there was a huge commotion at the bar. Edward turned around and saw that one of the teenagers, the young boy that he had bumped earlier, was staring defiantly at the face of the bartender.

"I said turn out yo' pockets, boy! I know you took 'em. I ain't stupid!" the bartender shouted angrily at the boy.

"I ain't took nothin'. You a goddamn lie!" the boy replied, but Edward knew he was lying.

The boy wore a baggy hoodie with deep pockets, and right away, he saw that the boy had three beer cans stuffed in his pocket.

"You got three seconds to put them cans back, or I'mma call the police," the bartender threatened as he reached for his cell phone.

"Yeah, go ahead, and call one. I ain't goin' nowhere," the boy replied.

Edward realized the other boys that the teenager was previously playing cards with had all vanished, leaving the beer thief by himself. When nobody stepped up to his defense, Edward stepped in. "Look, Jerry, it's all good. Put it on my tab," he told the bartender, who then put his cell phone down.

"Don't know what that lil' bastard's thinkin'. His ass too young to drink beer anyway. He showed me no I.D. or nothin," Jerry grumbled.

"Look, it's all good, man. I'll take 'em off your hands. Just let the kid go, alright?"

Reluctantly, Jerry dropped the issue, and Edward walked outside with the boy. They were followed by David.

"I ain't asked for your charity, Wall Street," he said as he turned around to face Edward.

"You gotta be a lil' more grateful than that, youngblood. I just saved you a trip to the precinct."

"Whoop-de-do, so what you want, a cookie? I never asked for you to step in for me. I got it," the boy replied harshly.

"So, where you stay at, kid?" Edward asked.

"Just a few blocks blocks from hea'. I could walk there. Hold up," the boy replied before turning off to the side of the bar.

A few seconds later, he emerged with a bookbag, which Edward was almost certain did not hold any books. Based on the boy's disheveled clothes and his uncombed hair, Edward perceived that he had either run away from home or had escaped from a juvenile center. In Queens, it was not uncommon for kids who felt abused by their parents to run away from home and spend days or weeks living elsewhere. But Edward knew that if nobody claimed the kids, usually the streets claimed them.

"Tone, you sure about this kid? I don't trust him," David whispered.

"Come on, man. Look at him. I bet you he a runaway, and he ain't got nowhere to go. Won't be long till the police catch up to him and put him in the system. I'll drop him back home. I'll hit you later, B."

After David went his separate way, Edward told the kid, "C'mon, man. I'll give you a ride."

Stepping into Edward's car, the kid looked around. "Nice ride, Wall Street. Better not leave this shit unlocked in da hood," he laughed.

"So where do you stay at?" Edward asked again.

This time, the boy lowered his gaze in embarrassment. "The Bayside Boys Group Home. But I don't wanna go back over there, man. Every day I gotta scrap for food. Then I gotta fight to sleep in a bed, or else it gets took. I used to live with a family in Cambria Heights, but they left, and now I'm back at the group home."

As Edward listened to the boy's story, he felt remorse, and it confirmed his suspicions about the boy's background. "Alright, I'll make you a deal, man. I'll let you crash at my place tonight, and then tomorrow I'll make some calls. I work in a law office, but I have connections to an adoption agency, and maybe we can get you to stay with a nice family. What you say?" he asked.

"You ain't gon' call the police?" the boy asked.

"Nah, bruh. I ain't no snitch. So, what they call you?" Edward asked.

"My name's Chris," the boy replied.

"That's it? Just Chris? You ain't got a last name?"

"Well, I never knew my real parents cuz I've bounced from foster home to foster home, but I stayed with this nice family whose last name is Pope, so I guess my last name is Pope," he replied.

"I'm sorry you never knew your parents, Chris. It's tough out here in these streets."

"You talkin' like you about that life. What you know about the streets?"

"More than you know, kid," Edward chuckled as he entered the highway to make his way back home.

He was determined to help this kid if he had anything to say about it. These were the type of boys that people such as Tadarius were looking for: fatherless boys, young men without direction that were easy to mold to do his bidding. With Tadarius out of prison, Edward could not let Chris wander the streets alone. What if Tadarius wanted to rebuild M.O.B.?

When they arrived at Edward's place, Chris stared inside the loft in awe. "Whoa. You live here, money?" he asked Edward.

"Yup. Not too bad, huh?" he asked.

"Eh, it's aight," Chris replied, changing his tone once again, shrugging his shoulders.

"Alright, so I got a guest bedroom that's down the hall, to the left, near the bathroom, so you could take your stuff in there, and I'll be there in a few minutes with some fresh sheets."

Chris made his way into the guest bedroom. The king-sized bed was still unmade, and all the drawers were empty. He wasted no time taking his clothes out and folding them neatly, the way his mother had taught him, before placing them in the drawer. Chuckling to himself, he looked out the window where he noticed that he was several stories up. He could have never imagined that his next mission would land him in the Upper East Side of Manhattan.

Wow, this sucka's got it made. Some people feast while others starve, and this rich boy's feasting big.

Chris knew he only had a few days before he had to report back to his street crew. He had to put his plan in motion immediately because it would not be long before Edward discovered that there was no such place as the Bayside Boys Home. The moment Edward found out about his fake background, he was sure that he would be kicked out or possibly arrested. But he was determined to gather as much intel on Edward and his friends before his benefactor suspected that something was afoot.

Chris's real name was Chris Jones. He never knew his father, and his mother never fully went into detail about who his father was, only that he was a sorry deadbeat that never made time to visit him and that he was a snake, the worst kind of snitch known to man. His mother had very close ties to some gang known as M.O.B., and the way she described them, they were angels to her, providing her with the necessary means to survive when her own family never stepped up to the plate.

With the primary leader of M.O.B. locked away in prison, the remaining affiliates of the gang stepped up to help Chris and his mother upon their return to the states. Then the news broke that Tadarius Hill was released from prison, and nobody was happier than his mother upon hearing the news, but as happy as she was, she was also fixated on one man that she had been endlessly tracking, some fool named David Anderson.

She had studied his movements and his daily habits, and she knew without a doubt that David would be at the bar. She did not count on him being with friends, but she sent Chris with a group of other M.O.B. potentials to the bar, where they would pretend to start a ruckus and get David's attention. Unfortunately, Chris drew Edward's attention, which was not what his mother had in mind. But his mother was specific with him before he went out.

Okay, Chris, T wants you to scope him out as much as you can. Find out what he does, who he rolls with, and get back as soon as possible.

Chris had never even met Tadarius Hill in his life, but if he was that important to his mother, and if what she said about him was true, then he knew better than to disobey her. With his mind wrapped in thought, Edward walked into the room with extra bed sheets and a towel with some toiletries.

"Here you go, man. Bathroom's just ahead. You can crash here for the weekend. Then on Monday, I'll figure something out." After handing the items to Chris, Edward began to turn around to walk back to his own room.

"Aye yo, Eddie. Thanks, man," Chris said.

"Don't mention it, boss. Just do me a favor. Please don't make a mess in my bathroom, okay? I spent a whole hour cleaning in there."

"I got you, man," Chris laughed. "Yo, so who was that that big dude you was wit' down at the bar?" he asked.

"You mean my homeboy David? Yeah, he cool. He is a big dude, huh? Used to play football back in high school. Man, we all thought he was gonna go pro."

"For real? Damn, what happened?"

"Knee injury in college took him out. So, he coaches high school football now. He's never really stayed out of the game. Anyway, it's gettin' late, man. I'mma let you do yo' thing. I'll see you in the morning."

Edward walked out of the room, unaware that the information he shared with the young boy was exactly what he was looking for to set his plan in motion.

Later that same Saturday night, LaToya and Andrea stumbled out of the nightclub, laughing hysterically. It was the second straight Saturday that they went out and LaToya had loosened up Andrea, who was typically reserved, by convincing her to drink and join in a karaoke contest.

The normal patrons at the club were excited that Adia had appeared, and they were very accommodating to the one-time R&B star. She even sang a couple of songs from her old album.

"Oh my God, girl, I haven't had this much fun in a long time. I told you to ease up on that fourth shot," Andrea laughed as she involuntarily snorted.

"Girl, you need to get a grip on yourself. But see how good it is to let loose and just have fun? Sometimes I think you be wrapped in yo' work, all stressin' out. It's givin' you split ends and all," LaToya remarked.

"Girl, stop. You know you lyin' about that. I keep mines on point all the time, you feel me?" she replied, slurring slightly.

"Yeah okay, keep tellin' yourself that. Hey, you remember back when you were ten years old, and you combed your hair to the side to try to wear you hair the same way Loree and I wore it?"

Andrea laughed as she flashed back to that fond memory. "Yeah, I definitely remember. Loree was so pissed that I used her comb, she told my mama she was gonna do my hair that night, and she ended up puttin' this perm on me. And girl when she used that hot comb, it was like she was holdin' a deadly weapon. I felt like she skinned my scalp or something."

"True, but she turned you into the 'it' girl when she did that, so a little bit of pain went a long way. Besides, I bet them lil' boys in P.S. 139 was eyein' you with your new style."

"Girl, you crazy. Now I see why Loree always hung out wit' yo' crazy self," Andrea replied as they walked to her car. She handed LaToya the keys. "You don't mind driving, do you? I don't think I can drive right now."

"Sure thing, girl. I got you," LaToya said as she took the keys and guided Andrea inside her car.

As they drove back to Andrea's house, LaToya felt her phone vibrate. She recalled New York's hands-free law and did not check to see who was texting her. When she arrived at Andrea's house, LaToya saw a man waiting at the front door.

"Oh God, it's Quentin. I forgot he was coming over tonight," Andrea said, putting her face in her hands.

She could not let her fiancé see her in her current state. After LaToya parked the car, she figured that she would play it off, and she hoped that Quentin wouldn't notice that she was slightly inebriated, but he knew better.

"Andrea, what's going on? Where were you? Did you forget that I was coming over for dinner?" he asked as LaToya guided her to the front door.

"Oh, baby, I forgot. I'm sorry. I guess when I was out, the time got away from me. Don't be mad. By the way, this is my friend LaToya Richardson. LaToya, this is my fiance' Quentin Stevens."

"Pleasure to meet you, Quentin. Drea's told me a lot about you," LaToya greeted, but Quentin was in no mood for pleasantries.

"Really? Cuz I don't know that much about you, LaToya. Andrea, how many drinks have you had tonight?" Quentin asked.

"Oh, baby, relax. I'm fine, okay? You always trippin' about something. I just need a hot shower and some sleep, and I'll be okay."

"Girl, you sure you'll be okay? I can walk you into your house if you need me," LaToya offered, but Quentin adamantly stepped in.

"I think you've done enough, LaToya. Nice to meet you. Have a good night," he replied, walking Andrea inside, hastily shutting the door behind them.

Such a response would have dismayed many, but LaToya grinned from ear to ear. Her devious plan was unfolding beautifully. Checking her phone, she saw three missed messages from Tadarius. He had another mission for her to complete.

Time to go to work.

CHAPTER 16

THE INTRICATE PLOT

Quincy Harvey walked in for a routine check-up on Friday evening. He had been seeing his physician due to his high blood pressure and choleric levels. A large burly man with a thick beard, Quincy attended his local clinic and waited at the reception area for his name to be called. When a nurse walked out and called his name, Quentin followed her into one of the doctor's offices.

Quincy, who normally hated visits at the doctor's office, perked up during this visit because his nurse was stunningly beautiful. A black woman with light red hair and curves in all the right places, she walked him to the doctor's office, making sure to sway her hips from side to side so she would catch his attention.

After she led him into the office, the nurse took her stethoscope and checked his heartbeat, per usual. Then she took his blood pressure, and to no surprise, his blood pressure was elevated.

"How are you feeling today, Mr. Harvey?" she asked.

"A little nervous when I first walked in, but since you've been with me, I've felt a lot better," Quincy replied, grinning slyly.

The nurse pretended to giggle and turned her back to him before rolling her eyes.

"Yeah, it's the first time that someone as fine as you is treating me before my physician."

"Well, I just started here last week," the nurse replied. "Sonya, the nurse who treated you before me, was transferred to another clinic."

Quincy chuckled. He had forgotten all about Sonya, the bow-legged wonder. "Oh yeah, Sonya. That was her name. It always escaped me. I was never good in remembering names. What's yo' name, by the way, sweetheart?"

Ignoring his question, the nurse had her back to Quincy the entire time because she was pulling a needle from the health receptacle. As she updated his chart, she pulled a vial from one of the drawers, and after preparing the needle, she dipped it in the vial, unbeknownst to her patient.

For the first five minutes, Quincy was completely relaxed, but as time wore on, he grew suspicious. His physician normally walked into the room after the nurse did her preliminary duties. "So, where's Dr. Robinson?" he asked.

"Oh, Dr. Robinson will be here very shortly. He's running a little late, but he will be here. So, Mr. Harvey, when was the last time you took your flu shot?" she asked.

"Um, it's been quite a while. I guess I'm supposed to take it today. Is Dr. Robinson the one who's going to apply it?"

The nurse tapped the needle tip. A few drops of the solution squirted out of the tip. "Dr. Robinson instructed me to administer your flu shot today, Mr. Harvey," she replied.

Quincy looked at the nurse as if she was a foreign being. In all his years of visiting his physician, the nurse had never administered his flu shot before. Typically, Dr. Robinson applied it, and there were certain questions he asked before he did.

"Don't worry, Mr. Harvey. I will be very careful. Just relax your left arm for me." She dabbed Quincy's arm with alcohol and gauze, preparing the location for the needle.

"That's a very interesting tattoo you got there. What's it mean?" she asked curiously as she stared at Quincy's unique body art.

Quincy thought of his next words carefully because outside of the crew, nobody was supposed to know the origins of the tattoo. Although it had been over seven years since he ex-communicated himself from M.O.B., he always felt it was a part of him. He regretted the crimes that were committed under the gang colors, but he didn't regret the sense of family and unity that the crew shared.

"It's nothin', just some unique body art...just me actin' a fool in my younger days. You know how it is."

Although Quincy lied about the origins of the tattoo, the nurse was not beguiled. She knew who Quincy was, and she knew he had walked away from the family years ago, betraying Tadarius Hill, and as a result, he had to pay dearly for it with his life.

"Anyway, enough about me. You never did tell me what yo' name was," he pointed out.

"Ebony Fatima. But everyone calls me Bunny," the nurse replied as she stuck Quincy with the needle.

What he originally perceived to be a flu shot turned out to be something more lethal. Bunny had dipped the needle into a clear arsenic poison solution, and she knew that Quincy had a little less than an hour until he would feel the deadly effects of the poison. She smiled at him, then proceeded to leave the office.

A few minutes passed, and Quincy began sweating profusely, his heart beating rapidly against his chest. A person who had normal weight for his height would have succumbed earlier, but due to Quincy's overweight status and girth, the effects were increasing in pain and affecting his mobility as his heart worked to fight the poison from the shot.

Then Quincy suddenly went into cardiac arrest, and gasping for air, he grasped at the door handle, which was locked. He attempted to knock at the door, but he was weakened by the effects of the poison and fell onto the ground. It would be more than an hour until another nurse would unlock the door and discover Quincy's lifeless body sprawled across the floor.

As for Bunny, she snuck to the back of the clinic, removed her nurse's jacket, and changed to a different pair of clothes. Removing the red wig, she smiled as she heard the frantic sounds of the doctors and nurses who were trying to revive Quincy, but she knew it was too late for him.

Another one bites the dust!

Just two days after rescuing Chris, Edward Reed searched for the Bayside Boys Group Home in the archives, but there were no results in his search. After trying different browsers to search for the location, he finally discovered that Chris lied to him about where he stayed. Enraged, Edward took the rest of the day off and rushed back home.

If Chris lied about where he stayed, what else could he have lied about? If he was not a gangbanger, he was probably a petty thief who fed his victims the same sob story just to get into their houses to rob them blind. Edward blamed himself for falling for the banana in the tailpipe. He saw so much of himself in Chris, and it blinded him from the reality that Chris may be more than what meets the eye.

After he arrived home, Edward unlocked the door and walked inside, preparing to confront Chris, but to his surprise, Chris was gone. He searched the guest bedroom and discovered that Chris had taken his bag and the rest of his belongings, but all his things appeared untouched. Breathing a sigh of relief, Edward walked into his closet and checked his clothes, shoes, and signature Nike and Jordan wear. Surprisingly, they were still in his closet. Edward was sure that those were the first items that a teenage boy would attempt to steal if given the opportunity.

Maybe he knew that I would find out he was lying about where he really stayed, and he left once he figured out the jig was up.

Opening his briefcase, Edward decided to work on his cases from his home office. Right before he got into it, his phone rang, and he saw David's name on his screen.

"What's up, man?" he replied.

"Yo, what's up, man? How you handlin' that lil' wannabe gangsta you picked up on Saturday?" David asked.

"You tell me, man. So, I ask the boy where he stay at, and he tells me he stays at some place called the Bayside Boys Home. I get to work today, and I look up that location, and guess what? It doesn't exist."

"Damn, so what you tellin' me is that he took you. I would've kicked his lyin' ass out my house."

"Well, I was coming back to do just that, but when I got back, he wasn't here. Looks like he just bounced. Probably knew I was gonna air his ass out for lying to me."

Edward heard David chuckle in the background. "What's so funny?"

"I could've told you he was gonna scam yo' ass. Better check to make sure he ain't stole nothing," David laughed.

"That's the thing though. Everything is still intact. He didn't even take any of my J's, and you know how kids feel about new shoes. You can't tell 'em nothin' when they want some new shit."

"Yeah, but at least he's outta yo' way now. Check it, did you watch the news this morning?"

Edward never opened his television on workdays, so all the news that he received normally came to him via phone notification. To him, the television was a distraction box, and the news always showed nothing but propaganda and negativity.

"Nah, what happened?"

"Remember that big kid that rolled with M.O.B back in the day, Quincy Harvey?"

Upon hearing the name, Edward nearly dropped his cell phone. Although he never spoke directly to Quincy, he remembered his wide frame always being sprawled all over the couch with either two women on either arm or he would be in front of a tray, where he would be cutting up weed. While Edward was in the gang, he never so much as said two words to Quincy and vice versa. He was not part of Tadarius's inner circle, but he was an informant that was very vital to Tadarius's operation.

"Yeah, what happened to Quincy?" Edward asked.

"Doctors found him dead in the clinic. They said that he had a fatal heart attack, but I've known Quincy for years, and even though my mans was big, he never had any type of heart attack, stroke, none of that."

Edward's eyes widened. Murdered. This had to be foul play. No way he just fell down and died like that. There has to be more to this story.

"That's crazy, son. You don't think that he was killed because of..." his voice trailed off.

"Nah, come on, man. I know where you're going with this. No way Tadarius could've gotten past all the security, doctors, or anybody at that hospital. Someone would've seen him."

"Fool, you don't think Tadarius could've had somebody on the inside at that hospital that poisoned him? Think about what happened. First, we hear that Xavier dies, under mysterious circumstances. Then, Tadarius gets out of jail, and now Quincy's dead. He's coming after us, David. I know he is." But Edward knew that David still did not believe him, and he noted a hint of sarcasm at his next response.

"Ain't you supposed to be a lawyer, Tone? You need evidence to back up your crazy claims about Tadarius coming after crew because he's holding some ten-year grudge for being locked up."

"Some things are happening a little too close to home to be just chance, man. I mean, who's next after Quincy? Me? You? If I were you, I'd leave town, or at least I'd get some extra protection until that psychotic bastard's back behind bars or six feet under."

"Whatever, man. Like I said before, I know Tadarius, and I know how he moves. Even if he comes my way, you think I sweat him? I got my piece in my car, and it got twelve fresh rounds. So, I'd like to see him try to fuck wit' me."

Edward then heard a click on the other line. David had hung up. Despite the points that he explained to David, he was not convinced that Quincy's death was accidental, and he was positive that Xavier's death was not accidental. Edward decided he would worry about Chris later. He began looking online and decided to open the details surrounding Xavier's death and the new information that unfolded around Quincy's death. If David was not going to help him, he was going to confirm his own theory that perhaps Tadarius had not gotten over being locked up, and he was out eliminating other members of M.O.B. who were seen as rivals or anyone that could potentially lock him back up in jail.

Andrea and Shania went out for their most favorite activity: shopping. They loved shopping for new clothes and new shoes. They were picking out wedding dresses from Sharon's Bridal Boutique in Long Island, but Shania sensed that her friend was distracted. Whenever she would ask her opinion on a specific pair of shoes or heels, Andrea would either mutter, "It's okay," or would just give a short nod of her head. She seemed withdrawn, and Shania was curious to find out what was up with her best friend. Andrea had just picked a pair of Jimmy Choo heels and was about to try them on, when Shania finally spoke.

"Okay, Drea, what's up? You've been quiet all day, even when I tried on them blue flats. You wanna talk about it?"

Andrea looked at her friend, smiling warmly. Shania and Andrea had a sisterly bond that could not be explained or rationalized. In many ways, she had replaced Loree as the wise, level-headed figure in her life.

"It's nothin', Nia, really. I'm okay," she lied.

"Starting to get cold feet about the wedding? Because, believe me, it's completely normal if you do."

"No, I wouldn't exactly call it cold feet. It's just that Quentin and I got into it the other night because I came back late from a party. He's always been pretty laid back about things, but lately I feel as if he's keepin' tabs on me."

"Really? When you first introduced me to him, he seemed like a real chill guy. I'm sure you two will work it out. Couples fight all the time, but as long as you don't let that spoil what you two have, you'll be fine," Shania reassured. "Why were you two gettin' into it though?"

"It really wasn't a big deal. An old friend came back into town, and she took me out a couple times, and I may have returned home a little late. But Quentin doesn't trust my friend and wants me to stop hanging out with her. Can you believe that? I mean, I'm a grown woman. I think I should be able to hang out with whoever I want, but he thinks my homegirl's a bad influence."

"Who's the friend? Anyone I know, or is it one of your celebrity friends, since you know I don't roll in the same circles you do, superstar," Shania cracked.

"Girl, bye!" Andrea laughed. "You know I don't hang with any celebrity friends like that anymore. But I think you know her. Remember LaToya Richardson?"

As Shania was putting away a pair of shoes, she tried to remember the name, but it took a couple minutes for the memory to register.

"I remember a girl named LaToya back in high school. She would hang with me and ReRe sometimes. She was a lil' rough around the edges the last time I remembered."

"Yeah, that's her. Loree and LaToya used to be best friends—well best friends—before she met you, I mean," Andrea replied, using her words with caution, but Shania did not take it seriously.

"Don't even worry about that. Yeah, LaToya and I didn't always get along back then, but I don't hold grudges from high school. We all grown out here, okay? So why don't Quentin want you going out with her?"

"Well, this past Saturday, we went to this new club and did some karaoke, and I may have had a few drinks, but it wasn't serious enough for him to put me on front street about it."

Shania listened to Andrea, and while she explained the details of the evening, she pulled out her cell phone and showed Andrea a picture that was posted through a celebrity paparazzi website. The picture clearly showed a drunk Andrea being led out of the club by LaToya and another girl. Andrea covered her mouth in shock.

Who had taken the picture, and how long had it been posted online?

"At first, when I saw this shot, I was like, that had to be some type of clone or just somebody messing with edit features, but it looks like somebody snapped you and ran with the image to publish it and post it," Shania explained.

"What the hell? How did they catch me though?"

"I don't know. Maybe Quentin had a reason to be concerned about you. But you gotta be careful out here, and tread softly because the image of a gospel artist leaving a nightclub half-drunk really ain't a good look for you."

"C'mon, Nia, did you think I planned for that to happen? I just let my guard down. That's all."

"I'm not saying you have to be perfect, Andrea, but you've gotta be mindful of who you surround yourself with. So, what has LaToya been up to since high school?"

"Nothin' much. She went to the Army, got deployed a few times, and after she was discharged, she came back to New York," Andrea replied.

"Does she know about, you know, the other you?" Shania asked, referring to Andrea's performing occupation.

"Yeah, she knows about me, and honestly, she says she loved me better as Adia, the R&B songstress."

Shania then pursed her lips disapprovingly. Although she had not seen LaToya in over ten years, the positive memories that she had with LaToya were few and far between. "Figures," she muttered.

"Come on, Shania, what's that supposed to mean? Just because she says she liked me better as a secular artist, don't mean I have the desire to go back to singing R&B. One day, I'm gonna reunite us, and we're going to hang out for old times' sake."

"Well, I got a lot of work to catch up on. Plus, I have to prepare little Ms. Loree Emiline for her first ballet recital. You know she won't ever give Mommy a break when it comes to buying ballet shoes, leotards, and the whole nine."

"I bet she is excited about that. How is my goddaughter doing these days?" Andrea asked of Shania's seven-year-old daughter.

"She's doing great. She loves school, and after being enrolled in ballet class, she's ecstatic about the recital. She can't stop asking about her godmother though. Maybe she needs to make some time on her schedule to visit more often."

"Don't worry. I'm working on it," Andrea laughed. "By the way, how's Bighead doing?" she asked.

"Oh, Trevor's just being Trevor. He likes his job, but sometimes I get the feeling that he misses the court. He loved playing basketball and really regretted not making it to the NBA. But you know what? I'm completely fine with it because I didn't want to be no NBA wife anyway. Can you imagine the women that would've thrown themselves at him? Knowing him, they would've locked me up for breakin' his neck if he eva' played me, okay?" Shania and Andrea laughed as they continued their shopping.

In Crown Heights, New York, Pooh waited for two young prospects of the new M.O.B. crew that he was forming.

They better not be late.

But two minutes later, he saw two boys walking in his direction. Chris and Isaiah "Zay" Carter were eagerly talking about the day's profits that they had taken in from a day of selling drugs. Together, both boys raked in over five thousand dollars, but they were counting the money too loud for Pooh's liking.

"About time ya niggas showed up. Can ya keep yo' muthafuckin' voices down, please? We don't need ya to bring any heat on us."

"My bad, Pooh. I was just schoolin' Chris hea' on how to handle his take. But I'm hearing he livin' large these days," Zay replied while ignoring an angry scowl from Chris.

Chris had hoped Zay wouldn't talk about where he currently resided.

"The fuck you talkin' about Zay? I thought lil' Chris here was still livin' wit' his mama down in the projects."

Since Zay opened his mouth, Chris had no choice but to explain his living situation to Pooh. "So, I was at the bar just chillin' and watchin' homeboy with crew, and then we got into that fake fight, and that's when the punk-ass bartender threatened me over a beer bottle. I was about to throw hands wit' him, but then this funny-lookin' cat in a shirt and tie came in and slowed shit down before anything popped off. I lied about being from some boys home and being homeless, so he let me crash at his crib."

"Yo, Chris told me this cat lives in the Upper East Side, so you know he loaded," Zay replied, excited.

Zay and Chris were two hopefuls that were vying to get inducted into M.O.B., and they were working and hustling to make it happen. For Zay, it was a chance to prove himself and climb the ranks to be the top man like Tadarius. But for Chris, his ties to M.O.B. ran deeper than anyone realized.

Since he was born, his mother had bounced from state to state, but no matter where she landed, she found herself struggling to financially support her son. His father never visited, nor cared to find him or his mother. But when they returned to New York, M.O.B. welcomed Chris and his mother with open arms. They used a quarter of the profits from the drug and gun-selling business to support Chris and his mother, and it afforded them a small flat in West Sayres, New York.

"Upper East Side? And the cat that you stayin' wit' is black?" Pooh asked as Chris and Zay paid him their earnings for the day, while waiting for their cut.

"No doubt. But he a bit sketchy though. He told me he was a lawyer or something like that."

"What? Oh, hell nah, you got to get up out of there, B. Lawyers deal directly with pigs, and if you lied to him, best believe he gon' have yo' ass arrested," Pooh warned.

Referring to them as "pigs," Pooh never trusted nor appreciated the police. To him, they were as cruel and ruthless as the other gangs that ran the streets, but the only difference was that their actions were deemed legal.

"Yeah, I got up out of there before he knew my ass was lying."

"How did you even end up there anyway? Your job was to scope out that snitchin' ass David. T wanted you to keep him in yo' sights—find out what he do, where his ideal spots are, then report back to us. We gon' move in on him."

"Believe me, I know everything about David Anderson. Coaches football at Townsend Harris. Has a wife and three kids, goes to the Cue Ball Bar every Friday, and shoots pool with that lawyer," Chris reeled off.

"Lawyer?" a voice asked, and out of the shadows, a girl named Sherika emerged.

A member of M.O.B., she was an informant but was considered one of Tadarius's "angels" with a sweet face and a nice body, but she was a ruthless killer. She had many different aliases, and with her extensive work background, she was able to infiltrate any location within the city to get her target. Each assignment Tadarius had given her, she had not failed.

Known by her street name, Bunny, Sherika was the woman who had killed Xavier Burrows. She also killed Quincy by posing as a nurse at the clinic where she previously worked in. Now she was working on a third victim, but this one seemed to be more elusive than the other two.

Bunny was instructed to go after Antonio Franks, but nobody had seen Antonio for more than ten years, so she looked his family up, and when she realized he had siblings, she made her move.

"Was this lawyer's name Edward Reed?" she asked Chris.

"Yeah, some square ass name like that. How'd you know?" he asked.

"Cuz we've met, fool. What you think? You sure you my nephew? My question is, what's this lawyer's connection to David?"

As Sherika started to connect the dots, another woman stepped out of the shadows. "Edward Reed is the man formerly known as Antonio Franks. He changed his name. Now we can move in on him. Welcome home, my son." LaToya Richardson replied, hugging Chris tightly.

CHAPTER 17

NO WAY OUT THE GAME

While Chris loved and appreciated his mother, he was not fond of the public show of affection. The last idea that he wanted to implant in Tadarius's head was that he was a mama's boy.

LaToya Richardson was barely nineteen when she gave birth to Chris, and as a single mother, she struggled to raise him. Resources were scarce, and even after LaToya was enlisted into the Army, she did everything she could to provide for her son. At first, she was traveling from one army base to another with him in her arms, and as he grew older, he went to different schools, but he always had a hard time fitting in.

Then after she was discharged, LaToya moved back to Queens with him, but she was barely surviving on government assistance and was running low on funds until she reunited with Pooh and the other remaining members of M.O.B. who stayed loyal to the family. LaToya herself had never wavered in her commitment to the crew that she joined with her best friend, Loree McAfee, years earlier, and when Tadarius was finally freed from prison, he went out of his way to support LaToya and Chris monetarily.

To LaToya, Tadarius defined what a man was in her eyes.

Chris's father never fit the bill. He was absent from his son's life the day he was born, and he strayed away from the responsibility of taking care of their son. The irony of it all was that he was the one who introduced her to Tadarius and the other members of M.O.B. years back, and he was one of the gang's main kingpins. But he betrayed the family, betrayed her, and worse of all, he betrayed Chris. There was no forgiveness for those types of betrayals.

It was no secret that Tadarius wanted David Anderson dead, but he was not the only one who wanted David gone.

LaToya had been tracking Chris's father for months and even had Chris scope him out. There was no doubt at all that David Anderson was Chris's father, for there were way too many similarities. Chris was a natural athlete, like his father was. He had a nonchalant demeanor about him that resembled that of his father. But he had never known his father on a personal level, and no matter how many times he showed up at the bar, his father would pay no attention to him. Chris knew that David would soon get what was coming to him, and it would be just as painful as his betrayals were to him and to the crew.

After LaToya revealed Edward's identity, Bunny laughed. As LaToya's younger sister and a fellow avenging angel, she was methodical and scheming in her approach to vengeance, which Tadarius found a useful trait.

"LaToya, Tone was like six-four with long hair that would either be designed into dreads or braided. He was a down-ass cat. The lawyer that Tony introduced me to was a straight-up square. Ain't no way that's Antonio."

"Bunny, I'm tellin' you it's him. I remember Tone's snitchin' ass better than anyone. I was in the Army, girl, and the one thing that they used to tell us all the time was to be analytical about shit. Just peep this photo." LaToya pulled an old photo out of her purse.

On the photo, which dated back to early 2002, were the original members of M.O.B. The gang was at a rec event at a local park, and a photographer took pictures of them. They wore throwback basketball and football jerseys, which were baggie. Other members posed with their middle finger to the camera. Included in the shot were Quincy, Xavier, Terrell, and Antonio.

"Now look at this," LaToya explained while pulling out another photo.

This time it was a newspaper clip, and the clip was an advertisement for Schorr Law Group. All the members of the group posed for the ad, and right there in the middle of the photo was Edward Reed, the only black man in the middle of the other white attorneys.

"Tell me you don't see the similarity. Just take out the braids and jersey, and that's him. Bastard thinks he slick."

After taking another look at the photo, Bunny shook her head in disbelief. "Damn, Toya, you right. This fool went from being down wit' the fam to being in a damn plantation."

"Yeah, he did, but that ain't the reason why I want him six feet under," Tadarius emerged from another door, a smile on his face.

For years he had been searching for Antonio and David without any success. He knew David was still around the area, and when his name resurfaced, due to his football coaching success, Tadarius had been plotting for an opportunity to destroy the man he once knew as his brother.

Antonio, on the other had proved to be more elusive than Tadarius anticipated. Although he had operatives, informants, and other people scope out Antonio's whereabouts, he had been unsuccessful in locating him. But when he heard that Antonio changed his name and was now working for the man, a government that did not care for its patrons, it strengthened Tadarius's resolve to find him and make him pay for the years he spent behind bars.

"I knew that he was still around. Bunny, I'm gonna go big game hunting now, and I'll take care of Tone. I want you to track him, and when you find him, don't kill him. I want to deal wit' that snake myself. As for David, I'll leave him in your capable hands, LaToya. After all, you have your own reasons for wanting that low scum dead. So, Chris, how did it feel, meeting yo' daddy again?"

"He barely said two words to me. He ain't even know who I was," Chris replied, shaking his head.

"That's cuz he don't claim you. But you always got family here within these walls. M.O.B. always got yo' back," Tadarius reassured.

As they walked back to living room area of the apartment, three hopeful potentials sat on the floor, and the other members sat on the couch, waiting for their leaders to address them. Pooh stood by Tadarius's right side, a side where David once stood. All the members were busy listening to music, playing video games, smoking weed, and playing cards, but when Tadarius walked into the room, raising his hand, the music stopped, and the commotion ceased at once. Chris, who was one of the hopefuls to join M.O.B., sat on one of the stools facing the kitchen next to his mother.

"Check this out, fam!" Tadarius's voice bellowed through the apartment. "The system thought they could take this muhfucka down, but they was dead wrong! I make it out, and I keep the shit going!"

He turned to the new members, the hopefuls who were sitting on the floor. There were four new members: three boys and one girl.

"To those who want to join the fam, welcome. If you're hea' you've sworn to take the M.O.B. credo and add to its legacy. You've committed to putting in work out in the streets and to keep makin' money for the crew." Emphatically pointing out the window into the streets, Tadarius continued talking his point.

"If you're here, you're lost, and you're searching for a home. Yo' moms and pops failed you. Yo' so-called society has failed you. You're getting yo' ass kicked by racist ass cops and Uncle Tom-ass niggas who swear they your family to your face and then stab you in the back the next day. You ain't got no one to turn to, but believe this: I protect my own, and I go to war over my own. If you got my back, I got yo' back. Simple as that."

Tadarius then lowered his voice and stared intently at the group. "But if any of ya snitch, or open yo' mouths about this operation, or if ya so much as whisper about the crew, you forfeit my protection, and then you're on your own out there. Don't make me regret makin' you part of the fold. I've been too trusting of my own in the past, and it got my ass locked up. Trust and believe I won't make the same mistake again, and you don't want me to make an example out of ya'll. I've done it before, and I'll do it again. You feel me?"

The new members, Key-Low, Vice, Charlene, and Dome, all listened to Tadarius.

"Most importantly, keep all personal relationships separate from business. If you find yourself needing to get some dick or pussy, keep that shit private, and take it somewhere outside of the fam. Don't bring any relationship drama over here. It's a mistake that I allowed in the past, and to this day, I'm still payin' for it," Tadarius stated, glancing over to LaToya, who felt her face turn red with embarrassment.

She hated when Tadarius put her on the spot in front of the new recruits. Reflecting back to her rendezvous with David, she couldn't help what eventually took place during that time that she sometimes wished she could take back.

Early the next morning, Edward woke up, showered, and got ready to go to work. His mind was still on Chris as he checked his suit and shoes. Before he headed out, he saw his cell phone vibrate. Checking his caller ID and chuckled to himself.

"What up, Tony? You know I get ready to go to work around this time," he replied.

"My bad, son. I would've hit you up earlier, but I've been busy as hell all week, cleaning up shit," his brother explained. "Two of my stores got hit back-to-back over the last couple days. They held my employees up at gunpoint and robbed hundreds of dollars in groceries, over-the-counter drugs, and prophylactics."

"What?" Edward asked, stunned.

"Yeah, man. The worse part about the whole thing is we couldn't even identify the bastards that did it. They all wore ski masks, and by the time my people got to the alarm to call the police, they were already out. It's bad enough that they robbed one of my stores, but to rob two stores, and no other spot was robbed? If I ain't know any better, I'd have thought somebody was targeting me," Tony replied.

"Damn. Are your people okay though?" Edward asked.

"Yeah, they're good," Tony replied. "Thankfully, nobody got shot during the hold-ups. The po-po still up in there looking for clues and asking all the graveyard shift workers to ID these fools. I'll be surprised if they get anything though. Some of 'em are too traumatized to give any information. I had some new hires ready to start this week too, and now they probably thinking twice about coming in."

Edward's mind started racing.

It can't be a coincidence. I know that crime happens everywhere, but ever since Tadarius got out, two former members of his crew are killed. Then a brawl ensues at the bar, and I meet Chris, who's pretty sketchy to me, and now this happens. Could Tadarius and the cronies that he keeps around him be responsible for the robberies? And why would they rob my brother's stores? Unless they've somehow made the connection between me and Tony... Do they know that we're related? Do they know my real name? Are they going to come after me or Tony or my brothers?

"Man, I hope they find the pieces of scum that hit your stores. So how are things going with Tina?" Edward asked. He heard his brother sigh over the phone.

"I ain't gon' lie to you, man. It could be better. I want us to work, but she's too damn mysterious, bro. Always got to run off somewhere. She told me she got two jobs, so she's mad busy, but we ain't gettin' it like we used to. I might have to break it off."

"Damn, sorry to hear that, bro. She might be creepin' on you, Tony."

"You know what, it wouldn't surprise me if she was seeing somebody else. That girl love to go out, and she got friends that are some real roughnecks—gangsta-type thugs. I don't cross any of 'em though cuz that's her business."

Before Edward replied, he heard a knock on his door. Checking the peephole through the door, he saw Chris standing outside. "You don't think that maybe them roughneck friends might have had something to do with them robberies?" Edward asked.

"Nah, man, come on. Tina ain't about that life. Okay, so she hangs out with some lowlife-ass dudes, but that don't mean she set me up," Tony replied.

"You sure about that?" Edward asked. When Tony failed to reply, he continued. "What you need to do is call her, and tell her to come correct. Ask her where she's been the last few days. If she can't account for nothin', then that makes her a suspect in my eyes."

Chris knocked on the door three more times during the brothers' conversation. "Yeah, but she wouldn't a motive though. Why would she wanna rob me?" Tony asked.

"Why? Because you got money, bro. You own multiple stores in the tri-state area. She knows you making ducats, man."

Or she could be workin' with Tadarius, and he figured out who I am, and these robberies are just a play to smoke me out and make me give myself up to them. Nah, I'm trippin'.

Brushing off his conspiracies, Edward said, "Look, man, I gotta roll. I'm late for work, so I'll check with you later." Hanging up, he looked at the peephole, but he dared not allow Chris back into his home.

"What you want, man? Shouldn't you be back at the Far Rockaway Boy's Home? That's where you came from, right?" he asked sarcastically.

"Look, man, my bad. Sorry for playin' you like I did. I just didn't know who to trust, and I had just met you, but you were the first one to hear me out when no one else did," Chris replied.

"So, where are you really from then, boy? You better not play wit' me cuz I won't hesitate to call the police on yo' dusty ass."

"Look, my mama raised me for a few years, and before that my grandparents. After my grandmama died, my mama took me back, but she got involved in some shady shit, and I didn't want to out her or nothin' like that. She ain't the most friendly person to be around after she works, and because I'm her son, she tryin' to keep me in the trap game, but I don't wanna do it."

"Why should I believe you?" Edward asked, grabbing his keys and his briefcase before heading out of the door.

Chris backed away as Edward closed the door after himself, and Chris followed him outside as he made his way to his car.

"Because if I was lying, or if I was tryin' to boost yo' shit, why would I come back and tell you all that?" he asked.

"I don't know. Maybe you tryin' to see if I'm a sucka that falls for the okie-doke. But you can't fool me, man. I've been playin' the street game long before you were born, so I know what's up."

"Probably, but the game done changed since your day," Chris said as Edward got into his car and thrust the key into the ignition.

"Is that so? And who are you to tell me what I know about the game?" Edward asked.

"I know that if you keep playin', you'll find yo'self in too deep, and you can't get out of the game," Chris replied wisely.

Realizing that this boy may know more than what he was leading on, Edward unlocked his passenger door so that Chris could get inside. "Look, I'll drop you off to the nearest subway station. Then after that, you on yo' own, dawg. I don't know what to tell you about yo' mama, but it ain't my business," Edward said.

"Oh yeah? Try me then. By the way, I know what yo' real name is, and it damn sure ain't Edward," Chris said, while Edward was driving.

Stunned by what he heard, Edward slammed the brakes on his car to prevent himself from rear-ending the one in front of him that had just stopped at a red light. "What did you say?" he asked.

"I know you ain't really who you said you were. I know what you and David did to Tadarius and the rest of the fam to get him locked up. I know that instead of facing Tadarius, you snitched him out to police."

Edward was happy he wore a suit because if he hadn't been wearing the suit, the perspiration that was dampening his shirt out of anxiety would have been visible. "How do you know about all that?" Edward asked, but internally he already knew the answer to the question.

Chris is a new member of M.O.B. Tadarius hadn't even been out of prison for a year, and he was already recruiting young boys to join the lethal group.

Edward wished he had not brought it up in the first place because he had his suspicions about Chris, and here he was being completely lucid.

"That ain't all I know. I know what happened to Xavier and Quincy, and I know that they want you and David dead and gone."

Edward shifted uncomfortably in the driver's seat. "How much more do you know, and are you gonna tell Tadarius about me?" he asked nervously.

But after thinking it over, Chris replied that he would not spill the beans to any of the other members.

But the awkward silence that followed his response did not sit well with Edward. "What else do you know about the crew, since you know so much?" he asked, hoping that Chris didn't pull a gun out to shoot him in broad daylight.

"The grocery stores that got hit a few days ago, it was planned by another member of the crew to get back at you through yo' brother. It was a warning from him. He wants you to show your face so you could get what's coming to you, or else all your brothers are dead," Chris revealed.

"Tell me, did a girl by the name of Tina have anything to do with the robberies?" he asked.

"Nah, I don't know anybody by that name, but she goes by the name of Bunny, and she's pretty much the brain behind the operation. She's Tadarius's right-hand femme-fatale, and she's high-key dangerous."

"Why you tellin' me all this, Chris?" Edward asked.

"Because I need a way out of this game. My mama's tryin' to induct me into M.O.B., but it's a foul game, and I ain't tryin' to die early. The way that I see it, you're the only way out of this."

Edward could not believe that this boy's mother was encouraging the involvement of her son in gangbanging and drug dealing, but he knew that there were people that saw the street life as a way out of poverty and would do anything to keep a roof over their heads.

"Who's yo' mother?" he asked.

"LaToya Richardson. Name ring a bell?" Chris asked Edward.

Edward almost did a double take on the road as he recalled LaToya, the girl who was part of Tadarius's female informant group.

"I also know who my dad is. I've been tracking him for months now, and I also know what really went down in '03 when Loree got shot."

With Chris willing to spill everything on the crew, Edward could not drop him back to his place in Queens. He had to find a secure spot for him before M.O.B. members found him.

Veering off to the nearest exit after driving the freeway, Chris asked, "What are you doing?"

"I'm taking you to my brother's place. It's a safe spot. Nobody'll know you're there." Edward replied as he drove about twenty miles over the speed limit.

The following Sunday afternoon, David Anderson drove to J. Foster Phillips Cemetery on Linden Boulevard. While his wife and kids stayed with his in-laws during the weekend, David had started routinely visiting places of his childhood. It gave him a chance to relive the places where he met his friends, where he first got in trouble with the law, and where he first fell in love with football. But on this day, David decided to visit someone that he hadn't visited in years.

Although it was a warm spring day, there was a chill in the air that David could not incubate himself. He searched by headstone until he found her final resting place.

LOREE ANNE MCAFEE. A LOVING DAUGHTER, SISTER, AND FRIEND.

They always said that you never forget your first. Loree, I've never forgotten the love we shared when you was still here on earth. Sure, we were young, but you gave me the love that nobody else, not even my own family, gave me. Anytime I was buggin' out, you always listened to me. I took you for granted, even pawned you off to a person who I thought was a brother. Worse of all, I wasn't there to protect you when you needed me the most. It's ironic because I have what I always wanted with you: a family. Don't get me wrong, I love Renee, but it wasn't the same with her as it was with you.

As he knelt before the headstone crying, David was unaware that he had been followed. A woman whom he had dealt with in the past was now just a few feet behind him, and he was so focused on pouring his heart out to Loree that he was oblivious to what was going on behind him.

"So you come by to visit her too, huh?"

The voice startled David, who believed that he was alone in the cemetery. "What's it to you? Who are you, anyway?" he asked, angrily brushing a tear away.

"Just someone who came to pay her respects to the dearly departed. Boy, you a creature of habit, ain't you? I could read you like a book, Heisman."

Upon hearing his nickname, David turned around, and no sooner did he turn around, he realized that he was surrounded by ten figures, and leading them was a woman whom David had not seen in years.

"How do you know that I go by that name?" he asked.

"I know everything about you, David. I remember when you took Loree and I to New York Jets games, and I remember how we used to try different pizza flavors at our favorite spot, El Manchini. I remember watching your games. You were a maestro on that field with the ball in your hands—the best QB ever. We all knew you was going pro, but that was before we found out what you really were."

David angrily turned around to face his verbal assault, and he felt his heart sink into his chest when he found who the speaker was.

"Surprised to see me, David?" LaToya asked as she approached him.

"LaToya? Is that you?" David asked, but internally he knew who it was, and it appeared that she still kept the same company.

Edward was right. It was only a matter of time before they caught up to him, and now he was surrounded.

"How long you've been trackin' me?" he asked.

"Oh, longer than you'll ever know, sweetie. I knew you'd crawl your ass back over here, and we were ready for your snitchin' ass. Too bad, it had to end this way," LaToya said as a cruel cold smile formed across her face.

David looked around, and he saw more dark figures emerging from behind bushes and trees with their hands in their pockets, ready to draw their weapons out.

"Just answer me this. Did Tadarius put you up to this? Look, LaToya, I'm sorry I left you when you needed me, okay? I was only eighteen. I lost Loree, and I didn't know what to do, okay? I panicked, and I left for college. I should've been around to help you raise our son."

"That's right. You should've been there to take care of him. But don't even worry because Chris is gonna be a better man than you ever were."

"I told you, Heisman, ain't no way outta the game," Tadarius said, suddenly appearing from the shadows.

"There's always a way out, T, even if you don't wanna admit it. I'm still done with M.O.B. Ya' killed a real one, and you gave the order for that shit," David replied.

"But I wasn't the triggerman, David. You know that, and my lawyers do too. Loree was in the wrong place at the wrong time."

"Yeah, because you gave the kill order to Antonio and Terrell to ice her!" David replied furiously.

"Yeah, only Terrell never pulled the trigger either."

David questioningly looked at Tadarius, wondering if he was delirious, but the split-second cost him because LaToya pulled out her firearm.

"I shot Loree, fool!" she exclaimed gleefully before firing the gun.

CHAPTER 18

SEPTEMBER 15, 2003

Terrell drove at speeds of nearly sixty miles an hour as he found himself contemplating his next move. Suddenly, he was starting to get second thoughts about the mission that he was set out to do.

Loree was still in the back seat, silent as a mouse, where just a few minutes earlier, she had been driving Terrell crazy with her sarcasm and pointless diatribes. They had just dropped Antonio off at a street corner after the two boys pulled their guns out against each other.

Unbeknownst to Loree, the incident caused Terrell to rethink his life and ponder over his next move. What if Tone's right? Is it worth going to prison for life? I personally don't want this girl dead. I don't want to kill her. She should be allowed to get up out of this car and go home.

But it was a direct order given to him by Tadarius, and he could not back out now. He had to get the task done...or did he? Maybe if he drove somewhere other than Queens, he could stop and let Loree leave and return to her parents. Unfortunately, it would not guarantee that he would not have a bullet in his temple when the crew caught up with him.

But Terrell had never killed or taken a life, and the task of carrying out murder without conscience required a mind that was not susceptible to compassion or regret. Tadarius seemed to fit the bill, and when his orders were not followed, it was open game against the person that failed to follow the leader's orders. He knew Antonio would get what was coming to him soon for escaping the vehicle, and he only hoped that Antonio wouldn't suffer as Theo Brunsen had.

Finally, Loree spoke. "I bet you feel real stupid. Don't you?"

Terrell turned around to face her with a menacing glare. "Shut the hell up, Loree."

But she detected the internal conflict that her captor was struggling with, and she knew that with Terrell being two years younger than her, he was in a place of panic, and she picked it up immediately.

"Don't you see what T has you doing? He had you pointing a gun at yo' boy's head. That is what Tadarius does. He's crazy and divisive, and he wants to drag all of ya down with him. Terrell, please do the right thing, and let me go. You ain't got beef with me, and I ain't got nothing on you. It don't have to go down like this. Please," Loree pleaded as the car slowed to a spot on 161st Avenue.

She's right. This whole thing was foul from jump. Why did Tadarius choose me for this? I can't do this. I gotta let her get out of this car. Then I gotta come up with an excuse for Tadarius. Hope he's in a listening mood.

Terrell began to drive through Jamaica Avenue until he reached Guy R. Brewer Road. He had reached the spot which Tadarius had instructed him to, but at that very moment, Terrell decided that he was no longer going to carry out Loree's execution. He was going to disappear for a few weeks and hoped that Tadarius was in a forgiving mood.

Stopping the car, Terrell said, "Look, you can go alright? I ain't gonna do nothin' to you. This shit's foul."

Loree, internally grateful that Terrell changed his mind, began to exit the vehicle, but not before she saw a friend walking towards the car. It was near twilight outside, and the street and sidewalks were empty, save for the young woman that appeared out of the shadows. She was walking towards the car.

"Hey, girl!" LaToya greeted as Loree got out of the vehicle.

"Hey, girl, what's up?"

LaToya stared Loree up and down as she was disheveled after the rough handling by Terrell and Antonio. "Girl, you look terrible. What's going on ova hea'?" LaToya asked as Terrell stepped out of the driver's seat.

"Nothin', we just chillin' down in the boonies," Terrell replied as he leaned against the hood of the car and lit his marijuana joint. His indecision was causing him to spaz out, and he needed to stay calm.

A few minutes passed and the girls were joking and laughing as they had done so many times earlier.

"Girl, are you serious?" LaToya asked after Loree told her about one of her romantic rendezvous with David.

"Girl, I'm tellin' you David knows how to work it. But he's so deep in Tadarius's pocket that we can barely do anything without his skinny scrawny boy in the cut."

While Loree believed that she was talking to her best friend, she had no idea that LaToya had her right where she wanted her at that very moment. For some time, LaToya had envied Loree, her beauty, her outgoing personality, and her budding relationship with David, whom she had coveted for weeks. Not to mention that Loree had the perfect family: a father and a mother and a little sister.

LaToya, who had been abandoned by her father and abused physically by her mother, grew up around dysfunction, and she could not bear to see anyone else happier than she was. The resentment for Loree was not immediate, but it had been building for quite some time to the point where LaToya hated her friend. So when Tadarius approached her and told her to finish the job that he knew Antonio and Terrell wouldn't have the stomach for, she felt obliged and honored to eliminate the woman that had enough information to bring down their family.

Slowly and deliberately, Terrell watched in slow motion as LaToya, who had her left arm wrapped around Loree's shoulder, reached into her back pocket and pulled out a small handgun. Time froze for Terrell as he was faced with a critical decision. Should he run and stop LaToya from murdering Loree, or should he allow the scenario to play out? Regrettably, he chose the latter.

"I'm tellin' you, Toya, ain't nobody out here that can be trusted," Loree said.

LaToya's mouth then curled into a twisted grin. You ain't never lied, bitch.

As Loree curiously looked at her friend, she realized what was about to happen a second too late. A shot rang out, and Loree held her stomach, which began bleeding profusely. A few seconds later, a second shot fired, and it was the fatal shot that penetrated a major artery. Loree dropped to the ground, barely stirring as the blood flowed out of her.

LaToya stuffed her gun in her back pocket and ran back to the car. Terrell was already at the driver's seat, and as soon as LaToya entered, they sped away from the scene. It would be almost thirty minutes before a woman named Cindy Crofton would drive to the scene and discover Loree and then place the 911 emergency call.

Over the next few weeks after Loree was declared dead, LaToya did her best to play the grieving best friend role, even going so far as to attend the funeral with Loree's family. While her family was all too convinced that David Anderson had committed the murder, they were unaware that the true murderer was in their midst, pretending to comfort and console them.

Then Tadarius was arrested, and the remaining members of M.O.B. disappeared, which left LaToya at the mercy of her abusive mother.

Donna Richardson, a tall, domineering lady, was an excessive drinker, and when she was inebriated, she often took her frustrations out on LaToya. As a result, LaToya did anything to stay away from her mother, whether it was to stay at a friend's house for a few days or work odd jobs to stay busy. M.O.B. gave her an excuse not to remain at home, but with the crew disbanding, LaToya was starting to feel isolated.

There were days where she regretted pulling the trigger, discharging the bullets that ended her friend's life, but Loree was beyond saving at that point, and Tadarius knew that Loree would ring the alarm about the crew's activities. In retrospect, her death was only a means to an end.

One day, LaToya walked into a corner store on 102nd and Liberty Avenue when she saw a familiar face. Wearing a blue New York Giants hoodie and a New Era cap, he did not notice her at first. His goal was to buy a quick snack, then leave the store as quickly as possible. Approaching him, she decided to strike up a conversation.

"David, is that you?" she asked.

David Anderson turned around to see who had addressed him. A young lady with her long black hair braided down her back looked at him. David recognized her at once, even though he wished she hadn't recognized him.

"LaToya? What's good? What you doin' hea'?" he asked.

"Just getting a couple things, no biggie. So how you been? I heard that Five-O had you on lockdown for Loree's murder but looks like you out and about now. Did you hear what happened to T and the rest of them boys?" she asked him, but LaToya was unaware that David was the reason that M.O.B. disbanded.

And David was unaware that he was speaking with the woman who shot his girlfriend. "Yeah, I heard about what happened to them. That's tough, but maybe it's a sign that the crew's history."

During their conversation, LaToya was not aware that David had led the sting operation that assisted in finally arresting Tadarius, and he had no intentions of telling her. For all he knew, she might have been communicating with Tadarius.

But LaToya had not been with Tadarius on Merrick Boulevard that evening because she was visiting her stepsister, Tina, whose nickname is Bunny. Bunny was at the cusp of being introduced to M.O.B. as another one of Tadarius's informants who would one day become his avenging angel.

"I'm sorry about what happened to Loree," LaToya replied as remorsefully as possible.

The grief was still fresh on David's face, and although he tried his best not to let his emotions show, he could not help but to brush away a tear when LaToya mentioned Loree's name.

"It's all good. I'm tryin' to move on, but my mind keeps going back to her. She always tried to talk me out of the set, but I didn't listen. I know it must hurt you more since she was yo' homegirl though."

"Yeah, she was. We damn near did everything together when we were kids. I was the one that got her into the game, and she played it better than I ever did."

What am I saying? I'm glad that bitch is dead. She never had to worry about nothing in her life, and she had the nerve to try to come up in here to try to change things. I was the one that got her in. I had my eyes on David long before she did. Well, guess what, Casanova? She dead, and she ain't comin' back, so deal with it.

"So, where you stayin' at these days?"

"Well, I'm chillin' at my cuz's crib right now. I had to drop by and grab some things."

After paying for their groceries, LaToya and David walked out of the store. "You know, if you ever wanna talk or just chill, you can hit me up," David said as they exchanged phone numbers.

"Appreciate it, David. Lemme ask you something though. Did you ever think about takin' it over?" LaToya asked.

"Taking what over?" David asked curiously.

"Look, Heisman, T is behind bars. With him gone, you got the Ninety-Nines, and the Serps that are gonna move in on his territory and take control, unless you take his place."

But David shook his head. He was done with the street life. He had the rest of his school year to complete, and he was anticipating college. He did not want to jeopardize his chances at the opportunities he had ahead of him.

"Look, LaToya, they can have it. I want no parts of that shit no more. Loree was right. There's more to life than this gang shit. I want to get outta hea' so I can give my grandmother, uncles, aunts, and cousins the life they never had."

"You can still give them all of that if you run the streets, Heisman. They'll respect you out here like they respected Tadarius. C'mon, what have you got to lose?"

Walking over to his car, David shook his head. "I hear you, LaToya. But I'm done with it. I don't want any more Lorees, Terrances, or Maliks on my conscience. Listen, do you need a ride back to your spot?" he offered.

LaToya smiled and entered David's car. This was the opportunity she had been waiting for. She had been infatuated with David Anderson for years, but he always had eyes for only Loree.

With Loree now gone, LaToya had a chance to embark on a relationship she felt they should have had for years. Over the next few weeks, the two teens drew closer together, spending endless hours talking on the phone. David did not initially plan on getting involved in a long-term relationship immediately after Loree's passing, but LaToya bore many similar attributes that attracted him. She was confident, flirtatious, independent, and she seemed down for him whenever he felt like he needed to talk.

The friendship would eventually blossom into something more one rainy day as David was completing his online assignments a few weeks before the upcoming Thanksgiving break. Suddenly, his phone rang.

"Hello?"

"Hey, David, it's LaToya. Can you come pick me up at the Q24 bus stop on Hillside?" she asked.

David couldn't help but notice that LaToya was fighting back tears. Her voice was shaking on the phone. "Yeah, I got you, LaToya. Everything okay?" he asked.

"No, everything ain't okay. Please pick me up. Are your cousins home right now?" she asked.

"Nah, they ain't home. They went to D.C. for some convention. They work wit' the government, so I'm flyin' solo at the crib this weekend."

After hanging up the phone, David grabbed his keys, and in fifteen minutes, he picked LaToya up at the bus stop. Completely drenched, LaToya stepped inside David's car as he covered her with his Giants hoodie. Turning up the heat, he drove back to his cousin's house, and when they arrived, David turned to LaToya, who was still shivering in the passenger's seat.

"Okay, do you wanna tell me what this is all about?"

Reluctantly, LaToya turned to face David, and he saw a dark bruise on the side of her face.

"What the hell happened?" he asked, examining the mark.

"My mama came back home more drunk than usual, and when she called me to buy her another bottle of Jack Daniels, I refused and told her she needed to stop drinking. Guess she didn't take no for an answer, and next thing I knew, the back of her hand hit me in my face. I just had enough, and I had to get out of there," LaToya sobbed.

David, who had regrettably been physical in his relationship with Loree, was adamant that LaToya reported the abuse to the authorities.

"LaToya, you gotta go to the police. She got issues, and she can't keep doing this to you. You don't deserve any of this."

"No, don't call the police. Please. She just gets out of pocket when she drinks, but she normally gets over it. She'll cool out after a day or two. I just can't be around her when she's doing this to herself."

"Where yo' sister at?" David asked.

"Bunny usually stays wit' my father upstate, so she doesn't know that Mama has these issues."

David guided LaToya into his kitchen. Taking a Ziploc bag from a cabinet, he opened the freezer and took out the ice tray. Filling the bag with ice, he gave it to LaToya to apply to her swollen face. They stared at each other for over five minutes, and LaToya could not help but to fawn over her rescuer.

Damn, he's so fine. Now I know why Loree was willing to risk it all for him. Ain't no man that would take the time to go out in the rain and pick me up for anything.

"You need something to eat? We don't have much, just some leftover pizza. I can throw that in the microwave and give you something to drink with it," David offered.

LaToya smiled. "You're sweet, David. I'm good. You know, Loree was so lucky to have a man like you. At first, I didn't see the hype, but now I know why she loved you so much. You have a good heart."

"Trust me, I ain't always perfect. I've done a lot of things I regret in life. I just wanted to make my grandmother proud of me. I don't want her to look at me and see the hood who could've made something out of his life but threw it away."

"You're more than that," LaToya replied, caressing David's face softly. "When we first got mixed up wit' the fam, there was something about you that was different from the other dudes that ran wit' Tadarius. You had a genuine quality, and that's the part I wanna get to know about you."

Before they could stop themselves, David and LaToya were kissing passionately.

Her lips taste so good. I forgot what it felt like for a minute.

As the rain fell outside, David proceeded to carry LaToya to his room and gently laid her on his bed. Removing his hoodie, her blouse and bra, and undoing her jeans, he kissed her neck before working his way down her breasts and belly button.

LaToya moaned in ecstasy as she licked David's earlobe. "Take your time, baby," she whispered in his ear as she took his T-shirt off, revealing his well-chiseled body and abs. The steady sound of the rain, accompanied by the low rumble of thunder, made a perfect art of noise as David and LaToya's bodies intertwined in one dance.

As wet as it was outside, it could not compare to the convulsing reaction of LaToya's body as David finally entered her moist walls. They were oblivious to everything else going on in the world as they wrapped each other in the warmth of their bodies.

It would be the first of many sexual encounters as LaToya and David solidified their relationship. During the first few weeks, they were as close as any committed couple. LaToya found unexpected solace in David when she could not bear to remain at home with her mother. But a few months passed, and David was waiting for news that he had been anticipating and he wanted to share with LaToya.

It was February 2004, and David had stopped by LaToya's house before her mother returned from work. With a wide smile beaming on his face, he held up an envelope, while LaToya sat on the front steps of her house. She had been anxiously waiting for him to arrive to share in his excitement.

"What's up, baby?" he greeted, kissing LaToya. "Guess what? Check this out. I just got accepted to Seton Hall on a full-ride football scholarship!" he exclaimed, hugging Latoya, but after realizing that she barely returned the hug, he asked, "What's wrong? Ain't you happy for me?"

"Yeah, baby, I'm happy for you. But..." she trailed off.

"But what?"

Taking a deep breath, LaToya decided to tell him immediately before she started hyperventilating out of anxiety. "I'm pregnant, David."

Excitement suddenly gave way to bewilderment as David looked at LaToya in disbelief. "What? Are you serious?"

LaToya nodded, confirming David's worst fear. David turned away from her, staring into the street. What was he going to do? He could not afford to have a baby, not at this time. This was his last chance to get into the

NFL. Having been nearly derailed by gang activity and false murder allegations, David knew his window of opportunity was closing, and he could not bear another hurdle that would prevent him from going pro.

"How long?"

"I've known for about a month now."

"Are you sure it's mine?" he asked.

"What you mean, am I sure? Of course, it's yours! You're the only man I've been with these last few months!" she exclaimed.

"And you've been with a hundred other dudes before that, so ain't no guarantee that it's mine!" David yelled back.

LaToya began sobbing. This was not the same man she fell in love with months ago, the one whose shoulders she leaned on for comfort while dealing with her mother's violent blows. "David, please don't do this! Don't leave me now, please! I need you!" she pleaded.

"I can't do this anymore, LaToya. I can't put my future on hold for you. I'm going places, and this is only gonna slow me down."

"Well this is yo' child, David!"

"Get rid of it!" David yelled irrationally, backing away from LaToya as if she was a strange and foreign object.

"You must be out yo' goddamn mind if you think I'm getting an abortion! I'm gonna have this baby, whether you like it or not!" she declared angrily, while David walked away furiously, holding his Seton Hall letter in his hands.

"Fine, but you gonna do it without me. I ain't sign up for all this!"

David left LaToya sobbing at her mother's house. They never saw each other again. David deleted LaToya's number from his contacts and prepared for graduation and Seton Hall.

Eight months later, Chris was born, and he stayed with his aunt Bunny while LaToya joined the U.S. Army. After many years, LaToya and Chris would reunite, and she would plot David's demise.

CHAPTER 19

I THOUGHT YOU WERE MY FRIEND

At the Queensboro County Prison, Terrell resumed his normal duties of stacking and filing police files. He had completed janitorial duties an hour earlier, and he was eagerly anticipating lunch hour at the dining hall. Due to his hard work and behavior, Terrell was given certain liberties within the confinement of the facility, walking freely through the cell blocks, going out to the recreational yard to lift weights and exercise during his free time. It was no surprise that Terrell had bulked up and gained over twenty pounds of muscle while incarcerated.

Three weeks earlier, he had received a visit from one of his cousins, who delivered unfortunate tragic news from his family. When he received the news, Terrell sunk in the chair. He wanted to die that day, to join the dearly departed, to apologize for ruining his life and ending up locked behind bars. For years, Terrell had believed that he was making a sacrifice for the crew, but the crew appeared to show little to no concern for his plight. Not one member of M.O.B. visited him, and he had not heard from Tadarius.

Before receiving his tragic family news, Terrell had heard that Tadarius was granted early parole from prison, and he was walking free, but not once did Tadarius pay his old comrade a visit to check on his well-being.

I guess everyone looking out for themselves these days.

But Terrell did not plan to die a fool in prison. He had begun frequenting the prison library and picking up a penchant for reading. He planned to educate himself and fill his mind with the knowledge that he had taken for granted before he was locked up. If he was not working garden duty or filing in the offices, he could be found at the library, poring over books.

He read books from various authors such as Alex Haley, William Shakespeare, Charles Dickens, Toni Morrison, Ralph Ellison, Maya Angelou, and James Baldwin.

Before he made his way to the mess hall one day, a guard came to him. "Washington, you got a visitor."

Wondering who could be visiting him at noon time, Terrell walked to the visitor's area, where he saw a black man wearing a suit, carrying a briefcase. He did not recognize the man immediately, but as he got closer to the transparent glass, he looked at the man's eyes. The last time the two had seen each other, they were in a car, and they both had guns pointed at each other as teenage boys.

Edward stared back at the man who had originally introduced him to gangbanging. He picked up the phone. Terrell did the same.

"What's up, Terrell? My name is Edward Reed, attorney at law. I was hoping I could speak with you for a few minutes."

Terrell snickered. He recognized the true identity of his visitor. He thinks I'm a damn fool. Well, he got the wrong one today.

"Edward Reed, huh? So that's where you went all these years? I should've known," Terrell replied. "You know, you could take a pig, change his name, dress it in a three-piece suit, and showcase him, but deep inside he still the same pig. You can wear whatever Armani knock-off from any suit store on the block, Edward, but you still Tone on the inside."

Edward sat back and took Terrell's sarcasm and insults. He expected no less, for had it not been for his testimony, Terrell might have not been locked away. He understood the level of Terrell's disdain towards him.

"Look, Terrell, I'm not proud of how things went down the last time we saw each other," he explained, without pretense. "I was a scared boy, and I panicked. I shouldn't have ditched you the way I did, and for that, I'm sorry."

"Look, man, you take yo' lil' apology, and shove it up yo' ass, B," Terrell replied. "You think sorry's gonna give back the years I lost in this piece? Is sorry gonna bring my mama back from the grave? I ain't tryin' to hear that, man. So, is that what you came all the way down here for? To say sorry?"

"No, I didn't come just to apologize. I came because I know you weren't the one that killed Loree," Edward replied.

Terrell sat back in his seat and chuckled.

"Wow, looks like Tone finally grew up and picked up some common sense. And what made you come to that conclusion?"

"I'm not gonna disclose him, but I have a key witness who told me the whole story. According to him, you started to get cold feet as well, and when she got to the spot, you met up with LaToya. She's the one that pulled the trigger, not you."

"She came out of nowhere, man. It was like she was hiding out, waiting for the perfect opportunity to blast her girl, and I didn't even think she had it in her to do some foul shit like that. I never drove so fast out of there in my life."

"So why are you taking the rap for her?" Edward asked. "Terrell, she's back in town. Look, I have access to the case in my position. If I can somehow re-open it, we can prove your innocence and get you out of here."

But Terrell shook his head and backed away from the glass that separated the men. "Nah, I'd rather not get involved with all that, okay? We both know Tadarius ain't the one to let anything go. Last thing I need is for him to come after me now."

Edward sighed. Here he was, offering an out for Terrell, but he did not want to take advantage. "But you and I both know you didn't commit the murder, and with Tadarius out, there ain't no doubt in my mind he's gonna recruit more boys to M.O.B., and there ain't nothin' we're gonna be able to do to stop it."

"That ain't my problem anymore, homeboy. Thanks to you, I'm in here for life, and that ain't gonna change. Besides, it's probably safer in here for me than it is out there when he's scheming. Who's yo' plug for this?"

Edward did not budge. He was determined not to disclose the name of his informant. "It's the son of an old M.O.B. member. He knows what went down. Look, Terrell, you could hate me all you want, and I understand that. But I'm throwing you a bone of opportunity to get out. This ain't a math quiz."

Quoting a line Terrell said to him during their first meeting, Terrell chuckled as he remembered the significance of the line.

"True. But in this case, it's more complicated than that, bro. I'm sorry. I can't help."

Edward hung his head. He couldn't believe how deluded his old gang comrade had become after these years.

Just when he figured that maybe he may have wasted his time, Terrell spoke again in hushed tones, looking around as if a nefarious person was listening to the conversation. "Okay, check this out. There is somebody out there that can use the information that you have. Actually, her life might depend on it."

"And who's that?" Edward asked.

"Andrea McAfee. Remember her?"

The name rang a bell, but Edward drew a blank for the first couple of minutes. "You mean Loree's sister?" he asked.

Terrell nodded. "Yeah, that's her. She became some type of singer now, so she has the extra ends that could help yo' investigation, and besides, she deserves some type of closure on this," he replied.

"Do you know where she stay at?" Edward asked.

"Nah, but you a lawyer though. I'm sure you got ways of finding her. But I'd do it quick because I remember LaToya and Loree were thick as thieves back in the day, and Andrea used to follow 'em around everywhere. If LaToya could cap Loree like she did, how long is it gonna be till Andrea's next on their hit list? You better also tell Heisman to watch his back, too. Tadarius is gonna be coming hard after both of ya'll," he warned.

Edward shook his head nervously. He knew Terrell was telling the truth, and it was only after he mentioned his name, that he realized David hadn't called him in a few days. Could David have run into Tadarius and met his fate? Edward planned on reaching out the moment he finished speaking with Terrell.

Standing up from the chair, he said, "Thanks, man, and for what it's worth, I believe that you're innocent, and I'm gonna prove it."

Edward hung the phone and walked out of the facility. Terrell watched his old friend walk out of the building. He knew they could never return to the old days when they were friends constantly arguing and bantering while playing video games, but he hoped that Edward, or Antonio as he knew him best by, would help the family find closure.

On Saturday morning, Edward drove into Queens Village, searching for the right address. With the help of reliable sources, he was able to find Andrea McAfee's address. He was keen on visiting her to explain the new information that may serve as the bombshell in the Loree McAfee case. After locating the house, Edward walked up the front porch steps and knocked on the door.

This is quaint. She definitely lives modestly for her earnings as a singer.

A few seconds later, the door opened, and a young lady appeared. She was putting on her earrings and appeared to be preparing to go to work.

"Hi, can I help you?" she asked.

"Hi, my name's Edward Reed, attorney at law, Schorr Law Group. Are you Ms. Andrea McAfee?" he asked.

"Yes sir, I'm Andrea. I'm sorry to be hasty, but I'm in a bit of a rush. I have to get to work," she replied.

"I understand, ma'am, and I promise I won't take too much of your time, but it's important that I speak with you. This is regarding your sister's homicide case and the possibility of having it re-opened."

Andrea suddenly stopped in her tracks. She clearly did not expect this stranger to know anything about her sister or the case.

"In that case then, please come in," she replied, inviting him inside. Leading him into the kitchen, she asked, "Can I get you anything, like orange juice, coffee, or water?"

"No, thank you. I'm fine. I just need to speak to you about Loree's case. It won't take long."

Seeing that Edward did not want to waste time, Andrea sat across from her guest.

Noticing the ring on her finger, Edward asked, "Are you married, Ms. McAfee?"

"Engaged actually, Mr. Reed. We're about to get married in two months. My fiancée, Quentin Stevens, just left for work shortly before you arrived."

"Wow, congratulations to you both."

"So, you said you had some information about my sister's case?" Andrea asked abruptly.

Edward shuffled his feet slightly under the table. He was unsure how he was going to begin the conversation. But he decided not to hold anything back from her. This was a woman who lost a family member at a young age, and she deserved to find out the truth.

"Yes, I have vital information about the case. I found out through a mutual source that Terrell Washington did not murder your sister," he explained.

Andrea stared directly at Edward, as if trying to read him. Since the case, she had built a natural distrust for the judicial system that had failed her family after Loree's murder, and she thought most lawyers, if not all, were crooked public servants who cared about nothing more than their bottom line and did not wish to see justice served.

"Would that mutual source happen to be Terrell Washington? Because you do know that the man is a pathological liar, right?"

"Well, yes, Terrell cleared himself of any guilt in the crime, but he wasn't the only one that corroborated his innocence. A young boy by the name of Chris, explained to me that his mother confessed the crime to him, and he was sworn to keep her guilt a secret. But I wanted to warn you because I don't know how close you are to the suspect," Edward explained.

Andrea rolled her eyes. This was not going anywhere. "Okay, and who is Chris?" she asked.

"Chris is the son of LaToya Richardson, who was Loree's best friend, if I'm not mistaken."

This time Andrea stood up from the table, her head swimming with all sorts of doubt and confusion. LaToya never told her that she had a son during her sabbatical. "Wait, wait. So, you mean to tell me that LaToya shot my sister?" she asked.

When Edward failed to reply and only nodded his head, Andrea buried her face in her hands. This could not be true. LaToya could not have killed her sister.

She was her friend. There's no way she would've done that to me. She was hanging out with me each Saturday. I was going to make her one of my bridesmaids at the wedding.

"Listen, Andrea, I know this is a lot to process right now, and I hate to be the bearer of this news, but I want to help you by re-opening this case and making sure that we..." he started but Andrea cut him off.

"Let me ask you something, Mr. Reed. What are you doing here?"

"I already told you. I'm here to help clear this case so we can arrest the suspect that is responsible for this crime," Edward replied, but Andrea was not buying his response.

She stared even more intently at him. There was something familiar about his eyes. The fear and apprehension in his face was something that she had seen before. "No, tell me the truth, Mr. Reed. What are you really doing here? Who are you?" she asked, forcefully. "Out of all the cases that you handle each day, and you come over here to tell me that you gonna re-open this one? Why are you so invested in my sister's case? What are you hiding?"

Finally realizing that Andrea could see past all pretense, Edward decided to tell her the entire truth before she got even more suspicious. Lowering his head and taking a deep breath, he said, "Okay, Andrea. I'll tell you everything. Before I was Edward Reed, my name was Antonio Franks, and when I was young, I made many mistakes in my life. The biggest mistake was joining M.O.B.," he explained while Andrea listened intently.

"I never had the ambition to become a gangbanger or a thug. I just wanted acceptance, respect, and sense of belonging. I just wanted to be part of a group that was just as ambitious as I was. I spent a year dealing drugs, making money under the table, and guys like Terrell, Malik, David, and Tadarius were like family to me."

"Then one day, Tadarius gave Terrell and me a mission to eliminate Loree because she was threatening his operation. I rode in the car that day with Terrell, but as you know, I got out. I couldn't go along with it anymore, and it nearly cost me my life."

As Edward explained, the tears slowly fell down Andrea's face.

"As I left the car, I could still see Loree's face in the back seat. Her eyes were begging me to save her, but I didn't do anything. I was scared. When I found out that she passed, I went to court, and I name-dropped Terrell because he was the only one in the car that day. But recently, over the past few days, I received new intel that LaToya intercepted Terrell that day, and she pulled the trigger that ended Loree's life. I'm not saying that Terrell and I are innocent by any means, and I'm not asking you to forgive me for the part I played in all this, but I just wanted to let you know that LaToya ain't your friend. She killed your sister, and that's the truth."

Andrea turned her back to Edward. Shaking with grief and rage, she closed her eyes and prayed for her feelings to subside.

Please, Lord, help me with my anger. Lord knows, I want to go off on him and everyone else who had something to do with Loree's death.

"First of all, if you really are Antonio Franks, prove it," she said, briskly.

Sighing, Edward took off his black blazer and unbuttoned his shirt sleeve before rolling it up, displaying the tattoo of the gang emblem. It was a tattoo that Andrea loathed, but she needed closure.

"So, if LaToya was a part of it, wouldn't she have the tattoo also?" she asked.

"No, only the immediate members of M.O.B. have the tattoo. LaToya and Loree were informants—call girls—and they worked for Tadarius, but they weren't in his inner circle."

"Okay, and where does this Chris boy fit into all this?"

"Chris is the son of LaToya and David Anderson, but apparently David doesn't know Chris is his son. Since, he's been out, Tadarius has been grooming a new crop of potential M.O.B. members, and LaToya has been helping him. She's been getting funds from M.O.B.'s operation since being discharged from the Army. She had been itching to get David back for deserting their son many years ago, and I'm afraid that they might have already gotten to him cuz I haven't heard from him in days."

"Even if I choose to believe you, how do I know you ain't lying to protect yo' boys?"

"They ain't my boys anymore, Andrea. I made my choice when I stepped out the car that day. But if we want to get LaToya, we'll have to get a confession out of her somehow," Edward replied.

"She's supposed to come by tonight. Leave it to me, I'll get her to fess up." Andrea thanked Edward for his visit and walked him to the front door.

After telling Andrea to be careful, he gave her his business card, and she closed the door behind him.

Later that night, LaToya stepped out of an Uber in front of Andrea's house, preparing for another night of wild fun with her late friend's sister. She planned to take her to Apple Kim's Gentleman's Club, a strip club in the city. Her plan was unfolding beautifully. Aside from vindicating herself of the hurt and pain of abandonment just hours earlier, she planned to destroy Andrea's reputation.

It was $1 bottle night at the club, and it was going to be filled with celebrities and paparazzi. One glimpse of Andrea at that club would bring headlines. LaToya could see them now: "Gospel Singer Partying Excessively at Strip Club."

Andrea would be dropped from her label and forced to suffer through life the same way LaToya had suffered. Then when the time was right, LaToya would reunite Andrea with her sister. LIttle Ms. Perfect would only be a memory.

"Come on, girl! We wastin' time. Got a new spot in town. With a few weeks before your big day, we need to get you lit, baby!" LaToya exclaimed, knocking on the door.

With no intention of letting her in, Andrea opened the door and walked out, only closing the door halfway behind her.

LaToya beamed at her, unaware that Andrea was repulsed by her very presence. "Come on, girl, what you waiting for? Night's young, and we got a whole of trouble to get into."

But Andrea only folded her arms and blocked LaToya from her front door entrance. "I ain't goin' nowhere with you tonight or any other night," she replied slowly, trying to stem the tide of fury bubbling within her.

"Okay, what's up with all the dramatics? Girl, you uptight. You probably got cold feet, right? You know, between you and I, this Quentin dude ain't yo' type anyway."

"LaToya, you got some nerve comin' up here like it's all good between us. Lemme' ask you something," Andrea continued while angrily brushing a tear away. "How could you do what you did and act like you down with me?"

"What are you talkin' about?" LaToya asked, bewildered.

"Oh, don't give me that BS! You know good and damn well what I'm talkin' about! You know, they should give you an award for being a phony ass bitch!" Andrea exclaimed angrily.

"Okay, Drea, you trippin' right now. I don't know what's goin' on wit' you, but…"

"Don't give me that! I want you to look me straight in the eye, and tell me that you didn't shoot my sister."

LaToya tried her best to remain clueless and acted as if Andrea was out of her mind, but she could see through the act.

"All I wanna know is why? Why did you take Loree away from me? I thought you were my friend. How could you do me like this? Do you know how many years of pain you put me and my family through?"

Turning away from Andrea, LaToya knew that her game was up. Somebody told her. Who would've dimed me out like this? Did Tadarius tell her? No, he wouldn't have gone out like that. Terrell? Nah, he ain't a snitch. He still in lock-up. I only told one other person about it, and there's no way he would've told her. He doesn't even know where she lives.

"Loree always had everything. Since we were kids, she always had it all, the best clothes. She had both her mama and her daddy. She was popular at school and in M.O.B. She was the little pampered ho' that everyone wanted," LaToya continued. "I got sick of it, and so did Tadarius. So after he told them two fools to finish her off, I knew they would freeze up, so T sent me to make sure it was done, and guess what? I made sure I put that bitch in her place."

Andrea backed away, shaking her head. LaToya was bordering on insanity, and years of jealousy and rage propelled by her mother's physical abuse, finally took its toll.

"So, who finally told you that it was me?" she asked, as a cruel cold smile curved her lips.

She reached behind her back for her gun. She had planned to keep Andrea oblivious to the truth until her reputation was ruined, but now she knew the truth, and before she blew the whistle, LaToya would have to silence her.

"Not that it matters anyway because you're gonna be joining Loree and her man very soon," she said as she took the gun out and prepared to fire but not before a figure stepped out of the shadows.

"It's over, Mama. Let it go," Chris said, stepping out from behind the house with Edward.

LaToya stared at Chris in shock. She could envision being betrayed by a close friend, but never in all her wildest dreams could she have imagined being betrayed by her own flesh and blood.

"Chris, after everything Tadarius and I have done for us, you go and do this? You betray the fam like this?"

"They're not my family. Not anymore. I ain't a pawn out here," Chris replied.

LaToya then turned to her son, the gun still in her hand. "Like father, like son, huh? Well, I guess you overplayed yo' hand, and you lost too," she said, firing the gun.

Instinctively, Edward dove at Chris, knocking him down, and the bullet missed Chris and Edward by inches.

"Freeze!" Detective Shawn Wells yelled, accompanied by two uniformed NYPD members.

Edward had tipped Shawn off before LaToya arrived, and with his assistance, Shawn was able to arrive without LaToya noticing them.

LaToya complied with the police, dropping the gun, and the two officers read the Miranda Rights to LaToya as they handcuffed her and led her to the car.

"You think this is over, Tone? You ain't nothin' but a bluff actin' like you some big-time lawyer. You ain't shit. You still the same punk ass that you were back in the day. A new name ain't gonna change that fact, Jack!" she yelled as the police guided her inside the squad car.

"I'mma get out of this cuz ya'll ain't gonna have no proof," she said from the back of the car.

Chris took out his cell phone and hit the playback button on the previous video of his mother confessing the crime to Andrea.

"Looks like we have all the proof we need. Get her out of here," Edward instructed the officers.

"You think this is over, Tone? It ain't over. You better watch your back cuz T's gon' come after yo' two-faced ass too. Just ask David."

As the car sped away with LaToya, Edward looked at Andrea. "The real work begins, now. I'm gonna help you get justice for Loree."

As he left the premises, he only had one thought in his mind. Where is David?

CHAPTER 20

IT AIN'T OVER

The arrest of LaToya Richardson provided little comfort to Andrea's family and the community. Queens, Brooklyn, Manhattan, and other boroughs were on high alert as soon as LaToya's arrest was reported. Traumatized after discovering her long-time friend was her sister's murderer, Andrea postponed the wedding indefinitely and took some needed time off from recording.

But beloved high school coach David Anderson had not been seen for over two weeks. His wife filed a missing persons' report as countless calls were made to David's cell phone, but each call went to voicemail. Renee assisted a city-wide search party to locate David, but no sign of him turned up.

Then one day, a sanitation worker made a grisly discovery. Human remains of a middle-aged man were located half a mile away from Springfield Park in a dumpster. The body was in an advanced state of decomposition, and as a result, the individual could not be identified immediately. Once the coroner transferred the corpse into forensics, the victim was positively identified as David Anderson.

David had been shot more than nine times at close, blank range in the head, chest, and pelvic areas. When the police broke the news to Renee, she was inconsolable in her grief, breaking down at the front steps after Detective Shawn Wells advised her.

Chris did not fare any better, going into a period of seclusion and depression upon hearing the news. He never had the chance to develop a relationship with his father, and there would be no chance to make up the years of lost time. As angry as he felt at David for abandoning him, he felt enraged that his mother turned him against his own father and used him to exact revenge on David.

Renee and her children were immediately placed under witness protection care, and they relocated to Renee's sister's house on Hempstead.

Not wanting to forsake the opportunity to bid farewell to their friend, father, dedicated husband and coach, Renee decided, against the advice of the police, to arrange a proper funeral for her late husband. With a closed casket, the service was held at Rock of Jacob Baptist Church in Queens, and Pastor Mike Hillman directed the service for the young man that he supported and assisted from being falsely accused and arrested. As requested in his will, David Anderson was laid to rest next to his grandmother, Willamena Anderson.

Along with Townsend Harris's entire football team, the coaching staff and some of the educational staff members that attended the funeral, David's old teammates from LIU Post, Seton Hall, and Richmond Hill High School also attended his homegoing service. But no member of M.O.B., except for one, attended the funeral.

Edward Reed, struggling to hold back tears, sipped some Jack Daniels from a little flask he had in his jacket pocket. At the gravesite, where the body was buried, after all the people had paid their last respects to David, Edward walked over to the hole, where David's casket was already lowered. He opened the lid off of the flask and poured the liquid onto the ground.

"See you at the crossroads, my dude," he whispered before closing the tip of the flask. While he was still facing the casket, he heard somebody walk toward him. Turning around, he realized it was Andrea.

"Hey," she greeted.

"Hey, how are you holding up?"

"Well, I'm hanging in there, Edward, but truth be told, I don't know what I'mma do. My relationship with Quentin is kinda on the skids right now. I guess he felt some type of way about me calling off the wedding."

"I'm sorry that you had to do that. I know how much you were looking forward to marrying him. I feel like I'm the one to blame for getting you mixed up in all this."

"Edward, you don't have to apologize to me. You saved my life, and you exposed a person who I thought was a friend. Quentin and I have no words to thank you for what you've done."

But at that moment, Edward did not want apologies or sympathy. He could not prove it, but he knew that he had been tracked for days before David's death, and there was no denying that he was the gang's next target.

The battle was far from over with M.O.B., and if Edward wanted to make them all pay for his friend's murder, he was going to have to step in the dark side of his crew. He was determined to make them all pay the price for his friend.

"Andrea, this ain't over. I'm gonna expose these guys, and I'm going to reopen your case, and I will make them work for us," he stated, but Andrea closed her eyes and shook her head.

"Edward, I've lost so many friends and family in the streets. I've lost my sister, David, my friend Omar. Please just let law enforcement handle this."

"I let law enforcement handle this solo, and look what happened. They let the ringleader go. No more, Andrea. I'm gonna make this right, believe me." Before walking back to his car, he said, "Andrea, Loree and I never saw eye to eye, but I never had beef with her. She didn't deserve what happened to her, and neither did David."

Andrea watched as Edward got into his car and drove away from the cemetery. As she prepared to walk back to her car, her cell phone rang, and when she viewed the number of the caller, it was not one of her familiar contacts.

Probably a spam caller.

"Hello?" she replied with every intention of hanging up if she heard any type of upsell pitch. But the voice of a young woman answered instead.

"Hi. Is this Andrea McAfee?" she asked.

"Yeah. Who is this?" Andrea replied, unable to identify her mystery caller.

"After all these years, girl, you still don't know me by now? The one who traded hair ribbon barrettes with you when we were six? Or going after the same boy back in I.S. 139? Clowning Sean all through high school?"

Tears filled Andrea's eyes as she recognized the voice that she had not heard in years. The guilt that she felt for isolating her friend at the height of her fame disappeared as soon as she heard her high school best friend on the line.

"Vanessa? Is that you, girl?" she replied, choking back tears.

"Yeah, it's really me, Drea." A moment of silence passed between both women before Vanessa spoke again. "I heard what happened to David on the news, and the first person I thought about was you. I'm so sorry for not hitting you up after all these years."

"No, Vanessa. I'm sorry for not checking for you after everything that went down at the club that night. I should've seen Slam for who he was, but he played us all, and I was blinded by the lights, girl."

"I saw that, and that's why I bounced after you blew up. But therapy, meditation, and prayer work wonders, girl, and I'm fortunate that I'm in a position where I can help other assault victims through their ordeals."

"I hear you, Nessa. Now one thing's confusing me though. How'd you get my new number? You know I stay changing contacts."

"Well, as luck would have it, I went shopping at Wal-Mart the other day, and I ran into your man, Quentin. It was like a blast from the past, and we caught up on high school events, teachers we couldn't stand," Vanessa explained. "Then he brought up the fact that he was engaged to you, and he admitted to me how he always regretted that we never patched things up, so I asked for your new number. I wanted to call you earlier in the week, but I kept hesitating because I wasn't sure if you were going to answer or hang up. Then, when the news about David came out, I knew that I had to hit you up, and I couldn't keep putting it off anymore."

"Well, I appreciate you for reaching out. It's true. Quentin and I are engaged. We were actually supposed to tie the knot this year, but with everything that went down, we decided to put it off."

"I don't know about that, girl. Didn't you watch the news about some kind of epidemic that's spreading out around in China? They're calling it the coronavirus, or whatever. They're saying it's a matter of time until it gets to U.S. soil, and if that happens, it'll be worse than the swine flu."

But Andrea laughed. "Girl, we always have those types of warnings, but it ain't gonna hit us. I guarantee that." As Andrea continued catching up with her friend, she hoped that this reunion with Vanessa would mark a milestone in their relationship.

After David's funeral, Edward returned home. Spending the day consoling David's family in their sorrow and Chris finding a home with them was nothing short of draining. Chris, who had previously been staying with Edward's brother Bruno, would ultimately be adopted by Renee. As a result, he too would be placed in witness protection. With his mother's court date approaching, Chris knew that he would have to testify against her to prove that she killed Loree in 2003 and had attempted to kill Andrea. But until the time would arrive, Renee was more than willing to provide a home for her stepson, and Chris would happily stay with her and get acquainted with David's other kids.

Hearing his phone beep, Edward checked and realized that he had a voicemail that was waiting. The voicemail appeared to be from David's phone number. Puzzled, Edward played the message, and he heard an ominous voice, one that he recognized all too well:

Yo, Edward, or should I say Tone because it don't matter what the fuck you change yo' name to, you always gonna be Tone, the punk ass snitch that couldn't face me like a man. I imagine, right now you back at home, workin' on a high-profile case or bending over for the man. What a way to go out, my man. You could've been next in line to take over the crew, but you turned yo' back on us. Then you dimed us out. I spent more than ten years in the pen because you opened your mouth one too many times. You went and snitched on LaToya and had her locked up. Well now, I'm itchin' to shut yo' mouth for good, and I'm waiting for you because I don't want anybody else to eliminate you. I wanna do that on my own. If you thinkin' about callin' the police or reporting this message, one of yo' brothers is goin' six feet under. Tony, I think, is his name? Him and Tina been goin' for a minute. Too bad he ain't know Tina already spoken for, and now I got yo' boy. Before you panic, he's still alive, but if you do anything stupid, that'll no longer be the case. You want to see yo' brother alive, meet me at this street, and we gon' settle this. Or Tony's gonna end up like David. You choose.

The line went dead.

THE END?

ACKNOWLEDGMENT

Wow, where do I begin? Book number eight, and my sixth novel is finally a finished product. I never thought I would reach this point and there are so many people that I need to acknowledge, for if it were not for them, I would not have made it this far. First, I would like to thank the Lord for giving me the courage and strength to continue writing, even on days where I have felt like giving up. Without Him, the series of books that I have written over the years would not exist. I would like to thank my editor, Dawn Goodwin, who is an accomplished writer herself and who has worked diligently with me every week to ensure the grammatical quality of this manuscript. I would like to thank my cover designer Clinton Holmes, who has taken the time to work on coming up with the ingenious cover design concept and my hope is that we continue to work together on future projects. I also would like to extend my heartfelt gratitude to my parents, Jean and Lineda Beausejour, for their continued support of my vision in this literary journey, a journey that I'm still learning to navigate, much like their journey as immigrants from Haiti to the United States decades earlier. I want to acknowledge my brothers, Jonathan and Daniel, who are walking their own paths and making a difference in people's lives, and I want to thank my church family, from Kennesaw, Marietta, and Jonesboro Georgia, to my first spiritual family in Queens, New York. Last, but certainly not least, I would like to thank all my readers, supporters, and mentors for inspiring me to continue writing during this challenging time. As the world struggles through a pandemic that has crippled so many people and have taken so many lives, my prayer is that everyone finds healing.

ABOUT THE EDITOR

Author D.A. Goodwin is a mother of two from South Carolina. She earned a bachelor's degree in political science with a minor in English Language and Writing from Francis Marion University. She went on to earn a master's degree in English and Creative Writing from Southern New

Hampshire University, and she is currently seeking her PhD in Education with a specialization in Curriculum, Instruction, Assessment, and Evaluation from Walden University. She is the author of the drama suspense novels. She is the author of the drama suspense novels, The Offender I Once Defended and Chants in The Darkness.

ABOUT THE AUTHOR

"Marc A. Beausejour"

Marc A. Beausejour was born on July 28, 1987 in Queens, New York to Haitian parents Jean and Lineda Beausejour. He discovered his passion for writing at the tender age of twelve, with poetry becoming his initial artistic expression. Beausejour showcased his poetic talents in various school talent shows and poetry reading events during his time at North Cobb High School and later at Kennesaw State University after moving to Kennesaw, Georgia in 2001.

Throughout the years, Beausejour continued to hone his craft, writing poems for diverse occasions such as weddings, funerals, and church events. In 2011, he took a significant step by self-publishing his first book, "Words on High," a compilation of spiritually inspired poems from his formative years. Building on this success, Beausejour released his second poetry book, "Rising Higher Than Ever," in 2015.

In the same year, he ventured into a different literary landscape by writing and publishing his first urban novel, "The Preacher's Web." This gritty morality tale marked a departure from his earlier poetic works, showcasing Beausejour's versatility as an author. Expanding his literary horizons, he created the *BlackCyrano* series, demonstrating a wide-ranging creative skill.

While continuing to share his literary work on blogs and social networks, Beausejour remains committed to his education and promotions, earning his associate degree in marketing management from Chattahoochee Technical College in 2018. As a multifaceted writer, Marc A. Beausejour continues to captivate audiences with his words across various genres and platforms.

ALSO BY, AUTHOR

"Marc A. Beausejour"

Title: The Preacher's Web | Publisher: SHE PUBLISHING LLC | ISBN: 978-1-953163-91-2 (paperback) Publication Date: February 2024 (*Second Edition*)

Set in the heart of the city, "The Preacher's Web" unfolds a gripping narrative of former All-City quarterback turned pastor, Mike Hillman, whose dedication to preaching love and forgiveness in Queens, New York is challenged by the return of an old friend seeking revenge. Amidst a community grappling with the scourge of drugs and gangs. As Mike puts his reputation on the line to testify for a young man accused of murder, the story converges with the adolescent struggles of Jamal Samuels on the basketball courts of New York City.

Now, standing at the crossroads of faith, family, and societal challenges, Mike faces a pivotal choice. Will he risk more than his reputation to uphold justice and fulfill his role as a public servant and father? The pages of "The Preacher's Web" beckon you to explore the complexities of morality and redemption. Can Mike Hillman rise above, or will he be consumed by the web of his past?

Title: Fires of Justice | Author: Marc A. Beausejour | Publisher: SHE PUBLISHING LLC | ISBN: 978-1-953163-93-6 (paperback) | Publication Date: February 2024 (*second edition*)

English professor Levell Thomas is ecstatic when he receives the opportunity to teach in a metro Atlanta high school. A native of Queens, New York, Levell moves to Georgia with his family and as they settle in their new home, Levell meets his neighbor, a mysterious girl named Raven Roberts. Despite being underaged, she doesn't hide her desires for Levell and pursues him relentlessly. Levell refuses her advances but would soon pay dearly for his decision. The spurned teenager accuses Levell of assault after a physical confrontation and Levell is found guilty in the court of law. Detective Isaac Sands leads the investigation to expose a plot of false accusation and imprisonment in a race against time. Will Sands help prove Levell's innocence by finding the conspirators, or would he put himself in harm's way?

"The controversies confronted, stirred, and then addressed in this story have no choice but to awaken you to new perspectives that might not have ever crossed your mind. Readers, all I can say is be prepared to feel the fire that Beausejour has ignited in this suspenseful masterpiece!"

—D.A. Goodwin, author of The Offender I Once Defended

Title: Adia's Ballad | Author: Marc A. Beausejour | Publisher: SHE PUBLISHING LLC | ISBN: 978-1-953163-92-9 (paperback) | Publication Date: February 2024 (*second edition*)

From the author of "The Preacher's Web", this coming-of-age story explores the life of young Andrea McAfee who struggles to cope with the tragic murder of her older sister. Then a chance opportunity lands Andrea into the music business where she shares a bond with other artists in the hip hop industry and learns she has more in common with them than she realizes. As Andrea immerses herself deeper into the life of recording, touring and partying as Adia, the new R&B princess, she begins drifting away from her family and her loved ones as her star rises too fast for her to absorb. With fame corrupting her relationships with those she loves, will Andrea find the inner peace and closure she seeks, or will she succumb to the draw of money and celebrity?

Title: Split Decision | Author: Marc A. Beausejour | Publisher: SHE PUBLSIHING LLC | ISBN: 978-1-953163-94-3 (paperback) | Publication Date: February 2024 (*second edition*)

Prepare to enter the ring as cultures clash in this adrenaline-filled drama! Under the tutelage of experienced trainer Jim Shaw, young boxer Sylvio Dominique has taken the middleweight class division by storm, winning bout after bout. Nicknamed "Wolf" for his boxing style and aggression in the ring, Sylvio works hard in the ring and plays even harder out of the ring and there is no shortage of women. Reuniting with childhood friend Valentina Cruz, the two become involved in an intense romance. But as Sylvio falls deep in love with Valentina, he realizes that she is more than what she seems. With a fight against the undefeated Dominican champion Felipe Maximo looming, secrets are revealed, and friends turn to foes as Sylvio later discovers that he may not be fighting only for the middleweight crown, but he may also be fighting for his life.

Title: Split Decision II - The Comeback |
Author: Marc A. Beausejour | Publisher: SHE
PUBLISHING LLC | ISBN: 978-1-953163-95-0
(paperback) | Publication Date: February 2024
(*second edition*)

After Sylvio Dominique's sudden retirement from middleweight boxing following a close brush with death, the former champion hangs up his gloves to continue running the Shaw-Dominique Community Center in Queens, New York. When Sylvio's hometown rival and current middleweight champion Barry Taylor; asks him to help train for his title defense against new contender and former MMA fighter Jun Zhang, Sylvio agrees to the proposition. But Taylor is defeated handily, and when Sylvio suffers a tragic death in the family and the center struggles financially, he makes the decision to return to the ring. Meanwhile, his girlfriend, Valentina Cruz find success as an actress and her relationship with Sylvio begins coming apart at the seams. Sylvio's trainer, Jim Shaw is reluctant to help Sylvio, as he finds himself struggling with his own personal demons. Jun Zhang then challenges Sylvio to fight him for the crown. As he prepares for his toughest ring battle yet, can Sylvio and Jim find the fortitude to emerge victorious while putting all their struggles behind them?

Title: Divine Vengeance | Author: Marc A. Beausejour | Publisher: SHE PUBLISHING LLC | Publication Date: COMING SOON!

After the murder of David Anderson, LaToya Richardson awaits her day in court while attorney Edward Reed receives a warning from Tadarius Hill, the gang leader of M.O.B. and sexy femme fatale Tina, who gives him an ultimatum. Realizing that he cannot use conventional methods to combat the tactics of his former gang, Edward pulls out all the stops to prevent Tadarius from wreaking havoc in the city. LaToya's son, Chris adjusts to his new home and new school while staying with David's family. Andrea McAfee's relationship with her boyfriend Quentin comes apart at the seams as lust and infidelity threatens to tear the couple apart. Can Edward, Chris, and Andrea summon the strength amidst the chaos in their environment to secure their futures?